THE TWELVE

THE TWELVE

A Novel

WILLIAM GLADSTONE

FIC
GLADSTO
2009

Vanguard Press
A Member of the Perseus Books Group

First published in the United States and
internationally in 2009 by Vanguard Press,
a member of the Perseus Books Group

Designed by Linda Mark
Set in 11 point Stempel Schneidler Light

Library of Congress Cataloging-in-Publication Data
Gladstone, William.
The twelve / William Gladstone.
p. cm.
ISBN 978-1-59315-556-8 (alk. paper)
1. Prophecies—Fiction. 2. End of the world—Fiction. I. Title.
PS3607.L344T87 2009
813'.6—dc22
2009012665
International ISBN: 978-1-59315-588-9

Vanguard Press books are available at special
discounts for bulk purchases in the U.S. by corporations,
institutions, and other organizations. For more information,
please contact the Special Markets Department at the Perseus
Books Group, 2300 Chestnut Street, Suite 200, Philadelphia,
PA 19103, or call (800) 810-4145, ext. 5000, or e-mail
special.markets@perseusbooks.com.

10 9 8 7 6 5 4 3 2 1

This book is dedicated to the twelve
who have carried the energy of the ancient prophecies
for the benefit of all humankind.

A Note from the Author

Dear Reader:

According to the Mayan Elders and scholars who have studied the Mayan Calendar, December 21, 2012, is the end of the Mayan Calendar and the beginning of a new era. This new era will have a different vibration from the present era. Greed and materialism will have a lesser role in this new era. There will be a greater emphasis on harmony among all living beings. Individuals may or may not perceive specific changes in their lives on December 21, 2012, but the changes will be enormous and grow over time.

Some scholars believe there will be specific galactic changes and even an altering of the magnetic and electronic poles of the earth. The majority of true Mayan experts do not believe that the changes will be in the form of upheavals that are harmful to the planet or human beings.

The Mayan Elders believe there is free will and, just as in my novel *The Twelve*, that humanity will choose its destiny on December 21, 2012. The decisions and affirmations you make on December 21, 2012, can create the tipping point that can lead to planetary harmony. The choice is yours.

In Joy,
William Gladstone

Preface

THE YEAR 2012 HAS BEEN HERALDED AS THE END OF THE MAYAN calendar. There are ancient legends from the Hopi, the Tibetan shamans, even from those who believe they channel the wisdom of the ancient worlds or myths of Lemuria and Atlantis, all pointing to 2012 as the beginning or the end of life as humanity has lived it over the past several thousand years.

Christianity has long awaited the second coming that will be heralded by end-times of fire, as well as the promise of "heaven on earth." The Jews wait for the coming of the Messiah, and many aboriginal spiritual traditions have anticipated the transformation of the planet in some magical way.

All in or around this sacred year of 2012.

If you have come upon a copy of this book and are drawn to reading it, then without doubt you are one of the chosen many who may help determine whether these end-times result in planetary destruction or the transformation of all humanity.

The Big Bang

MARCH 12, 1949

THE BIG BANG THAT OCCURRED ON MARCH 12, 1949, WASN'T the event that led to the creation of life in the universe—the one described by Stephen Hawking and many other scientists—but the one that created Max Doff.

On that auspicious, star-filled, winter evening at exactly 11:11 P.M. and forty-five seconds, in the bedroom of their ranch-style suburban home on Benedict Avenue in Tarrytown, New York, Herbert and Jane Doff experienced the most joyful mutual orgasm of their forty-five-year marriage.

For Herbert it lasted fourteen seconds.

For Jane, it was much more significant. While her physical body quivered with waves of sensual pleasure pulsating deep within her soul, she simultaneously had an out-of-body experience, wherein she was surrounded by magnificent colors of purple and blue.

Time stood still, and she entered a state of complete surrender. She'd never experienced anything like this in her life and knew for a fact that at that precise moment in time, she and her husband had created the child they desired.

Herbert and Jane already had an 18-month-old son, Louis, who had been born with the umbilical cord wrapped around his neck. It was only through the heroic measures of the hospital staff that he had survived the trauma of his birth.

From the start, Louis was colicky, irritable, hyperactive, and uncontrollable. Fortunately for Jane, Herbert owned a successful book publishing company and was able to provide a full-time maid/nanny to help her care for the child, but even so, he was still a handful. And both of them still longed for a normal child.

Thus it was that by 11:12 P.M. on the night of March 12, 1949, Herbert was able to relax, completely satisfied, and observe in awe Jane's pulsating state of bliss. He held her for three full minutes, while she experienced a full body orgasm far deeper than any climax of his own.

The Argentine writer Jorge Luis Borges has written that, if a single couple made perfect love, the entire universe would change, and that couple would become *all* couples. The Dalai Lama of Tibet has called the Tantric path to enlightenment the path of laughter and of touching. His belief also posited that two people loving each other perfectly would save humanity and bring all beings to nirvana.

To his knowledge there has never been such a couple, nor such a coupling.

※   ※   ※

On December 12, 1949, at five past 4:00 P.M., Max Doff was born with both eyes open and a smile on his face.

Because of the chaos surrounding the birth of Louis, Jane had been advised to schedule a Caesarean section. While creating trauma for Jane, it provided the easiest possible birth passage for the baby, establishing for Max the precedent of a life of comparative ease.

There was, however, a dark shadow hovering over the blissful circumstances of his birth. That shadow was embodied in his brother, Louis, who was twenty-seven months his senior and strong enough and mobile enough to be completely dangerous to his younger sibling's well-being.

❋　❋　❋

On Max's third day of life, Jane and Herbert brought him home and, sitting on the large bed in their master bedroom, introduced Louis to his new brother.

Within seconds and before they could react, Louis grabbed Max and began squeezing him tightly around the neck. Recovering from the shock, Jane quickly broke Louis's vice-like grip and pulled the older child away, while Herbert moved to shield the newborn.

Upon being restrained, Louis let out a series of loud shrieks and began hitting first Jane and then Herbert, who had to remove him from the bedroom altogether.

Max survived this overzealous introduction to his older brother, but it was the beginning of countless such explosive episodes. It was clear from the start that he found such violence strange, frequent as it was and always focused upon him.

In all other respects, however, his life was relatively trauma-free, and he was a peaceful child.

As a young boy, Max was adorable. He had reddish brown hair, long, black eyelashes, deep brown eyes, and a face of almost perfect proportions, especially when he smiled—which was most of the time.

Max was neither heavy nor skinny, but well-proportioned. He was athletic and strong, though small boned, with delicate wrists and ankles.

He showed no alarm in the presence of strangers and seemed to trust that everyone who met him intended nothing but love and affection. And except for the aberration with Louis, this proved to be true throughout his infancy.

For some unknown reason, however—whether due to the trauma of Louis's attacks or some genetic predisposition—Max did not develop normal speech abilities. He was able to make sounds like any other infant but could not form words.

Indeed, he seemed to understand what people were saying to him and had an almost telepathic way of conversing with his mother and even with his tormentor, Louis, but that was the extent of his communication skills.

This condition provided his older brother endless hours of potential for abuse.

"Retard, get me another cookie from the kitchen," Louis would command.

"Hey simp, come here, or you're cruisin' for a bruisin'," he would shout.

He thought himself clever to have shortened "simpleton"—which was his pet name for his younger brother. And though Jane and Herbert drew the line at "retard," at least in their presence, they reluctantly allowed "simp" and hoped in vain that he would grow tired of it.

Out of his parents' hearing, Louis had no regard for their rules, regularly saying things like, "If you don't give me that truck, retard, I'll beat you to a pulp." Or, "Get out of my way, retard."

✳   ✳   ✳

Jane and Herbert also inferred from Max's lack of language development that their son was mentally impaired. When he was four years old, they decided to employ a speech therapist to work with him, and the therapist quickly realized that she was dealing with an extremely bright little boy who seemed to comprehend everything.

Nevertheless, it wasn't until he reached the age of six that Max began talking in full sentences and immediately exhibited a complete command of language far exceeding his years. One day, seemingly as if by magic, Max simply spoke up.

"I think when we go to Martha's Vineyard this summer, we should rent the yellow house that has its own pond and boat," he said. "I loved going on that lake last summer and would love to be able to go every day."

When they recovered from their shock, Jane and Herbert were overjoyed.

At the same time, Max achieved extremely high scores on intelligence tests, putting to rest any fears his parents had harbored.

While this turn of events came as a complete and welcome surprise to Herbert and Jane, it was beyond annoying to Louis, who became even more intense in his role as Max's childhood nemesis.

※　※　※

Max knew from the beginning that there was a purpose to his life and an important destiny that he had been called upon to fulfill. This understanding wasn't something tangible, however, There was a voice in his head that spoke of a reason for which he had been born, yet there were no words—just colors and powerful vibrations. His inner world, this secret playground, was filled with beauty and elegance, and it made Max very happy.

He seemed to be able to summon knowledge on any subject but had a particular attachment to the art of mathematics and exhibited an uncanny ability and proficiency with numbers, which constantly swirled around in his mind, vibrating in a multitude of colors. Even before he could talk, he was able to multiply triple-digit numbers in his head.

And this talent adopted a three-dimensional component. He imagined boxes placed vertically and horizontally and at tangents without end. He envisioned each box as a universe complete unto itself and would contemplate the shape, direction, and lack of beginning or end within each box and collection of boxes.

Such exercises afforded him great pleasure, as did most things in life. However, there remained one constant reminder that all was not perfect.

Louis.

Despite the violence and sadism he experienced at the hands of his older brother, Max considered Louis his best friend. Their uncanny link caused Max to feel great empathy for his sibling, and it seemed as if they both remembered that blissful paradise that had been the womb.

From the moment of his birth, Max accepted that wherever he was, he was exactly where he was supposed to be in life and was completely at peace with the idea.

Louis, on the other hand, was angry that he had been forced to leave that perfect state of being and that the world had greeted him with a stranglehold. Thus, he had come into this world kicking and screaming and remained in a constant state of revolt.

That Max felt no such thing angered Louis even more, and he was determined to make his brother's life as miserable as his own by virtue of force and fear. Even as toddlers, Louis would attack Max, pinning him to the floor and choking him, and then retreat as soon as Max started to cry. When the adults came running, he had achieved a safe distance, and they never realized the level of the violence. Since Max couldn't express himself, they remained utterly ignorant.

Eventually Max learned to play dead. He found it otherwise impossible to resist, since Louis was filled with such superhuman strength when enraged that it would have taken more than one adult to subdue him, had they even been aware of the need.

And despite his inherent inclination to be optimistic, Max found that the constant violence began taking its toll. He never felt safe at home and knew that whatever success he achieved at school, or in any aspect of life, he would suffer for it.

As the attacks increased, he seriously considered ending his life in order to escape his tormentor.

At the age of seven, he contemplated stabbing himself in the stomach with a butter knife. While in his secret, inner world, he had seen the potential for his existence and was excited at the possibilities that lay ahead, the outer world presented him with a very large, seemingly unavoidable obstacle.

His decision made, he picked up the knife.

Yet as he pushed the soft-edged blade into his tummy, he remembered that quiet, inner voice from early infancy. So he put the knife aside, realizing in that moment that he had a purpose—a true mission—and even though there might be obstacles in his path, he would have the courage to face whatever came his way.

Once he'd learned how to escape his brother's choke holds.

❊   ❊   ❊

As a toddler, despite his lack of coherent speech, Max exhibited leadership qualities by taking charge of any group.

As he grew, he excelled in every subject at school and had real joy in learning. He was very good in sports and at twelve years old was Westchester County's fastest runner in the fifty-yard dash. Max joked that it was running away from Louis that had led him to become such a fast runner.

When he graduated from eighth grade, he was valedictorian, president of the student council and captain of the football, wrestling, and baseball teams. He had an extraordinary sense of anticipating where the ball or opponents might be headed, he always seemed to be in the right place at the right time, and the idea of making an error never occurred to him.

He expected himself to be perfect in every thing he did, . . . and so, he was. Yet these expectations didn't yield the anxiety experienced by most children.

There was no question that he was loved by his parents, and thanks to his father's success, he had material abundance. So, despite the torments leveled in his direction by his brother, Max managed to survive his early adolescence.

Then when he was fifteen years old—on Thursday, February 19, 1965, at 3:15 P.M. in Dr. Howard Gray's medical office—Max Doff died.

The Death
of Max Doff

1965

JANE AND HER SON MAX ARRIVED AT THE TARRYTOWN MEDICAL Center complex of offices at precisely 2:44 P.M. that fateful February afternoon. It was cold, and there was snow on the ground—not a clean, fresh snow, but a melting-then-refreezing snow that became less inviting by the moment.

The roads were mostly clear, although from previous salting and plowing, they had a film of crunchy dirt that was unappetizing to the eye and ear.

It was a good thing the roads were clear. Jane Doff was an awful driver. She had no confidence at all behind the wheel of a car and had been in a terrible car accident just two years previously—an event that had changed her life.

✳   ✳   ✳

Jane Lefkowitz was a beautiful woman. Standing five foot five inches with perfect skin and a perfect figure, she had dark, curly hair, incredibly soft, dark eyes, and a captivating smile that was irresistible. She reminded those who met her of Mary Pickford, Norma Shearer, and the other movie stars of the 1920s and 1930s.

She was just sixteen, and accompanying her twenty-four-year-old sister Mona on a boat cruise to Cuba. As the daughter of Russian immigrants, Mona was perceived to be an "old maid" with few chances left to marry. The eldest of three sisters, Mona was not beautiful like Jane and did not attract suitors easily. But this was 1939, and her parents were from the old world, so she had to be the first to marry, or her siblings could not.

Such was the tradition of Russian families, or at least of the Lefkowitz family.

Jane's father, Arnold Lefkowitz, made a modest living as an egg seller in Newark, New Jersey—a profession that his wife, Gladys, looked down upon. A deeply intellectual man, he was an expert on the Torah and became well regarded by rabbis throughout the world. But this wasn't enough to compensate for the degree to which Gladys felt she had "come down" in the world.

Her own family had owned their own store in Europe, and her father was a medical doctor, which was quite prestigious. So Gladys considered herself worldly, and sophisticated, and much too good for her humble husband.

Gladys never worked but was an excellent homemaker and managed and controlled all the money generated by her husband, Arnold. Despite the expense of the cruise, she went to the "for a rainy day" jar she kept hidden in the third drawer above the kitchen icebox, pulled out the necessary amount—almost completely depleting the fund—and sent not just Mona, but also her sister Jane, on a ten-day cruise from New York City Harbor to Havana, Cuba.

Jane was to serve as chaperone for her sister, with whom she really didn't get along. But she wasn't about to object, for this was an opportunity for Jane to see a little of the world. She had a dream of traveling, of being a writer, and of living in a thatched-roof cottage in Devon, England.

And it wouldn't have been proper for Mona to travel alone, since there would have been the potential for people to gossip as to her behavior and moral character.

This was serious business.

Mona needed to find a mate on this "singles cruise," although no one dared call it that. Time was running out, and Mona's future—and the future of Jane and her sister Miriam—teetered in the balance.

The cruise was designed so that there would be interaction among the many single men and women on the ship. At the first cruise dinner Jane and Mona were assigned to the captain's table.

Herbert Doff, who was a dapper, good-looking twenty-four-year-year-old—the same age as Mona—was also seated at the table. He was five foot eight, with dark, wavy hair and sparkling, brown eyes full of playful mischief, a little pudgy from overindulgence of wine and food, but generally fit and physically strong.

* * *

A brilliant scientist, Herbert had seemed headed toward a promising career as a professional chemist. But an explosion in the chemistry lab at Union Carbide had left him partially deaf and required him to take a six-month, paid leave of absence from the lab. During that time Herbert spent his time going to ball games, dating curvaceous young women, and generally attending to the necessities of life— such as renewing his driver's license.

This last activity had led to a turning point in his career.

Herbert observed that driving test booklets were in short supply and, having time on his hands, took it upon himself to print copies and sell them to prospective drivers.

Since a fair number of people failed the written exam of the driver's test and were forced to reapply, he hired a secretary to type up and mimeograph one hundred copies of the booklet, with the answers to the multiple-choice questions included.

Herbert then presented himself at the entrance to the license bureau of Manhattan and quickly sold every single booklet—for a dollar a copy. He printed thousands more of the booklets and recruited friends and students to sell them all over New York City, for which they each would receive a quarter for every copy sold.

This arrangement continued for several months, with Herbert accumulating a profit of several thousand dollars a week—which was very good money in the mid-1930s and far more than he could ever hope to make as a chemist.

Unemployment was still high as the country struggled to come out of the Great Depression. Military service at that time was not a requirement, but rather a privilege and a solution to unemployment. The Army inductee's level of pay and opportunity for continuing education was determined by his performance on the Armed Forces Entrance Examination. Since the examination—just like the driver's manual—was a public-domain document produced at the taxpayers' expense, Herbert saw another opportunity to make money while helping others.

He completed what were for the most part basic math and English questions, then duplicated the exam paper, and thus was born the booklet titled "Practice for the Armed Forces Test." And Herbert was on the way to making his first $1 million.

In 1938 $1 million was practically a fortune and certainly more money than a single man could spend without getting into mischief—something at which Herbert excelled. He loved the high life—lavish meals, good wine, the company of beautiful women—the latter being the reason he was on the cruise.

He had been dating Lisa, a voluptuous, blue-eyed blonde for six months, and she was expecting him to place an engagement ring on her finger, guaranteeing her a life of comfort and pleasure. Even though he was fond of Lisa, Herbert *didn't* want to marry her.

First of all, he wasn't ready for marriage. And besides, while she was a fun party girl, she wasn't someone with whom Herbert saw himself settling down and having children.

Yet he couldn't seem to summon up the courage to look her in the eye and tell her that, so he decided to disappear. It was the cowardly route, but he believed that his absence would heal Lisa's desire for marital bliss—at least with him—and he would continue to play the field.

So, he told her he had to go to Havana on business and prepared a quantity of pre-written postcards that would be sent to her from Cuba for six full months, detailing the ever-more-complex business entanglements he would encounter, preventing his return.

Herbert would, of course, be back in New York and hoped that, by the end of six months, Lisa would have given up on him and found another man.

Thus he found himself at the captain's table, and the moment he sat down at the captain's table next to Mona and Jane, he fell madly, hopelessly, completely, and forever in love . . . with Jane.

Her beauty was overwhelming, and while she seemed to know that she was beautiful, she didn't flaunt it. However, it did cause her to emanate a sense of confidence and comfort that automatically drew him to her. During the course of dinner, he learned her age and realized that she was too young to enter into a courtship with him. He subsequently paid more attention to the age-appropriate Mona, who was clearly delighted with his charm.

When the ship docked in Havana, newly matched couples strolled down the streets and visited the beaches and casinos of the sultry capital. Herbert arranged for the sisters to accompany him on horse-drawn carriage rides through the city. He took them to shows, treated them to dinners, and bought them flowers and gifts. They were an inseparable threesome throughout the stay and resumed their position at the captain's table on the return trip, Herbert seated firmly between the two sisters, being ever attentive to Mona.

Upon their return, the Lefkowitz family was regaled by their two daughters with tales of a potential suitor for Mona. Thus, it came as a shock when Herbert came calling and asked permission to court Jane.

Neither Gladys Lefkowitz nor Mona ever forgave Herbert for rejecting Mona. Even years later, when Mona was married and had two children, Herbert was considered a scandalous cad who had misused her to gain access to her young and beautiful sibling.

As she got older, Jane became more stunningly beautiful. In 1953, when she was already the mother of three children, she and Herbert were dining at La Mamounia Hotel in Marrakech, Morocco. Winston Churchill was sitting at a nearby table and couldn't take his eyes off her. He finally invited Jane and Herbert to join him, a gesture she took in stride. Although she had enjoyed a simple upbringing, she was comfortable around people of any stature.

She had a gentle soul and an uncanny, almost telepathic empathy that gave her the ability to put people at ease, no matter who they were. Such was the case with the elder statesman. They talked as if they'd known each other for years, while Herbert sat back and glowed with pride.

*   *   *

It all ended for Jane on June 16, 1963, at 4:22 in the afternoon on Sleepy Hollow Drive in Sleepy Hollow, New York, about twenty miles north of New York City.

She was driving Louis to pick up refreshments for the party that would celebrate Max's graduation from eighth grade. Max had been chosen to give the valedictorian's address to the students and their parents the following day, and since both the upper and lower schools of the private Hackley School would be in attendance, there would be hundreds of people in the audience. Jane felt she should make some gesture of acknowledgment to Max for his striking academic success.

Max was home preparing his speech. Jane stopped her white station wagon at a stop sign where three roads intersected. A brown Chevy approached, driven by Mrs. Allison Broadstreet.

Jane had the right of way, but she hesitated.

Instead of coming to a full stop, Mrs. Broadstreet mistakenly confused the accelerator with the brake, thrusting the car full throttle and reaching a speed of forty miles per hour—which thankfully would not be fast enough to kill Jane and Louis, but would be enough to throw Louis from the car and leave his mother with wounds to the head and face.

They were rushed to the hospital, and Jane required forty-three stitches to close the wound above her left eye. According to the doctors, the only other result was a concussion.

Max went ahead and gave his speech the following day, as planned, at the Hackley School commencement ceremony. His brother, Louis, unhurt by the accident, was the only family member in attendance since he, too, was a Hackley student and was required to be there.

Herbert chose to stay at the bedside of Jane. She returned home shortly and was still as beautiful as ever to her husband and indeed to all others, but not, unfortunately, to herself.

Jane was afflicted with a minor flaw—the inability to control the nerves on the left side of her face. She still had her smile, but it had changed, and she was unable to ignore this anomaly in her features. She had never been vain and almost took her beauty for granted. Life had been good to her. She'd been blessed with Herbert, her children, a comfortable home, friends, and abundance.

She had always felt nurtured, loved, and living in a perpetual state of grace. In the aftermath of her accident, however, all that disappeared. She became despondent and lost her zest for life.

Forty-one at the time of the accident, Jane began to doubt her worth. Her dream of England remained unfulfilled. Her identity was inextricably linked to Herbert, whom she loved dearly, but living in the shadow of this powerful and successful man had given her a sense of inferiority, and she began to resent him.

She lost all belief in herself. She had never been religious and harbored doubts that God existed, especially as a result of the accident. As feelings of regret and disappointment rolled over and over in her mind, she began to chain-smoke cigarettes and drink vodka to numb her pain.

❋   ❋   ❋

Her primary physician was Dr. Howard Gray. His children also went to Hackley School, and Howard and his wife, Zelda, often dined and met socially with Herbert and Jane. Since this friendship had been of many years' standing, it seemed only natural that when Jane returned from the hospital and was diagnosed with clinical depression, Howard would be called upon for advice and assistance.

When she was a young girl, Jane spent two weeks every summer at the Jersey shore. She loved those outings, and as a young mother she would always arrange the summer holidays for herself, Herbert, and the children on Cape Cod, Long Island Sound, or even Martha's Vineyard—anywhere she could spend hours staring at the waves. It didn't matter what time of day or night, the hypnotic trance of the sea—its sounds, its swelling, rushing water, its retreat, its constant movement—engulfed Jane and placed her in a state bordering on bliss.

Thus, when he heard the diagnosis of depression, Howard Gray wisely recommended that Jane rent a cottage for a month and enjoy her love affair with the ocean.

Jane agreed on the condition that no one would see her in what she felt was her "defective" state, afflicted by her nerve-damaged smile and her depression. She didn't want any visitors—not her children, not Herbert, not even a cleaning woman. She wanted to be completely alone, with no one checking on her.

But Dr. Gray *did* check on her from time to time. He indicated that as much as Jane needed rest and the sea, the isolation she had insisted upon was not healthy for her. Since he was also providing her with painkillers and sleeping pills, he made the trip to see her every weekend.

At first he stayed in a nearby beach motel, but soon he took to staying Saturday nights at the cottage, taking Jane out for meals and walking with her on the beach. He slowly influenced her to interact once again with people, enabling her to realize that she was still beautiful and still worthy of the love that had always filled her life.

The inevitable occurred, and Howard fell in love with Jane. Love blossomed into a spontaneous state of arousal that neither he nor she could resist—nor did they desire to do so. Howard was unhappily married, but with two children and family responsibilities, he wasn't the kind of man to have affairs or abuse the sanctity of the doctor-patient relationship.

He justified what they were doing as an act of healing, a way to reaffirm to Jane in the most intimate way that the accident had not diminished her beauty. She was still a vibrant, sexy woman who needed reassurance—even love—from a man other than Herbert, who, until that summer, had been the only man with whom she'd made love. Howard would have left his wife and children had Jane desired him to. Yet she did not. Her love for Herbert was not diminished. Her love of her children was not diminished.

But Jane's love for herself *was* diminished. Her affair with Howard was over at summer's end—a hot and sultry Indian summer that lasted from September until mid-October. A healing of sorts had taken place in her, and she returned to normal life, although life was never really the same for her again. She was never again as much a part of her own family, and with Max in particular there was a distance that hadn't been there before.

The cigarette smoking, the heavy drinking, and the loss of wonder and of living in a state of grace changed Jane in ways that were observable to all—*especially* to Max. The strong bond he and his mother had shared was gone, leaving a lonely void.

* * *

When their mother returned, Max and Louis knew only that something had changed.

Their mother took up knitting, and she produced all shapes and sizes of hats and mittens, even sweaters, which more often than not were somewhat imperfect, but always warm and full of love.

Dr. Gray continued to attend to the Doffs, and to the boys he was smart and always making witty comments. He was the kind of family doctor who was well-acquainted with the medical history of every family member. He made house calls at a time when few doctors still did.

Then on February 19, 1965, Max suffered from a severe case of the flu, with bronchial symptoms that made his every breath painful. He had been held out of school for three days, but his symptoms were getting worse, not better. The juices, soups, and pills were not helping.

"You'd better bring him in," Dr. Gray said, when Jane called on that fateful afternoon. It was exactly 2:44 P.M. when she and Max entered the waiting room to the doctor's office.

Sick as he was, Max's senses seemed heightened, and as he sat there he noticed every detail—the reproduction on the wall of George Washington crossing the Potomac River with his men, the *National Geographic* magazines, with their yellow covers, the brown table on which they lay, the green chairs on which he and his mother sat for what seemed like hours, but were only minutes, and the fresh white uniform of nurse Ethel who greeted Max warmly as she led him into the doctor's office.

It took only a few minutes for Dr. Gray to examine him. He held a stethoscope to Max's chest and asked him to breathe. Max wheezed and then coughed in pain.

Nurse Ethel took his temperature and noted that the fever was only moderate.

Dr. Gray decided to give Max a penicillin-based shot that he had been using on patients with similar symptoms. It had been able to knock out the flu in at most two days, he explained. Then he asked Max to roll up the sleeve of his shirt.

Max hated shots but was tired of the pain in his throat, and so he resigned himself to the needle in his arm.

There was a prick, pain, and then it was done.

"Sit here," Dr. Gray told Max. "I'll be back in just a minute."

Max had no idea how long Dr. Gray was gone, or if he ever left the examining room at all. What Max remembered was that he was suddenly in a state of bliss.

He experienced a sense that he was a creature of pure light, floating with other light beings in the brightest glow he'd ever known. His body pulsated with feelings of love, and every pulse brought even more light around and within him.

He entered a state of complete euphoria.

Suddenly, through the bright light came an array of beautiful colors, vibrating and floating around him, like individual objects. As the color vibrations became stronger, Max saw a person's name embedded within each one of them. He counted twelve colors and twelve names—none of which were known to him.

Then, just as quickly as the names and colors had appeared, they receded, and the pure white light returned. With the change Max had a sense of beings he had known long ago, who surrounded him with love and greeted him as if he were a dear friend or a relative now returned home.

It was a state of quiet calm, euphoric yet still, gentle yet pulsating with joy—active and effortless movement without constriction of any kind—a sense of self, but without a physical body.

And thus Max died.

Max Lives

1965

MAX DOFF MOVED ENTHUSIASTICALLY TOWARD THE TUNNEL of light.

As he did, his floating consciousness was distracted by a series of loud noises, and his attention was drawn to a man flushed with emotion and fear. The man was speaking loudly.

He was on his knees with his hands pressed against a body that lay on the floor of a small room. Max wondered why the man was so upset, then realized that the man was a doctor, and he was distressed because the body wasn't responding to his words or attempts to resuscitate.

Then Max saw that it was his own body that lay there. Disturbed by the doctor's anxious state, he made a conscious decision to return.

So, in a courageous act of selflessness, he turned away from the tunnel of light that offered what seemed a familiar and comfortable world and returned to the human drama of being Max.

As he reentered his corporeal form, he opened his eyes, and the fear and panic subsided in Dr. Gray's face.

"I thought we had lost you," Dr. Gray said, and he had no idea of the sacrifice Max had made out of compassion for the doctor.

Yet the doctor's pain wasn't the only thing that had motivated Max. More than ever, he was propelled by something even bigger—by a mission of greater importance . . . and one that required him to live.

Max still felt sick and was somewhat dazed from the experience of dying. He remained in the medical center another two hours under observation, and Jane stayed with him.

"Mom, you have no idea how beautiful it was to be out of my body," he told her. "There were these light-beings, and they were full of love."

"I can only imagine what you experienced," Jane replied, and she hugged him close. "It sounds a little like what I feel when I gaze at ocean waves, where I imagine each wave as a force of love and life.

"But tell me more about these twelve names you saw," she asked.

"Well, they were names I had never seen before, and some seemed to be in foreign languages. The only name I remember is the last one, which was a strange one—Running Bear.

"Each name had its own specific color and vibration," he continued. "And when they combined there was a full rainbow of colors and a symphony of vibrations. It was all so magical and wonderful.

"Do you think I was supposed to remember the names?" Max asked, suddenly concerned that he may have missed a grand opportunity for knowledge.

Jane reassured him.

"They may have no importance whatsoever, and even if they do, there's no sense in allowing it to cause you pain. Just live your life, and see what unfolds." She paused and looked into his eyes. "The world is wide and vast and strange, and you will never understand all that occurs."

With that she gave Max a kiss on the forehead, then a hug, and waited until Dr. Gray felt it safe for him to return home.

❀   ❀   ❀

Once the doctor was convinced that there wouldn't be a repeat of his untimely demise, Max was released from the clinic.

He took his mother's advice to heart and got on with his life, continuing to shine in sports at school, gaining outstanding leadership skills in all activities and excelling academically, particularly in mathematics.

However, his achievements came so effortlessly that he began to look for additional challenges, and with this in mind he applied for the School Year Abroad program to study in Spain. That country had long fascinated him, in part due to the influence of his Spanish teacher, Fernando Iglesias.

Señor Iglesias, as he asked his students to address him, was the most unlikely man to become a teacher, let alone inspire students the way he did. He was the youngest son of the fifth wealthiest family in Cuba. Along with the other four clans, the Iglesias family controlled the politics, owned the sugar mills, the railroads, the casinos, and everything else worth owning. Fernando had hot and cold running servants who attended to his every need. He excelled at partying in a way he said only a real Cuban would understand—a variation on the Brazilian *Carnival* with outrageous enthusiasm and intensity, a love of beauty, and an appreciation for great art.

Though he did not need to do so, Fernando went to law school because it was considered a dignified career for him to pursue while waiting to inherit his fortune. However, he was an idealist and wanted to see reform—in particular the removal of Fulgencio Batista, Cuba's dictatorial and repressive ruler. As a student, he provided significant funding for a young idealist named Fidel Castro. It was only after Castro came to power that Fernando realized he had backed an equally totalitarian dictator.

By the time Fernando was ready to flee Cuba, he was only permitted to take $5.00 and the clothing on his back.

He landed in Miami and got a job as a soda jerk in a Howard Johnson's restaurant. He spoke eloquent English, and with his cultural background, he applied for the position of Spanish teacher at various private schools on the East Coast. His upper-class upbringing suited the requirements of the Hackley School in Tarrytown, New

York, so in 1964 he found himself teaching ninth-grade Spanish at this private, boys-only, day and boarding school.

❋   ❋   ❋

Señor Iglesias had no experience as a teacher, but he possessed a rich knowledge of life in his Latin culture. Consequently, Max found his teaching methods were rather unorthodox but always dramatic, exciting, and magical. His philosophy was that nothing was impossible. He took his students to New York City to attend parties with other Cuban exiles where the wide-eyed young men were exposed to exotic foods, exciting music, and beautiful women.

When the Spanish Pavilion at the 1964 World's Fair opened in Queens, New York, Señor Iglesias organized a trip for the entire class, including backstage passes to meet the gypsy flamenco dancers. Max was amazed that this simple teacher, who had virtually no money, could find such joy and excitement in everyday life.

Fernando's love of his native culture was thoroughly contagious, and Max soon adopted a deep affection for all things Hispanic, including stories about the Incan and Mayan civilizations and how the Spanish conquistadores had vanquished those highly evolved civilizations so quickly and seemingly effortlessly. And thus, on September 9, 1966, at the age of 16 and full of enthusiasm and wonder, Max set sail with a student group on the USS *Aurelia* for Southhampton, England, en route to Barcelona, determined to learn more about the culture that had spawned Cortes and Pizarro.

Upon his arrival he was assigned to the Segovia family, which consisted of the matriarch, the widow of Segovia, her three children, and their maid and cook, Julieta, who had been with the family since the birth of the eldest son, Alejandro.

Alejandro was an extraordinarily handsome twenty-eight-year-old party boy who hobnobbed with models and artists, including Salvador Dali. He was an architect but not very successful and constantly fought with his mother about money and his less-than-stellar career accomplishments.

Roberto, the second son, was twenty-four and also studying architecture. He did not have Alejandro's fabulous good looks but had a pleasant face, although he was somewhat on the chubby side. He became engaged to his high-school sweetheart while Max lived with the family. Her name was Cristina, and she was much taller and thinner than Roberto. They made an amusing couple, but both were sweet, intelligent, and kind.

Max spent a good deal of time with Roberto, playing cards and discussing food, music, and architecture. Since Roberto loved to eat, he introduced Max to a great variety of Spanish, Catalan, and Basque delicacies.

However, Max spent most of his time with the youngest child, Emilia, who was twenty years old and thus closer to his age. She was studying literature at the University of Barcelona, so they talked for hours about the great authors and poets of the world and ventured deeply into philosophical subjects. Emilia was a true sister to Max, and the idea of a romantic relationship never entered the picture. Indeed, she had a very wealthy boyfriend, Quitano, who lived in Madrid but visited every weekend and treated Emilia and Max to the theater, ballet, fine restaurants, and concerts.

But la señora, the widow of Segovia, was the real showstopper.

Her husband had created a highly successful medical insurance business but had died prematurely, leaving her with three small children ranging in age from four to eight. In 1956 Spain did not grant equal rights to women, and few—if any—owned businesses. Since Spanish law prohibited single women from owning businesses at all, la señora kept her formal name as the widow of Segovia.

She was a natural entrepreneur, and in addition to running the insurance company, she had purchased a laundromat, several small general stores, and a weekend beach home on the Costa Brava—the Spanish coast north of Barcelona. She believed in hard work and had inculcated this work ethic in Roberto and Emilia, but not in Alejandro, who was more attracted to glamour and the world of art.

In every way that Max's own mother, Jane, had been weak, the widow of Segovia was strong. She was not beautiful but had endless energy and excellent aesthetic taste.

Julieta, who served as the family's maid and cook, was almost a second mother to the children. From a poor family in a small village in rural Aragon, she had started working for the family when she was only 16 and was in her late forties when Max came to live with them. She frequently took Max shopping at the open-air market, teaching him how to choose fresh vegetables and pointing out which of the live chickens would make the best meal.

"Este chico es mas listo que el diablo," she would say to all who would listen. "This boy living with the señora is more clever than the devil!" She said it with such pride, clearly enjoying having this young American boy as her charge, and it made Max smile.

✻   ✻   ✻

In his nine months in Barcelona, Max learned to speak Spanish with an accent as pure as that of any Castilian. He felt a heart-to-heart connection with the Spanish people in a way he never could when speaking English—which for him always remained a language of logic and mental gymnastics, but not of deep emotions.

He traveled throughout Spain to every major city, became an expert on the Barcelona architect Antoni Gaudi, visited the birthplace of El Greco, marveled at the creation of La Alhambra in Granada, ate goose barnacles in Galicia, walked the ancient streets of Unamuno's Salamanca, and became even more enamored with the Spanish culture and its love of life, its intensity, and its passion. It all seemed very familiar to him. He felt at home.

He believed this was where he belonged. In Spain, Max learned to live without fear. He could walk anywhere in the city at any hour of the day or night in complete safety. Franco ruled with an iron hand, and even the red light district had no crime other than prostitution, which was semi-regulated, with condom shops on every corner and cheap hotel rooms above every bar.

Although Max turned seventeen that winter, he still looked fourteen, and even the prostitutes thought he was too young to touch. One night he and three of his friends decided it was time to lose their virginity. His friends were all successful, and, despite their condoms, they took away infections to prove it. Because of his appearance, Max was turned down by the prostitutes, and he was happy that he'd been rejected.

Max slept well in the house of the widow of Segovia and had pleasant dreams, except for one night when he drank far too much cognac following a baseball game. After two years of a losing streak and aided by Max's prowess, his Spanish team won a game against their archrivals. Every member of the ten-man team insisted on buying a round of cognac for the entire team, leading to ten cognacs each in the space of two hours.

That night Max dreamed he was fighting a stream of fire-breathing, green dragons. He had a sword, and he was able to kill each dragon as it approached him, but there was an inexhaustible stream of the creatures.

After killing what seemed like hundreds—if not thousands—of dragons, Max looked to the sky and saw a godlike presence, which bellowed at him.

"Do you want to stop fighting the dragons?" it asked.

"Yes. It's tiring, and I'm somewhat exhausted already," Max admitted.

"Well, you can just stop whenever you want."

"But if I stop, the dragons will just keep coming and destroy the world."

"Your thinking is correct," the godlike presence acknowledged, speaking in Spanish. "But you will never be able to defeat all the dragons. They are infinite in number.

"Are you sure you want to continue?" it asked.

Max just shrugged and returned to killing dragons.

Then he woke up.

Max had been told that he would know that he was proficient in Spanish when his dreams would be in Spanish, too. Since Max never remembered his dreams, this was an unusual and pleasant experience.

It also signaled that he had achieved his primary goal of learning Spanish before heading back to conquer whatever dragons might await him as he prepared to complete his education and ready himself for college and adult life.

"Understanding Understanding"

1968

MAX ATTENDED PHILLIPS ANDOVER ACADEMY FOR HIS SENIOR year, and he achieved but did not stand out—particularly in terms of his extracurricular activities. Instead he focused on his studies, college applications, and learning about sex and love.

He had little difficulty getting into any college he chose, and after receiving a number of acceptance letters, he decided to attend Yale.

Meanwhile, Max developed a sweet and wordless relationship with fifteen-year-old Lizzie, whom he met at a dance at an exclusive country club in Sleepy Hollow. Max danced with many of the vivacious and brightly dressed young girls that evening, but Lizzie was different. When he asked her what her favorite book was, she said *Candy*—a rather outrageous, almost pornographic novel that was on bestseller lists at the time.

Max was intrigued that such a young girl would be so bold with him and found himself attracted to her mystical eyes, gentle, feminine body, and alluring smile. Before the evening was done, he decided to pursue her.

She lived within walking distance of Max's home but since he was away at Andover most of the time, their meetings were restricted to school vacations. Nonetheless, the romance bloomed.

They would take long walks or go to Max's bedroom, which was above the garage, boasted a separate entrance, and offered complete privacy.

He considered their relationship "wordless," because he and Lizzie rarely spoke when they were alone. They would kiss and stare into each other's eyes for up to five hours at a time. But they were both virgins and neither of them was quite ready to explore too quickly the next level of intimacy.

This long-distance courtship lasted Max's entire senior year at Andover. Then the summer before Max went to Yale, the two of them enjoyed a weekend visit to New York City, staying in his father's empty apartment on 18th Street and Irving Place across from Pete's Tavern. That was when Max and Lizzie mutually decided to explore the ultimate physical intimacy of what was already an intense and emotionally charged love.

Once they began making love, they never stopped. The Beatles' song of the day was "Why Don't We Do It in the Road?" and, of course, Lizzie and Max did so—there and almost everywhere else.

When Max entered Yale the following September, it became harder to arrange to see Lizzie, but he wrote to her regularly. She wasn't as diligent in her responses, so he was blissfully unaware when it became apparent that she was no longer interested in him.

She was still only sixteen and in high school, and having a college boyfriend made no sense to her. She wrote Max a goodbye letter, which he received on December 12, 1968, his nineteenth birthday.

Max was devastated when he received this letter. He fell into a state of utter despondency.

His depression was exacerbated by the fact that he hadn't taken well to Yale—hadn't enjoyed being in a dorm that bordered College

Avenue, with trucks changing gears all night long, waking him up or keeping him from falling asleep altogether. He hadn't enjoyed having a girlfriend who was far away and unavailable. He hadn't enjoyed classes with as many as six hundred students and professors who didn't even know their names.

As a math major, he didn't appreciate going to math classes where his Australian math professor used mathematical notations that were different from the ones he had learned in high school. In a world that was turned upside down by the Vietnam War and the proliferation of recreational drugs among his fellow students and even the professors, he questioned the relevance of being a math major altogether.

His other studies offered little solace. He studied Piaget and learned that according to Piaget's stages of development it was impossible for a young child to hold and examine abstract concepts. This left him baffled, for he could not dismiss the reality of his own childhood visions and experiences.

Then there was the political unrest—the assassination of the Kennedys, Kent State, Abbie Hoffman, and finally the assassination of Martin Luther King. Amid such chaos, his one significant emotional anchor had been removed, and he had no way to cope.

※　　※　　※

That fall Herbert and Jane moved from Scarsdale, New York, to Greenwich, Connecticut, so they were actually closer to Max—only a forty-five-minute drive from Yale.

Consolidation was the buzz word of the day, and Herbert had been courted by Litton Industries, one of the large companies that had decided to incorporate publishing into a broader media business model. Litton began buying up smaller publishers, and Herbert received one offer . . . and then another.

Competing offers followed from other companies. The prices were high. Finally, one of the buyers found a way to break down Herbert's resistance. Perfect Film, an instant photo company, promised to appoint

Herbert the head of the publishing division. He would be able to use Perfect Film money to buy *other* publishing companies.

Herbert had no desire to actually sell his own publishing company, but he very much liked the idea of running a larger organization, so he began to make preparations. These included moving out of New York State and into Connecticut where—in 1968—there was a much lower capital gains tax and no state income tax.

※　※　※

Consequently, Max no longer had his room above the garage, or any real base, emotional or otherwise, when he returned "home" for Christmas. Jane was often inebriated or asleep, and because of his focus on the possible sale of his company, Herbert was rarely available to Max either.

Max was forlorn.

It was an unsettling time, and many young men were afraid of being drafted and sent to the constantly deteriorating situation in Vietnam. Since Max's draft number was 321, he wasn't concerned with the military, but he also didn't see much reason to stay at Yale.

"Mom, I really don't see any point to it. The teachers aren't as good as those I studied with at Andover, School Year Abroad, or even Hackley," he complained. "I mostly just go to three or four films a night at the film societies, and the rest of the time I'm pretty much bored with my classes."

"Put a little more effort into connecting with your teachers and the other students, and I'm sure you'll have a better experience," Jane advised. "The important thing is not to give up—your education is too important."

"I'll stay if it makes you happy," he conceded, "But it just seems like a waste of time and money."

"Trust me on this," she implored. "You'll have more power in your adult life if you see this through and graduate. And believe me, you *will* want that power.

"So promise me you'll stay and graduate. Please, Max."

Not wanting to disappoint his mother, he promised.

❋   ❋   ❋

Despite his sense of alienation, however, Max did have friends at school, including Archibald Benson—who had been part of the student group that went to Barcelona—Chris Garvey, and Carl Becker.

At the beginning of the ten-day spring break, Chris and Carl approached Max with the suggestion that he try some of their hash brownies, and he felt there was little to lose.

A huge proportion of students at Yale in 1968 dabbled with drugs. It was part of the college culture, which also embraced the radical changes in music and fashion.

Much to the delight of Chris and Carl, a hungry Max devoured the brownies, though unexpectedly, instead of getting high, he fell into a deep sleep that lasted a full forty-eight hours.

❋   ❋   ❋

Max woke up filled with energy and alive with new ideas. Over the course of the ten-day break, he devoured all of the textbooks required for his five academic courses. He felt no need to sleep and would nap for twenty minutes or an hour at a time, but no more than that.

Max returned to the Yale campus, and the night before his philosophy exam he wrote the final draft of a paper that had been assigned by his professor Robert Fox, with whom he shared many physical characteristics. The instruction was, "According to Whitehead's Modes of Thought, Write a Critique of Yale's System of Education."

Alfred North Whitehead was considered the world's leading systems thinker and had explained how all knowledge was contained within the limits and possibilities of the systems in which human beings interacted. Max saw in a flash that the ultimate limitation was being human.

He also realized that it was only by being *fully* human, and allowing feelings and emotions to enter into the analytical realm of scientific investigation that true understanding could be achieved. Clearly Yale was underperforming in this regard, he concluded. The university had compartmentalized every aspect of every subject, dividing them into specialties, with the instructors and lecturers talking with each other but not with anyone outside of the closed system. The students were learning more and more about less and less and were coming no closer to—and indeed farther and farther away from—Whitehead's goal of "understanding understanding."

At the same time as he was preparing to write the paper, Max finished reading Eldridge Cleaver's *Soul on Ice*, the account of the Black Panther movement and the rage felt by blacks who had been oppressed under the restrictions and injustice of the legal system in the United States in the first half of the twentieth century. Some of the language used by Cleaver was caustic, even violent.

Influenced by such language and finding it effective, Max wrote his eighteen-page philosophy essay in equally strong terms and incorporated elements of his own emotional state, including details of not sleeping, of his descent into despondency, and how those factors related to his breakthrough of "understanding understanding."

The essay was carefully constructed. He reviewed Yale's purpose and practices. The university's motto—*Lux et Veritas*, light and truth—was in his estimation a good one, and in keeping with Whitehead's critique of education. If one could understand understanding, Whitehead proposed, then one could understand anything.

As a mathematician, Max believed that the only way this could be achieved would be by escaping the human system, and expressed that theory in his report.

Then he closed with the formulation that "A is and is not equal to A" as the ultimate equation in explaining how to penetrate the impenetrable intellectual domain of "understanding understanding." It was like an alchemist's magical stone, the one that would turn lead to gold or turn any situation of ignorance into one of knowing.

Whitehead believed that in every educational moment students and teachers should focus on the highest possible learning experience.

Thus it was clear to Max that the highest possible learning experience for his fellow students would be for him to read and then discuss his breakthrough paper.

First, however, he thought he should discuss this with Professor Fox, who also chaired the philosophy department, to see if perhaps he would choose this higher course of action and simply postpone the exam. With this in mind, Max arrived at the examination room early, and stepped on the wooden stage. He stood by the podium, facing the large lecture hall.

Because of his resemblance to their instructor—brown unkempt curly hair, glasses, and good casual, but carelessly assembled, jacket, preppy pants, and shirt with no tie—many of the students assumed Max was Professor Fox. One or two approached him with questions about the exam. Max calmly told them to just take their seats and not to worry.

"There might not even be a final exam," he said cryptically.

As a result, a steady buzz had spring up throughout the room by the time Professor Fox showed up, a minute or two before the exam was to begin. While the puzzled students looked on, Max triumphantly handed him the "A is and is not A" essay.

"I've been up all night writing this essay," Max explained in a matter-of-fact way, "and I think I've reached Whitehead's ultimate goal of 'understanding understanding.'"

As the professor leafed through the paper, he continued, "The class will benefit more from the reading of this essay than from taking the exam," he declared.

Professor Fox listened quietly and then replied.

"You may have, in fact, experienced this amazing breakthrough," he said, "but I have not had an opportunity to read the paper yet, and so just as you are following Whitehead's dictate that each individual must in every moment follow what they believe the highest course of educational learning, I must continue with the exam."

Though it wasn't what he had hoped, Max received this news calmly and replied.

"I understand. Perhaps there will be another time. I just wanted to offer you the opportunity."

"Well, you needn't take the exam at this time, if you don't wish to do so. You've written a much longer essay than was required, and having been up all night—as you say—to complete it, might put you at a disadvantage."

"No, I'll be fine," Max responded. "I can sit for the exam now— I'm not really that tired."

Yet as he went to take his seat, moving along the stage, he realized that in order to be true to Whitehead's modes of thought, he really *should* spend his time contemplating the insights of understanding understanding and not wasting his time just answering questions about Spinoza and Kant, just so he could get an A that would impress others.

So, Max turned to Professor Fox and spoke.

"Yes, I think you're right. Probably best that I skip the exam for the moment. Thank you, sir."

With that he headed out of the lecture hall.

※   ※   ※

As he left the building, he mulled over the details of his paper, and enthusiasm grew within him. He bumped into his sociology professor, Eugenio Rodriguez. Bubbling over with his revelation and anxious to share, Max stopped him and began to talk enthusiastically.

"I've just figured out Whitehead's modes of thought, and have uncovered the secret to 'understanding understanding,'" he said rapidly.

Taken by the young man's enthusiasm, Professor Rodriguez was intrigued, and he adopted the role of devil's advocate.

"Will that understanding get us to the Moon or allow us to solve any of our current social problems?" he asked.

Max hesitated for a moment and then, coming from a level of abstraction that suggested that those who refused to limit themselves to the human system could accomplish anything, he cheerily replied.

"I need to think about it a little more, but I think it *will* address those issues and more!"

"Keep thinking, then," Professor Rodriguez replied, "and let me know what you come up with." With that, he continued into the building.

Intrigued by the professor's suggestion, Max decided a walk in the fresh January air would help him sort out his thoughts. With the sound of snow crunching under his every step, he began to contemplate the varied applications of "A is and is not A" and what "understanding understanding" might really mean to each and every human on the planet.

There could be practical applications. The law of impenetrability that stated that no two objects could exist in the same place at the same time might no longer always be true. This would alter the nature of physics and might allow the development of new technologies that could overcome the limitations of the speed of light and other constants, resulting in great advances in space travel and the colonization of other planets.

The realization of "A is and is not A" changed the parameters for all logic, and the conclusions that purely logical theory could provide. The realization changed the axioms upon which general mathematics were based, and thus would have an impact on all hard scientific investigations.

Max's mind started spinning.

It could be the answer to our very existence . . . our life's purpose, he mused. *We're all connected and not just in superficial ways.*

As he contemplated these concepts he was approached by Professor Fox, who revealed that he had been searching for Max. The professor looked him in the eye with both admiration and trepidation.

"Your paper is brilliant, Max, but I'm not sure I understand it," he said. "I've asked Gordon Howell, the graduate student in charge of your philosophy section, to take a look at it.

"He wants to see you in the dean's office as soon as possible."

＊　　＊　　＊

"This doesn't make sense to me," Gordon Howell said sharply. "I don't understand your thesis at all. You state that somehow feelings must be part of any left-brain, analytical analysis. This is neither logical nor practical."

He looked Max straight in the eye.

"And you seem very angry—angry not only with Yale and your instructors and fellow students, but with all of humanity."

"You're missing the point," Max said, exasperation entering his voice. "I'm angry with the *hypocrisy* of this institution, not the institution itself. There is much at Yale that is wonderful, but I'm talking about the highest levels of truth. You need to reread my paper, and you will see that according to Whitehead, what I say is true—that 'A is and is not A.'"

At that point another man entered the room, and Max recognized him as Dean Bridges. He handed Max a form.

"Max, I've spoken with Professor Fox and Mr. Howell," he said quietly. "It seems to them that you could use a rest, and perhaps take some time off from your regular classes, as well." He gestured toward the piece of paper Max was holding. "Please sign this withdrawal form, and you'll be able to return to Yale whenever you are rested."

Max hesitated for a moment, then realized that he would rather study independently the effect of "A is and is not A" on all of human learning. So he looked back at the dean.

"Where do you want me to sign?" he asked.

A moment later he had officially withdrawn from Yale.

A large man with curly, black hair then entered the room and introduced himself as Dr. Weinstein from Yale's Mental Health Services. He told Max that he had arranged for him to stay at the infirmary, where sleep medicine would be prescribed.

While Max considered this, Dr. Weinstein explained that he had seen the effects of drug abuse in many of the students, with their erratic behavior and forced insomnia due to overuse of uppers to help them through exams.

Max, he said, was a classic case.

So without any fuss, Max followed Dr. Weinstein to his car. He was taken to the infirmary, where he was given sleep medicine.

Thirty minutes later he called for the nurse and asked if she could get him some books from the library. She informed him that it wouldn't be possible, and said that he needed to sleep.

"At least bring me paper and pen," Max entreated. "I have some ideas in my head that I need to get down. It can only help me sleep."

She didn't seem comfortable with the idea, but she did as he asked.

Thus he spent the next four hours writing and analyzing how "understanding understanding" could alter all human action and thought. He expressed his ideas on the nature of human relationships.

If "A is and is not A," then all relationships are and are not what they appear. A man may be a son but at the same time not a son. A wife may be a wife but at the same time not a wife. A student may be a student but at the same time not a student.

The statements at first just seemed to be obvious, but Max saw how most wouldn't understand at all what this implied. For Max it meant that all human programming was based on false premises, false axioms that led too often to confusion and missed opportunities for the highest and best interaction between humans.

He could see how "understanding understanding" would help resolve political and economic conflicts. Once false premises were revealed, completely new structures could be created—ones that would not require hierarchical distinctions.

He continued to focus on the implications for mathematics and philosophy. "A is and is not A" resolved fundamental philosophical knots. It explained away paradoxes and enabled a higher level of abstraction for ever more complex mathematical systems.

Max was in a world of his own, delighted with his mathematical formulations and the excitement of his ideas. These continued to prevent him from sleeping, despite the strong sleep medications he had already consumed.

Dr. Weinstein came by to visit him and prescribed an even stronger dose of sleeping pills, which finally did the trick. Within twenty minutes of his visit, Max fell into a fitful sleep.

He woke the following morning and was ready to leave the infirmary. He started to get dressed, but the nurse stopped him.

"Please wait for me to call Dr. Weinstein," she said quickly. "You can't just walk out the door without his approval."

"But I feel fine," he protested. "I got some rest, and I want to go to the library to investigate the impact of what I have discovered."

The nurse insisted he stay, and seeing how distressed she was becoming, Max got back into bed. He didn't want to upset her any further.

When Dr. Weinstein arrived, he told Max that he would have to stay in his room until his parents—who were in Europe—picked him up when they returned in a couple of days. He informed Max that if he resisted in any way, his parents had given them authorization to restrain him, and even take him to a mental institution, purely for his own safety and protection.

"If you make any more attempts to leave, that's exactly what is going to happen," Dr. Weinstein said, and his tone indicated that there would be no debate on the matter.

Max was aghast.

"But my parents would never authorize such behavior," he asserted.

"Well, they have," the doctor replied, "and I will commit you if I must." Then his voice softened. "We'd really like to keep you out of a mental institution, if at all possible. Max, you've had a psychotic break. This happens and ironically often with our best students. There's a lot of pressure in coming to Yale, and you don't need to feel embarrassed by this, but you *must* cooperate and allow yourself to be treated."

"You are being given Thorazine and some other antipsychotic drugs," he continued. "They will help you sleep, and will get you over your delusions. You must cooperate," he repeated, "and as long as you do, no doubt you will be able to reregister next fall and continue your college career without any loss of credits."

Still, Max couldn't accept what was being done to him.

"But I'm not delusional. I just happen to understand understanding. This is entirely unfair," he protested.

With that, however, it became clear that the conversation was over. The doctor gave him a vague look as he left the room, and it dawned on Max that Dr. Weinstein really *did* think there was something mentally wrong with him.

Calming his internal turmoil, he reflected on the mental health issues inherent to his family. His mother's younger sister Miriam had been placed in a mental institution as a young girl. As fate would have it, that's where she met her husband Michael, who was also a patient. Michael had been deemed unstable, but he ended up buying a large swamp outside of New York City, in New Jersey, which he sold for millions of dollars to the company that eventually built the Meadowlands football stadium.

Max's great-grandmother on his father's side committed suicide by throwing herself off the roof of the Brooklyn apartment building in which she lived when she discovered that her son-in-law, Max's grandfather, wasn't "keeping kosher" and was actually bringing bacon into her kitchen.

There had been other extended family members who were considered unstable, although, except for his aunt, none of them had been institutionalized.

In the light of his musings, Max did pause to consider if perhaps he actually might be mentally unstable. While he concluded that he was not, he did recognize that his theorem of "A is and is not A" had an inherent schizophrenic element to it—more a kind of controlled madness, but what might be considered madness none the less.

❋　❋　❋

In his three-day stay at the infirmary Max experienced sluggishness and other side effects of the medication. He did start sleeping longer and longer periods, but his enthusiasm for the potential of his equation remained undaunted.

His father arrived to pick him up, and as soon as he entered the room, Max tried to discuss his breakthrough, but Herbert showed no interest. He spoke in a matter-of-fact way and gestured to Max's belongings.

"Just follow me to the car and let's get out of here," he said briskly.

When they arrived home, Jane greeted him with warmth and love and explained that Dr. Weinstein had arranged for Max to meet with a local psychiatrist. She further explained that neither she nor Herbert were to talk with him about "understanding understanding" or any of his philosophical insights, for fear of exacerbating the problem. Only Dr. Austin, the psychiatrist who had been selected, would be permitted to discuss his breakthrough.

These conditions frustrated Max, but rather than upset his parents, he agreed to them, then went to his room to get settled.

The next morning Jane drove Max to meet with Dr. Austin, a portly man with gray hair and glasses. His son was a professional musician who had worked with Jerry Jeff Walker on the album that included one of Max's favorite songs—"Mr. Bojangles." This singular fact created a rapport between doctor and patient that would otherwise have been sorely missing.

Dr. Austin had written a well-reviewed book about the psychological forces that had created Adolf Hitler, and that, too, intrigued Max. The doctor was proud of the fact that his home in Tarrytown had once been owned by Mark Twain, who no doubt had written some of his masterpieces in Dr. Austin's own study.

Dr. Austin explained that he had dealt with grandiose thinkers before, and there was no doubt in his mind that Max was suffering from a condition known as "grandiosity." Nevertheless, Max spent their first five sessions together trying to explain the nuances of his "A is and is not A" equation and why it was such a breakthrough.

But Dr. Austin wasn't buying it.

He kept increasing the dose of Thorazine, until Max felt groggy most of the time. And he was to visit with Dr. Austin five days a week until further notice.

*   *   *

It was late May before Dr. Austin felt any significant progress had been made and reduced the sessions to three days a week.

Max also felt that progress had been made. He had learned how to answer questions in such a way that Dr. Austin would no longer think he was delusional or suffering from "grandiose thinking."

He never mentioned his near-death experience or the twelve colors and twelve names. He simply didn't think it was necessary. Max knew he was on his own wavelength, and that was perfectly acceptable to him—even though other people just didn't get it.

So, that's the way he left it.

Despite his apparent improvement and acceptance, he never ceased thinking that "A is and is not A" was anything other than brilliant and never considered that the insights he had gained were less then world changing. Max *did* understand that he needed to show greater discretion in sharing his ideas. However, this didn't mean the ideas were any less valid.

By September, Max was reenrolled at Yale. There was only one stipulation:

He could not take any courses in philosophy.

Detained in Bolivia

1970

CAUTIOUS ABOUT BEING SEEN TO FOLLOW ANY BUT THE MAINSTREAM path at Yale, Max kept much to himself, completed his course work, played intramural sports, and generally conducted himself in the low-key way that would please his parents and professors and those who feared for his mental stability.

Of course, he knew he still understood understanding, and all that it entailed, but as directed he avoided philosophy courses. He did manage to sneak in a cultural anthropology course on Claude Lévi-Strauss and structuralism, which provided a devious route to the contemplation of the singular continuities of the human brain across cultures and time.

*　　*　　*

In the spring of 1970 Max met Paul Hazelton, a political science major with a special interest in Latin America. Paul had participated in a program in Peru called *Projecto Amistad*, or Project Friendship, composed of American college students who had decided that they wanted an even more direct program than the Peace Corps to allow immediate contact between North American students and the people of Latin America.

The idea was to send forty college students to Arequipa, Peru, to work on building schools, implementing social service programs, and generally assisting in whatever way was advised by their hosts at the Peruvian-North American Cultural Center of Arequipa.

The students would be housed with Arequipian families as part of the cultural exchange.

Since Max was already fluent in Spanish, he thought Project Friendship would be an ideal summer program for him. He would be able to experience new adventures while keeping his Spanish fresh.

The trip could not have begun more auspiciously. The family in Arequipa to which Max had been assigned was similar to his Barcelona family, in that Señora Rodriguez was a widow and had two sons, Alberto, who was fifteen, and Javier, seventeen. Señora Rodriguez's sister also lived with them. They were all intent on learning English and maintaining the economic freedom, which their upper-middle-class standing had ensured them while Señor Rodriguez was alive. Like all but the poorest families in Arequipa at that time, they had several servants—two gardeners, a cook, and two maids—even though the house was not large.

Max's bedroom offered him a full view of the bright white center of Arequipa with its colonial architecture. By law, all buildings had to be painted white, and when the sun was shining, the city virtually sparkled with a blinding light that was breathtaking. Sunsets with the oranges and pinks of the early night sky left an equally indelible impression.

With the spectacular El Misti volcanic mountain in the background against the ever cloudless, brilliant blue sky, Arequipa was one of the most visually striking cities Max had ever seen. As in Spain, he felt a deep connection to this country and its people, and a great level of comfort.

He hadn't altogether overcome the loss of Lizzie, but he was no longer in a state of emotional devastation when he met the incredibly intense and exotically beautiful Carolina, who was twenty-three years old and lived just a five-minute walk from the Rodriguez home. Carolina was a cousin to Javier and Alberto, and the only daughter of their mother's brother, who had had twelve sons before she was born.

Despite her age, Carolina had never been alone with a boy. Her father was a professor at the university and was writing a mathematics textbook. He met Max at a party thrown at his sister's house to welcome their visitor to the community. He was intrigued that Max was such an accomplished mathematician and arranged for him to teach algebra at one of the local high schools.

Pleased with Max's teaching skills, the professor decided that Max would be the ideal person to translate his textbook into English. Thus Max gained access to Carolina's home and eventually to Carolina.

His interest in their sister drew suspicion from her brothers, who were certain this could not be a good thing, but their father was so taken with Max's ability that he overrode their concerns. Even when Carolina suggested that she take Max sightseeing, he consented, though of course one of the brothers went along as a chaperone.

After two such expeditions Carolina asked Max to accompany her to the movies. The film was Robert Altman's *M*A*S*H*, a new release. The brothers weren't available for chaperone duty, yet Carolina's father gave his consent. It seemed innocent enough for the young couple to see a film together, and at Carolina's suggestion, Max purchased two tickets in the *butaca* section of the Colonial Palace music theater.

Unbeknownst to Max, the *butaca* turned out to be a private room with curtains completely concealing them from all other theater attendees. Carolina and Max could see out to the screen if they chose to, but no one could see in.

Max didn't remember a single scene from the film.

Carolina sought in those two hours to explore every inch of his body and to assimilate what she had been prohibited from observing and experiencing the first twenty-three years of her life.

Thereafter Max was overwhelmed by Carolina's intensity and during his eight-week stay in Arequipa could not keep his hands or mouth or mind focused on anything other than her Peruvian beauty. The sheer intensity of the affair brought him to a state of euphoria, but with a detachment he found both disconcerting and liberating.

❋　　❋　　❋

It was in this strange state of detachment that he was approached by fellow Project Friendship participant Rolf Ines, who asked Max to accompany him to the wilds of the Bolivian jungle in search of jaguars. Rolf was Dutch, had already completed his military service in Holland, and at twenty-six, was the oldest member of the project contingent. He was over six-feet tall and a bit gangly, wore glasses, dressed sharply, and was always neatly groomed with his brown hair cut short, which made him stand out because long hair was more common at the time.

Rolf was a civil engineering student attending graduate school at Vanderbilt University in Tennessee, and his engineering knowledge had proved particularly helpful in designing the schools and homes that the project group had helped to build throughout Arequipa that summer of 1970.

It was the year of an earthquake that shook northern Peru, and Rolf had taken a two-week leave to assist with the devastation there. He was fun-loving with a daredevil streak. One of his personal goals for this trip was to hunt jaguars following the completion of the Project Friendship assignment. Thus he was seeking a companion who spoke Spanish, since his knowledge of the language was practically nonexistent, even after weeks of interaction with the locals.

He considered Max an excellent candidate to accompany him and had already mapped out two possible locations for the hunt. One was the Peruvian city of Iquitos on the Amazon, and the other was the Yungas region in nearby Bolivia.

"Max, have you ever thought about hunting jaguars in the jungles of Peru or Bolivia?" Rolf asked Max as they drank their Pisco Sours at the bar in the Peruvian-North American Cultural Center in down-town Arequipa.

"Can't say that I have," Max responded. "I've never held, let alone shot, a gun, but I love the idea of visiting a real jungle. What do you have in mind?"

"I've scoped it out," Rolf said enthusiastically. "I visited the Bolivian Consulate, and they told me about this place in the jungle called Caranavi, where you can rent guides and equipment and hunt jaguars. It's not very expensive, so I would cover the hunting expenses if you care to join me.

"You know my Spanish isn't very good, so it would be great to have you along as my interpreter, and of course we always have a great time together."

"Count me in," Max responded impulsively. "It sounds like a blast." They clinked their Pisco Sour glasses to seal the commitment. "But I only have $100 for the whole two-week trip, so it'll have to be low-budget travel all the way," Max added.

"Except for the money I set aside for the jaguar hunt, I'm on a tight budget, too," Rolf admitted. "Not to worry, though. I've planned it all out, and we can even visit Cuzco, Machu Picchu, and some other great places along the way."

"Excellent," Max responded, beaming. "I was really hoping to get to Machu Picchu, Lake Titicaca, and Tiahuanaco if possible."

"They're all on the itinerary," Rolf affirmed as he downed the remainder of his drink.

✳   ✳   ✳

Two days later, the duo departed on the train to Puno, and after a day there, proceeded on to Copacabana.

The least expensive mode of transportation from Puno to Copacabana was via *collectivo*, a private car service of Volkswagen minibuses that could cram up to twelve passengers into each van. However, when Rolf and Max showed up at the departing station, the nine vans were completely full.

One of the drivers sized them up and announced that he would make room in his van. He started speaking rapidly in Quechua to the riders who were already seated, and suddenly two of the Indians stood up, exited the vehicle, and climbed on top—most likely for a reduced fare.

The road was unpaved, dusty, and full of holes—a truly wild ride that required the half-priced riders to hold on for dear life.

The occupants in the van hailed from small villages surrounding Lake Titicaca. These were the homes of the ancient peoples, the original Incas who had ruled the Andes and much—if not all—of South America for centuries.

They didn't speak a word of Spanish, only the indigenous languages of Aymara and Quechua. Many were headed for the two-day music festival held every August at which they would play the same instruments, chant the same songs, and repeat the same dance steps as their grandparents' grandparents and even more remote ancestors had long ago.

The Indians believed in the sacredness of all of life. They worshipped rocks and trees and did not see any distinction between animate and inanimate objects. For them, there was life in every object, and they sought to defeat time through the ritual recreation of their sacred music. They also sought to have an uninhibited orgy of dance and song and *chicha*—corn beer—and coca leaves.

Everyone on the bus was already inebriated or high before they even sat down.

With the exception of the driver, Max and Rolf hoped.

✳   ✳   ✳

As the van crossed the border from Peru into Bolivia, Max asked the driver to stop so they could get their passports stamped. The driver told them that the border guards weren't checking passports.

"They know that hundreds of our people will cross over and return following the end of the festival tomorrow," he explained. "They know us and know that all is well."

This made sense to Max and Rolf, so they didn't question it.

Two hours later the van pulled to a stop on the shore of Lake Titicaca in the town of Copacabana. It was near nightfall, but there were crowds of people on the beach and in the plazas, with musical performances and dances occurring everywhere. The flutes and stringed instruments created extraordinary vibrations that made everyone want to dance, not with the wild abandon of Carnival in Rio, but with a deeper more soulful step, a kind of mystical sadness that contained the essence of joy that seemed to embody these proud, yet subjugated peoples.

Men and women were wrapped in brightly colored blankets and ponchos they had made with wool from their alpaca and sheep. The women all wore hats of different shapes and sizes. Each small town was known by the uniqueness of its hats—the style was a mark of identity and of the private heritage of place and purpose.

Hypnotized by the music and the energy of the people, Max and Rolf moved through the highly charged atmosphere as if in a dream. They ate roasted corn, guinea pig, and other delicacies from the food vendors, and eventually felt the need to sleep.

Since all of the hotels were full, an accommodating farmer allowed them to sleep in his barn with the alpaca goats, making their bed on the straw. He threw in a couple of beautiful, multicolored blankets.

Rolf thought these would make great ponchos, and knowing they would need warmer clothes for their trek through the mountain passes before descending into the jungle, they paid the farmer a nominal amount for the blankets.

The next day, Max and Rolf roamed back to the center of town, wearing their colorful new ponchos. They bought large Mexican sombrero-style straw hats to complete the picture and looked pretty ridiculous. Far from blending in, they stuck out as the gringos they were.

Wandering down to the beach they met two attractive seventeen-year-old girls who had come with their families and friends to celebrate the music festival. They lived in La Paz and had arranged for the school bus to drive them up and back.

As the conversation continued, the girls flirted with these two gringos who represented worlds they could not even imagine. They invited Rolf and Max to join them on the bus for the return trip to La Paz, and the two jumped at the opportunity, knowing the company of the girls would make the trip all the more enjoyable.

The next morning, shortly after sunrise and after another night spent sleeping with the farmer's alpaca goats, Rolf and Max boarded the school bus. The trip was uneventful, though there must have been at least twenty checkpoints along the road to La Paz. The checkpoint guards always recognized the bus and the driver and waved them through without incident.

They reached La Paz by late afternoon, said their goodbyes with thanks to the girls and their families, and decided to stop at the outdoor cafe near the bus station. As a native of Holland, Rolf was particularly fond of beer, and the Bolivian beer was a superior brew created by Germans who had been brought to Bolivia specifically to create breweries.

With the freshness of the mountain water throughout the Andes, the local beers were extraordinary and served in bottles double the size of their American counterparts.

"These are the best beers I've ever had," Max asserted. "Even better than the Peruvian *Arequipeño* beer." He and Rolf ordered another round to go with bar-food delicacies they were enjoying.

"I think you're right," Rolf agreed as he downed his glass.

Suddenly Max jumped up from the table.

"Oh my God," he said. "It's Archie Benson.

"Archie, Archie, over here," Max shouted as he gestured wildly to draw Archie's attention. "What in the world are you doing here?" he asked as his friend walked over to the table, an attractive, young woman at his side.

Introductions were made, and Archie explained.

"I don't think you ever met my wife, Elizabeth, did you Max? We were married in June, right after classes got out, and are down here in South America on a special fact-finding mission for the United Nations. We're both taking the fall semester off to complete our project.

"But what are *you* doing here?" Archie asked.

"Just visiting, but Rolf here wants to go to Yungas to hunt jaguars." Max smiled as he spoke.

"Well, we just returned from Yungas ourselves," Archie noted. "The best way to get there is to jump on what they call the 'banana boat.' It's a truck that comes in from the jungle loaded with bananas, and when the delivery has been made, the truck goes back empty the following day. The locals just hop on board, and for about a penny a mile, you can go all the way to the end of the line, the town of Caranavi.

"From there I'm sure you can arrange guides for your jaguar hunting."

To Max's surprise, Archie then handed him a hotel-room key.

"We have two extra nights paid for. Why don't you take the room, if you need a place to stay."

This delighted the duo. Yet again they had found lodging for the best possible price—in this case, free.

Since Bolivia was a country of many revolutions, and the laws were clear that all foreigners had to be registered, every hotel had a firm policy of reviewing each foreigner's passport and making note of each visitor. Thus Rolf and Max entered the modest hotel very surreptitiously and settled into their free room.

The next day a strike was declared by all communication services— every media worker walked out and shut down each and every newspaper, radio, and television station.

Anxious to set out on their jaguar adventure, they walked to the final gas station heading east on the road from La Paz to Yungas and boarded the "banana boat," an open-bed truck, where they squeezed in next to fourteen native Indians, including three mothers nursing children ranging from a few months to one who must have been close to five years old. The Bolivian women believed that their best form of birth control was to nurse their children as long as possible, so it wasn't unusual to see a six-year-old child suckling at its mother's breast.

The Indians had brought food and drink with them, and they shared it with Rolf and Max, who they scrutinized with some amusement in their faux native garb. There were checkpoints every twenty kilometers or so, but the banana boat never even slowed down. The driver, Jose, was known to the guards, and they seemed to think there was no reason to check the truck.

The ride was one of the most breathtaking Rolf and Max had ever taken—and could easily have been their last. Jose knew every inch of the road, but the drop-offs, ruts, and curves were so severe that no sane person would ever have attempted to navigate it.

Over the next six hours, all the other passengers jumped off the truck as they came to their homes and villages tucked into the sides of the mountains they traversed.

Jose invited Max and Rolf to join him in the cab, asking questions about America and sharing his knowledge and love of his own jungle town of Caranavi. When they reached the final military checkpoint entering Caranavi, the young guard on duty could see that Max and Rolf were not ordinary passengers. He peered at them suspiciously and demanded to see their identity cards. Max handed over their passports to the puzzled soldier, who had never seen such foreigners—or even a passport—in this remote outpost.

"These are international identity cards, just like the ones you use here in Bolivia, but better," Max explained.

The guard looked at Jose, who smiled and spoke up.

"These boys are okay," he said. "They have been with me the entire trip. They will not make any trouble, Jorge. It's okay to let them through."

The guard turned out to be married to Jose's second cousin, and just like that, Rolf and Max passed the thirty-ninth and final checkpoint since entering Bolivia, all without being stopped and questioned, defying all the security precautions of the Bolivian military government.

The banana boat continued into the town of Caranavi, and Jose dropped Max and Rolf off at the nearest bar while he headed home to his wife and children. As the two young adventurers enjoyed their beers and meal, they chatted with the restaurant owner, who promised to arrange for the hunting rifles and serve as the guide for finding the jaguars.

That accomplished, they sat back and observed their surroundings.

Although they were in the middle of the South American jungle, they felt as if they were in a John Wayne Wild West movie. There were wooden shacks on either side of the main road, which was dry and dusty, and an elevated walkway almost eight feet above the street that served as a sidewalk. From what they gathered, during the rainy season the road turned into a river, and most of the buildings were built on stilts to protect against flooding.

As Max and Rolf each finished their third beer, a uniformed officer came up to them, saluted, and spoke in Spanish.

"*El dice* wants to see you. Can you come with me?" the man said.

Max had no idea who he was talking about, and when he pressed the uniformed guard, he was informed that *el dice* was the equivalent of the director, mayor, and governor of the region, all rolled into one. He had the impression that no one should mess with *el dice*, so he and Rolf finished their beers and followed the man to the small wooden shack across the street that served as government offices and jailhouse.

El dice was a heavyset, imposing man. The first things he asked to see were their passports, which he examined carefully. Then he questioned Max quietly and without emotion. When told that they were there to hunt jaguars, he smiled and said that he would have his guard take them to the only hotel in town, and that in the meantime he would hold onto their passports for as long as they were in his jurisdiction.

Aware of their dwindling funds, Rolf indicated to Max that he should tell *el dice* that they weren't ready to go to the hotel yet because they wanted to explore the town first. In fact, their plan was to camp by the river and avoid paying a hotel bill, which was the way it worked out.

Unfortunately, Max and Rolf lay their blankets on top of an anthill, and in the morning when the ants woke up so did the duo, nursing several major bites.

The morning was ferociously hot, and as they walked back to town for lunch and to meet up with their jungle guide and restaurant owner, Rolf turned to Max and confessed that between the heat and ant bites, he had lost his enthusiasm for the hunt.

"We've gotten to see this exotic jungle, and plenty of rare birds and animals," he offered. "That was really my main goal. It's not that important to me that we actually shoot a jaguar, and our budget is pretty tight already. Maybe we should just head back to La Paz and then have some extra time to visit Cuzco and Machu Picchu."

"That's fine with me," Max replied.

So with their sombreros perched on their heads and their heavy decorative ponchos tucked under their arms, they headed back to town and sat down to eat.

They ordered two *platos americanos*—thin steaks served over rice, fried bananas, eggs, and a type of bean indigenous to Bolivia. Of course, this was accompanied by several beers, and after a leisurely meal ordered some of the rich Bolivian coffee. Just as they were finishing their first cup, a Jeep drove up and stopped smartly in front of the restaurant, kicking up a large cloud of dust.

A uniformed guard stepped out of the jeep, entered, and walked over to their table.

"There seems to be some irregularities with your papers," he said brusquely. "The lieutenant at the military barracks wants to talk with you."

Max just looked at Rolf to see what he should do or say. Rolf smiled and called the waiter to come and pour him a second cup of coffee.

Not knowing what else to do, Max ordered a second cup as well. He then turned to the guard.

"Just let us finish our meal, and we will be right there."

The uniformed man left, and ten minutes later Rolf ordered a third cup of coffee. So did Max.

"Rolf, what are we going to do?" Max asked nervously. "I can't drink a fourth cup of coffee, and I think those guards in the jeep are getting fed up waiting for us."

"Don't worry," Rolf responded confidently. "They'll wait as long as they have to. I've been in the army in Holland, and this is just fun and games to them. The lieutenant probably just wants to check and see what plans we have since we never showed up at the hotel last night."

So the two leisurely paid their bill and headed to the front of the restaurant, where four uniformed military men had patiently remained seated in the jeep with heavy rifles at their sides.

The sun was still high, and it was hot. Rolf peered at the bumpy, dusty road and turned to his friend.

"Max, tell them that after such a big meal we need to walk. They can just follow us in the jeep, but I know we will both feel much better if we walk the two miles to the barracks and not squeeze into that bumpy jeep."

He relayed this to the head guard, who had been patiently waiting, and it was at that moment Max realized that it was no longer a game.

The commander barked an order, and all four guards leaped out of the jeep, then trained their rifles on Rolf and Max.

"You will get into the jeep, and you will get in *now*," the commander informed them in a loud, firm voice against which there would be no resistance. Max was now frightened, but Rolf still seemed to think it was a big joke.

"Relax," he said. "This is just what they're trained to do. No one is actually going to shoot us." He smiled, and they climbed into the vehicle.

It only took five minutes to reach the military barracks, the largest military outpost in all of Yungas. More than four hundred men were stationed there, but at that particular moment there seemed to be a lot fewer on hand.

When a young lieutenant greeted them upon their arrival, Max asked him where the rest of the men were. The lieutenant explained that they were hot on the trail of the final members of Che Guevara's rebels. The entire region had been closed to foreigners the very day he and Rolf had jumped on the banana boat—something they hadn't known, thanks to the media strike. Upon hearing this news, Max and Rolf shared worried glances but said nothing.

The lieutenant was a well-groomed young man with an easy air. He practically apologized for being there, while all the senior officers had joined with the general in the expedition to round up the last of *los banditos aquellos*. After all, he said, there would be glory in making these final captures.

He explained that they had no formal jail, so he would have Max and Rolf placed under guard in the officers' quarters, where they would spend the night. He further informed them that they would be dining with him and the general's wife that evening, since that would be the most convenient way to keep track of them.

Given their sombreros and gaudy blankets, he seemed to think that they were actually who they said they were—tourists who had wandered off the beaten track and had managed to avoid thirty-nine separate checkpoints, completely unintentionally.

But it was a hard story to believe, and since all of the senior officers were off-site, he had no choice but to wire Section 5—the highest security section of the Bolivian central army headquarters in La Paz—and ask for orders.

He said he would let them know their fate at dinner.

❊   ❊   ❊

On the drive over, Rolf had noticed that there were some beautiful clay tennis courts, no doubt reserved for the use of the officers. He goaded Max into asking if it would be all right to play some tennis later that afternoon. Seeing no reason to object, the lieutenant granted permission.

As a result, a short time later they had two guards chasing after the tennis balls—serving as ball boys as if they were at a tennis club—while two others kept machine guns trained on Max and Rolf to ensure that there would be no attempt at escape.

Later that evening, over one of the most delicious meals Max had ever eaten, with pleasant conversation from the general's wife, the lieutenant told them where they stood.

"Section 5 doubts the veracity of your story," he revealed. "They have asked me to send you to La Paz tomorrow morning, so they can question you properly. As long as your story checks out, you have nothing to worry about."

"Well, we certainly aren't spies," Max confirmed anxiously.

"I know that," the lieutenant acknowledged. "I will be sending Raul with you as your guard, on the 6:00 A.M. bus to La Paz. The bus will be free, but you will have to buy your own food along the way."

With that, he rose.

"I have enjoyed our dinner together and hope all goes well in La Paz," the lieutenant said.

As they left, Rolf shot Max a wry look.

"Wow, this is even cheaper than the $2.00 we paid to get here," he commented. "You can't beat a free ride!"

Max was less certain that this ride was really going to be free, but he smiled and remained in good spirits.

He found it difficult to sleep, however.

✽   ✽   ✽

The bus ride proved to be much more comfortable than the banana boat had been, and there was a small town where they stopped and had lunch. They were given an opportunity to choose from baby mountain trout swimming in natural holding tanks among the rocks along the river, and once chosen, the fish were barbecued. The taste was exquisite, and the guard—Raul—was very happy, since this assignment had generated an opportunity for him to take a quick three-day leave to La Paz, where he could visit with his fiancée.

All was well until the bus reached La Paz and Raul introduced them to Juan, their new guard, who would take them the rest of the way to Section 5. Juan was proper enough, but clearly he wasn't buying the Mexican sombrero, brightly colored blanket "lost gringo" routine. He led Max and Rolf to a military jeep with a driver and an armed guard.

At 4:00 in the afternoon the two "gringos" were inside Section 5, the headquarters of Bolivia's security organization. Rolf pulled out his Minolta mini camera and began snapping pictures. A guard grabbed it out of his hands and before he could protest, ushered them into a large room. They were told that a General Anahola would be meeting with them as soon as he was able.

By 9:00 P.M., they were hungry. They asked Juan if they could eat and were surprised when he instructed a guard to accompany them to the officers' club, where he told them they could order a meal—though they would have to pay for it themselves.

After a short walk from the holding area, they stopped at a nondescript military building. Once inside, the elegance of the officers' club amazed both Max and Rolf. It resembled an English country pub, with dark, wood tables and tasteful decorations. There were only eight tables, but with four waiters the service was flawless. Three of the tables had other diners, but neither of them thought it wise to strike up any conversations under their present circumstances.

During the meal, Juan was replaced by a new guard, Jorge. At the end of the meal, Rolf still seemed to think this was nothing more than a playful, military exercise, and suggested that Max explain that they were "guests" of General Anahola and that the general would pick up the tab. Against his better judgment, Max offered this explanation, and the waiter smiled as they enjoyed their free meal before being taken back to the holding area by Jorge.

It was close to 11:00 P.M., and still, no sign of the general.

❋　　❋　　❋

As the night dragged on and fatigue set in, Rolf's ever jovial *c'est la vie* attitude was replaced with agitation and concern. His Dutch accent became heavier and harder to understand.

"Max, ask Jorge if we can call the Dutch and U.S. consulates and see if they can help us," he said, the strain apparent in his voice. "We don't want to spend the night in jail. There has to be a way out."

"*Señor, nos permite una llamada?*" Max asked Jorge. The guard sat at a desk in the waiting area where they had been held for the last several hours. There was a phone in plain view.

"Let me check with Captain Morales and see if that would be allowed," Jorge responded.

Five minutes later permission had been granted, and Max was on the phone with a clerk at the U.S. Consulate.

"The consul went home hours ago," he was informed. "I will bring your situation to his attention first thing in the morning, but there's nothing I can do this evening."

With that, the clerk hung up the phone.

When Rolf called the Dutch Consulate, however, he was immediately put through to the diplomat at his home. The Dutch consul spoke with the head officer on duty at the holding facility, Captain Morales, and arranged for Rolf and Max to be transferred to the responsibility of the Dutch Consulate. He also said that he would guarantee that neither would attempt to leave Bolivia until their case had been resolved.

Within forty-five minutes—just before midnight—the Dutch consul himself arrived at Section 5, signed the necessary documents, and Rolf and Max were escorted to a modest hotel, where a Bolivian army guard remained seated outside their door to ensure that there would be no attempted escape.

The following morning they were awakened at 6:00 and taken back to Section 5. After only a moderate wait of an hour and a half, General Anahola called for Max.

He entered a small room with a single light bulb hanging from the ceiling—exactly as he'd seen in the old movies he loved to watch. He was prepared for the worst, even torture, but the only element of torture was an old manual typewriter sitting on a desk that made an ear-splitting racket every time it was used.

The general was sitting in front of the typewriter and started to ask him questions immediately.

"How long have you been a member of the NLF?" he demanded.

"What's the NLF?" Max responded sincerely.

"*Los banditos aquellos*," the general replied. "Those who support Che Guevara and his animals."

"No, I'm not a member of that group. Until this moment, I didn't even know what it was."

"Then you must be a member of the CIA," the military man countered brusquely.

"No," Max answered, trying to keep his voice steady. "I don't think I am even old enough to join the CIA, and I wouldn't anyway."

"What is your political party?" the man demanded.

"I am too young to vote in the United States, but I would probably be a Democrat, if I were older."

The questioning continued for seven hours. Every movement Max and Rolf had made was questioned, every possible motivation was broached. Every person—from the first Bolivian official at the consulate in Arequipa to the bartender in Caranavi—was noted in the report.

At the end of the seven hours, General Anahola produced a two-page, single-spaced document with forty-four points covered. Max read the document and then signed it, asserting that everything written was a true and authentic "confession."

It recounted exactly how Max and Rolf had slipped through security, how they had worked with Project Friendship, how they had decided to take the *collectivo* van from Puno, how they "bumped" into Archibald Benson on the street of La Paz, and every other detail of their improbable journey.

Reading it in black and white, even Max found it difficult to believe, but he signed the document and—exhausted—returned to the waiting room where Rolf was waiting anxiously, holding his Minolta mini camera. He looked distraught and explained that it was because all of his film of the locals and animals in the jungle had been ruined.

Max wasn't overly sympathetic. He was exhausted from the

seven hours of questioning he had endured. Now it was Rolf's turn, and astonishingly he was gone less than five minutes, returning with a broad smile on his face.

"What happened?" asked Max incredulously.

"Well, you know my Spanish is not very good, so they just asked me if everything you said was true. I said 'Max never lies,' and signed the same confession as you."

※　　※　　※

Despite the signing of their "confession," Max and Rolf were kept under military surveillance for seven days. They were allowed to spend their nights in the hotel, with the military guard waking them every morning at 6:00 and transporting them back to Section 5 for further questioning.

The only one who was really being questioned was Max, but Rolf was now brought into the interrogation room with him.

Every detail of their story was checked and double-checked. The hotel in La Paz was called and had no record that they had ever been there. Investigators were sent to Arequipa, to Copacabana, and to Caranavi to verify every detail, every name, every "coincidence."

At night they could go where they chose—since both had been vouched for by the Dutch and U.S. consulates—but always under guard. They went to the soccer match one evening, much to the delight of their guards, all nine of whom showed up at the same time—despite their rotations—just to make sure Max and Rolf would not attempt to escape.

And, coincidentally, they were able to enjoy the big match against neighboring Peru.

At the end of the week, unable to find any holes in the amazing-though-improbable declaration of the foreign detainees, Max and Rolf were told that they would be free to go the following morning. They would be taken to the bus station and driven to Tiahuanaco, the ancient mystic site, and from there to a boat that would take them back to Puno in Peru.

Their passports would be returned to them in Puno when they debarked. Two Bolivian army officers were provided to accompany them on the final leg of their Bolivian adventure.

Both guards were pleased to have such an easy assignment, and took extra time while Max and Rolf visited the ancient Incan ruins in Tiahuanaco. Now that the worst of their "adventure" was over, Max felt a sense of comfort at the ruins, as well as a sense of wonder. He had read about the ancient sun god, Viracocha, who was believed to have come out of the waters of the nearby Lake Titicaca and created the civilization of the first indigenous people.

The ruins in Tiahuanaco were monuments to this great teacher and leader, and the legends spoke of his arrival and departure. There was a magical quality to the ruins, as if the rocks themselves were still breathing and communicating the ancient lessons of the mythical Viracocha.

The guards confirmed their own beliefs in the ancient legends, and the local belief that Lake Titicaca with its rejuvenating waters was the birthplace of humanity. There were those who believed that in the times to come the lake would once again become the center of spiritual power for the entire planet, ushering in a new era of humanity.

✳   ✳   ✳

Upon reaching the immigration control offices in Peru, Max and Rolf were greeted by two smiling officials who already had their passports.

"We have been waiting for you. Welcome back to Peru." They handed over the passports and in large, red letters on the page where the Bolivian stamp had been placed were the words *PERSONA NON GRATA*. Beneath lay other words in Spanish that made it clear that these were suspicious individuals who were not acceptable visitors to Bolivia, under any circumstances.

Persona Non Grata

APRIL 1973

WHEN MAX WAS TWENTY-TWO YEARS OLD, HE GRADUATED FROM Yale and began working for his father's book publishing company, his Bolivian adventures just an exciting memory.

The job allowed him to support himself and learn the ropes of the publishing world. And his father had recently suffered a minor heart attack, so his new position allowed Max to stay in close touch with him as well.

He had worked for his dad for nine months when he took on a special assignment rewriting and updating the test preparation title, *How to Score High on the Medical College Admission Test*, carrying on his father's successful tradition of helping students on their road to success. Max knew nothing about medicine and hadn't even taken a science course since high school, but he knew how to research, and he knew a lot about creating tests.

He was now living in Westport, Connecticut, and every morning would make his way over to the public library to start his work for the day.

By noon he would be ready for a break.

Since the YMCA was next door, and the paddle ball league was looking for new players, Max signed on. That's when he met George Hardy, an independent film producer and writer. Although more than twenty years his senior, George was a fit and competitive player and he and Max became regular opponents and partners in doubles matches.

Max always looked forward to his time at the Y with George. After a game they often spent time talking, and Max shared his passion for Latin America, the culture, the people, and the language. He glowed with excitement as he recounted his experiences and George, who wasn't easily impressed, was caught up in Max's youthful enthusiasm.

George had agreed to produce a film for Ralph Cohen Productions entitled *In Search of Ancient Mysteries*, and was looking for someone to scout locations in South America. He liked Max, thought the young man had a good work ethic, and was impressed that he could speak Spanish and knew the Latin American culture.

"What the hell," he said one day, "It's not brain surgery." So there in the locker room, after a particularly challenging game, George offered Max the job.

"Ever heard of Erich Von Daniken and his book *In Search of Ancient Astronauts*?" he said as they sat over a cup of coffee.

"No," was Max's honest reply.

"He's the guy who thinks that astronauts from outer space colonized the Earth thousands of years ago, and created some of the unexplainable mysteries from ancient civilizations. Rod Serling narrated an NBC television special based on his books. It was a huge success, and now they want to create a sequel. A lot of the locations he's mentioned are in South America, and I thought you might be a good choice to help select the location list for the film.

"Do you think you would be interested?" George asked.

Without hesitation, Max jumped on the opportunity.

"Sure, sounds like fun," he replied.

❋   ❋   ❋

The next day George handed Max a fourteen-page outline of the film, together with a preliminary list of locations that included Tiahuanaco in Bolivia, Cuzco in Peru, and other exotic places that boasted unexplainable mysteries that might be indications of the presence of ancient astronauts.

George was quite blunt about the shakiness of the film's concept.

"It could just be all smoke and mirrors," he admitted. "There's no telling if Von Daniken is right, or if he even believes it himself."

"Well, after you told me about his theory, I checked out his book from the library and I have to say that much of it seems far-fetched, to say the least—if not outright fabrications," Max confided.

"Well then, I guess this project doesn't interest you," George said with a tone of disappointment.

"No, exactly the opposite—I find this a fascinating project and would be delighted to help you out. I love exploring ancient myths and ancient civilizations. Working with you would be a blast."

"Great!" George responded. "Your initial salary will be $125 a week, and I think you'll do a great job. In addition to fleshing out and adding to the location list, I need you to figure out how we get our crew and equipment into each of the countries where we plan to film. Do you think you can handle that?"

"Absolutely," Max replied confidently.

So he took a leave of absence from his father's book publishing company and threw himself into the project with intensity and enthusiasm. He began with basic research and within four weeks had read every issue of *National Geographic* ever published and had a location list that encompassed mysteries and ancient sites from Bolivia to England, Syria, Israel, Greece, India, and Japan.

When next they met, George was impressed with the job Max had done thus far, and offered him the position of production coordinator on the project, which meant he would be involved in the everyday aspects of filming in all of the countries. George also bumped Max's weekly salary up to $150.

Suddenly word came down that the shoot dates for *In Search of Ancient Mysteries* had been moved up. They would be forced to scramble in order to meet the new dates and be prepared when the crew arrived.

"Can you get down to Peru in the next two weeks?" George asked Max.

In fact, Max was ready to go—but there was a problem. The necessary permissions hadn't been received from embassies around the world, allowing the filming to take place in the various countries.

To Max's surprise, George didn't seem too concerned, and he expressed confidence that everything would fall into place. Max wasn't so sure, but within days he was on his way to Lima, Peru, where he checked into the Sheraton Hotel, the tallest and most luxurious hotel in Lima.

It turned out that George always traveled in style—five-star hotels and the best restaurants wherever he went—and he expected his crew to be treated the same way. Years in the entertainment business had taught him that a content film crew made for a happy film set, he told Max.

Since Max was now a member of the crew—the advance guy—he also reaped the benefits of deluxe accommodations. Yet he still had a Herculean task ahead of him: The rest of the crew would be arriving in five days, and he had to make sure that all their needs were met.

The first step was a meeting with the Undersecretary for Peruvian Cultural Affairs, Señor Altamontana, and it did not go well. Altamontana, a short, bespectacled man moved with intense energy, and as he greeted Max he revealed that he knew nothing about the film production.

Max was stunned, but he recovered quickly.

"But didn't you get my letter?" he asked. "I sent it more than two weeks ago."

The undersecretary replied that he had certainly *not* received the letter, and even if he had received it, along with the application to clear equipment through customs and film in the country, the turnaround for such approvals was at least twelve weeks.

As Max became increasingly concerned, Altamontana explained calmly that a new law had been created just that year to protect the Peruvian film industry. In accomplishing its mandate, it was making it impossible to secure permission any sooner.

"There will be no exceptions," the undersecretary told Max in a matter-of-fact tone.

Max was stumped.

Now what? he thought, his mind racing.

At that moment the undersecretary's assistant entered the room with a small stack of envelopes perched on a silver tray—the day's mail.

There, on the top of the stack, Max spotted a familiar object. The letter he had sent with extra postage for speedy delivery

"There's my letter," Max cried jubilantly. "Please, just open it. You'll find everything you need right there."

Though wearing an expression of doubt, the undersecretary opened the envelope and read the letter typed under the Future Films banner.

Although impressed at the timing of the letter and having confirmed the validity of the project, the undersecretary was adamant that it was impossible to grant permission on such short notice. He explained to Max that the special committee for cultural affairs would need to review the shooting script and petition. He reiterated that the soonest they could process the requests would be September.

It was now June.

"But my crew arrives in five days," Max protested.

"Be that as it may, neither they nor their equipment will be permitted to enter," Altamontana responded firmly. "So you'd better tell them not to come."

The meeting was at an end, and Max left dejected. His meteoric career in show business seemed to be ending before even getting started.

George was scheduled to join him in Lima, but he couldn't wait for him to arrive. He immediately called one of the producers and his point person, Dan Brandon in Los Angeles, and told him "there is a problem."

"Don't worry," came Dan's cheerful response, and Max's brow wrinkled with confusion. "We anticipated that when the schedule had to be accelerated, we might have a problem with the Peruvian officials. Fortunately, one of Ralph Cohen's close friends from USC is Julian Jasper."

When Max didn't recognize the name, Dan continued.

"Julian was on the swimming team and competed in the Olympics. He's a good guy and runs the film industry in Peru. He even owns the main bus company in Lima and several other businesses. He's agreed to meet with you.

"He lives in Miraflores and is expecting you for lunch."

As cheerful as Dan was about all this, Max still had strong doubts when he hung up the phone. Julian may have been a "good guy" and a powerful film producer, but the undersecretary had been quite clear—approvals were required, sample scripts had to be submitted, twelve weeks minimum.

Still, Miraflores was the Beverly Hills of Lima, so at least Max would have a nice lunch.

When he arrived at the Jasper estate, he was greeted by an immaculately dressed house servant who escorted him to the garden, where Julian, his wife, and daughter were sitting down to an elegant lunch. The table was set with flowers and fine china, and the garden itself was full of fruit trees and myriad flower beds planted in exotic shapes.

Julian was a large and cheerful man. He rose and gave Max a hug and introduced him to his family.

The food was excellent and the conversation was light and full of suggestions for sights they thought Max should take in while in Lima. Despite his concerns over the imminent arrival of the film crew, Max actually began to relax.

It wasn't until after lunch, when they retreated to a gazebo in another part of the garden, that Julian finally brought up the main topic.

"You don't need to worry," he said cheerfully. "I have taken care of everything. Your crew and equipment will not have any problems getting permission to shoot."

Max was stunned.

"But how can that be? I left the undersecretary's office only a few hours ago and was told that the new law will not allow for any exceptions."

Julian revealed that he had written the film code and laws himself, and they were basically written to protect him and his friends. Since Richard Cohen was a friend, they had agreed that *In Search of Ancient Mysteries* would be a coproduction with Jasper Productions.

It was therefore now a Peruvian production, and would not be subject to the new laws. He added that there might be a minor problem with the customs issues because it was a national law that all such equipment must remain at least one week in quarantine, as protection against unscrupulous smugglers.

However, Julian had recently been awarded a medal as Honorary Mayor of Lima for providing bus service as part of the public works. The medal entitled him to exemption from all laws governing city employees, and since some of the custom officials were city officials, he felt certain that his honorary position would get the equipment through.

Julian was correct on all points, and the day was saved.

❋ ❋ ❋

With the Peruvian situation well in hand, the next stop on Max's location schedule was Bolivia, and it was time for Max to tell George of his *Persona Non Grata* status that would prevent him from heading south to La Paz, where he was supposed to set up the filming for Tiahuanaco and Lake Titicaca.

George arrived in Lima, and they met in the lobby of the Sheraton. Before long George was imbibing from a pitcher of Pisco Sours, the indigenous Peruvian hard alcohol, so the meeting went better than Max had expected.

"Well, as long as you have people there to meet us, and the schedule set up, I guess it will work out," George said between sips. "This does give you an extra day or two here in Peru. Why don't you go up to Trujillo to survey the pyramids and see if there's anything we might film, or anyone we might interview."

It Starts with Love

JUNE 1973

MAX GOT OFF THE PLANE IN TRUJILLO AND TOOK A TAXI TO THE local hotel. Although the largest city in northern Peru, Trujillo was still recovering from the earthquake and had only one major luxury hotel.

Upon check-in Max revealed his mission to the hotel clerk, whose name was Jose, and asked how far it was to the ancient pyramid and ruins. Jose was only too happy to help, and soon a taxi was waiting to take Max to scout the Huaca de la Luna—or Temple of the Moon—pyramid.

While touring this massive and mysterious structure, just two and a half miles outside of the city, Max was approached by several "amateur archeologists" who offered to sell him ancient relics and sculptures. And the pyramid itself, while impressive for its elaborate murals, did not contain secrets significant for the chosen Von Daniken storyline.

Upon his return to the hotel, he found a dark-haired and energetic young man waiting for him. The fellow introduced himself as Eduardo and explained that he worked for the local television station.

"We have never had a U.S. film crew come to Trujillo, except for the earthquake coverage, and we would like to interview you," he announced.

Max was honest with Eduardo and told him that it wasn't certain that filming would take place in Trujillo. However, the eager young TV reporter didn't seem to care too much about that, and he departed to fetch his film crew.

Max had to assume that it was a slow news week.

Minutes later Eduardo returned accompanied by his cameraman, Reginaldo, and the most beautiful and captivating woman Max had ever seen.

Her name was Maria, and she was twenty years old, slim, with dark hair and deep brown eyes. She had an easy and vibrant smile and an intensity of focus that was almost disconcerting.

Maria was dressed simply in a silver blouse and slacks. She was the production assistant on the news show, Eduardo explained, and did a little bit of everything. She smiled at Max and seemed as intrigued with him as he was with her.

After the interview had been completed, she left with Reginaldo and Eduardo. Moments later, however, she returned to ask Max to write out his name, the name of the production company, and some of the other details he had mentioned during his interview. After getting the needed information she turned to go and then suddenly stopped and looked at Max.

"Are you here alone?" she asked him, and his heart leaped in his chest. "Would you like some company for dinner? I know the best restaurants in Trujillo."

Max quickly recovered his composure and said that he would be delighted to join her. Before long they were in a cab on their way to a small restaurant where they sampled the local *antechuchos* (skewers of spicy pieces of calves' hearts), followed by roasted guinea pig, accompanied by exotic vegetables he couldn't identify but enjoyed nonetheless.

Throughout dinner Max couldn't stop himself from peering into Maria's eyes. They were dark and endless, and no matter what the topic, he found himself losing his train of thought.

Maria seemed similarly intrigued with Max, and she admitted that he was the first U.S. tourist she had ever met.

"Are all gringos as interesting as you?" she joked. "And do they all speak such pure *Castellaño*? I almost feel as if I am talking with the king of Spain. Your Spanish is so much better than my own that I am almost ashamed." At that, she laughed.

Ever serious and lost in Maria's beauty, Max just stammered his reply.

"I . . . I have been fortunate to travel throughout Europe and the Americas at a young age, but I'm not really all that interesting. Your world fascinates me as much as mine does yours, perhaps more. I love the way you speak. Your voice has a softness and natural melody that's pure music to my ears."

The more Maria spoke, the more Max felt as if he was losing control of his rational self.

They stayed at the restaurant until after midnight when the restaurant finally closed. Neither wanted the night to end, so they had the cab driver take them to the park next to the hotel where Max was staying. As they walked hand in hand among the trees, under the starlit sky, a bond formed between them.

To Max, it seemed as if they had known each other for many lifetimes. Maria told him about her family and her indigenous Inca roots. She spoke of her belief in a spiritual power beyond human knowing, and how she knew that all objects possessed life—"even the rocks and trees have consciousness," she said.

She revealed her belief that some day the ancient Incan deities would return, and the true Inca people would once again rule their native lands. She talked about her quiet acceptance of Catholic rituals and practices that dictated sex only in marriage.

Sitting by her side on a wooden bench, Max unexpectedly found words tumbling out of his mouth uncontrollably.

"I know this will sound crazy, but I am completely in love with you," he said. "I desire you as I have never desired any woman in my life, but even more, I love you with a holy, pure love that I have never experienced before . . .

"I know this is complete madness . . . "

And suddenly Maria kissed him passionately on the lips, a long, enduring kiss. They stared into each other's eyes, and he witnessed in a flash of no more than thirty seconds an entire lifetime spent together. The look on her face told him that she was gripped in the same experience.

They heard a baby crying as it was being born.

They experienced growing old together and becoming grandparents.

They saw identical futures and did not speak.

The clarity of the experience was beyond words; the shared emotion indescribable. It took their breath away.

Finally, Maria spoke.

"I love you equally. I am equally mad. This is a love that can never materialize but is a love that our kiss has consummated in the fullness of time and will live in my memory forever."

Max remained silent, shocked by this confession of love and yet confused and bewildered, as well. He had seen a life with this woman. He knew her, and he wanted her for all time.

Just as certainly he knew that Maria was correct and that their circumstances would not allow a lifelong commitment of the kind that Maria had been raised to fulfill.

In just a few hours he was to phone George in La Paz and report on what if anything he had found in Trujillo. He was booked on a flight later that afternoon from Lima to Quito, Ecuador, and then on to London. He would barely have time to shower and get to the airport in Trujillo for the flight to Lima.

With these and other thoughts racing through his head, Max looked at Maria and with a combination of joy, sadness, and resignation held both her hands to his heart.

"This has been a magical night, and I shall never forget you."

He took out a pen and paper and asked Maria to write down her name and address so that he could stay in touch.

Maria handed him the paper on which she had written her full name and mailing address.

> Maria Magdelena Ramirez
> 224 Calle de las Flores
> Trujillo 9490 Peru

Max went into a state of shock.

This was a name he had seen years ago and had been unable to retain, no matter how hard he tried. Yet now, as it stared back at him from the piece of paper he clutched in his hand, his memory of it was utterly clear.

Maria possessed the first of the twelve names he had been given during his near-death experience.

He looked at Maria in her silver blouse and then at the paper again.

Silver had been the color in which her name had appeared to Max eight years earlier. It could not be a coincidence. There had to be a deeper meaning—perhaps a connection that was in fact supposed to alter their lives. Perhaps Maria truly was his soul mate and that was why he had been given her name.

He tried to explain to Maria this new level of connectedness.

"Perhaps the only reason I came to Peru was to meet you," he suggested. "Perhaps we truly are meant to be together, or perhaps we have an important destiny that links us."

To his relief, she didn't act as if he had gone insane. She remained calm and accepted the strange synchronicity that had gripped them.

"The world is wide and vast and strange, and we will never understand all that occurs," she asserted. "If we are meant to be together, somehow that will happen, but if you do not leave now, you will miss your plane, and I will never hear the end of it from my parents.

"I love you. I have always loved you, and I will always love you," she continued. "I do feel a deeper connection with you than anyone I have ever known. Deeper than any boyfriends, deeper than my own brothers, and even my mother and father, and I do not doubt but that our lives have crossed for a reason. Yet I do not see how we can alter our present destinies."

With those words Maria gave Max a final kiss, stood, and walked out of the park, leaving him alone in front of his hotel pondering how it was that she had spoken the exact words his mother had used, after his near-death experience.

The Search
Continues

JUNE 1973

EASTER ISLAND.

Stonehenge.

Glastonbury.

The Museum of Man in London, the caves of Lascaux in France, Athens, and the Greek island of Santorini.

Max set up meetings in each of these locations with scientists, archeologists, and crackpots, all of whom had information to add to the ever evolving search for ancient mysteries.

However, he couldn't stop thinking about Maria Magdalena Ramirez in the few minutes a day in which he was not arranging the rental of cars, boats, planes, and whatever mechanisms would most assist the production team.

As he worked, a pattern evolved. Max would arrive in each city first, contact government officials, museum officials, and other persons with whom he needed to arrange permissions. He would scout locations and then greet the incoming crew upon their arrival at each international airport.

The cinematographer on the crew was Uri Ulick, considered in those days the best rough-terrain cameraman of his generation. Uri was in his thirties, Norwegian, thin, fit almost at the level of a professional athlete. He enjoyed steam baths and saunas and other fitness and health practices that would help him relax.

He was tenacious and confident in his filming. He would go anywhere to get a shot and was fearless. Because he was so fit and agile, he could climb around the top of buildings, perch on railings, and always get the shot. He did all of the helicopter and airplane shots and had no trouble with heights, often leaning out or strapping himself to the outside of the small planes they rented for filming the mysterious Nazca lines in the Peruvian desert or the ruins in remote locations.

Uri was easy to get along with. Everyone treated him with respect, and his services were always in demand. He had a wife and two young children at home in Los Angeles but was on location more than eight months a year.

Russ Arnold—their second cameraman—was in his twenties and big and burly. *In Search of Ancient Mysteries* was a big break for Russ, the most important project of his young career. He enjoyed his beer and was slower moving than Uri, but he was competent, professional, and showed a strong work ethic.

As their camera and lighting expert, Russ was meticulous. He loved to eat and joke, although, unlike Uri, he was less focused on fitness and often went on a binge when work was done.

Orlando Summers was twenty-nine, and as the line producer for the shoot, he was responsible for the budget. He gave Max his per diem and kept track of the equipment and expenses. He reported directly to George, who trusted him completely. Orlando aspired to be a producer and director himself, and Max had more interaction with him than with any other members of the crew.

They worked closely together to organize travel for the equipment and crew, and Orlando learned to rely on Max's judgment on tradeoffs they had to make concerning the costs and the importance of selecting the priority of the shoots.

The final member of the crew was Andy Munitz, who was twenty-seven, thin, and angular, and who, as sound technician and grip, reported directly to Orlando and Uri and helped each of them set up shots and do whatever else might be needed in any situation.

For Max, who had never served in the military, *In Search of Ancient Mysteries* was his male-bonding equivalent. The small team worked almost nonstop and relied on one another in every way.

The stakes were high for each of them—the project could propel their careers forward in a major way. They thrived on the pressure of negotiating foreign countries and going to exotic, out-of-the way locations where few people had ever been before, all in search of ancient mysteries.

There was urgency to the work that Max didn't think existed in a regular 9 to 5 job. It was utterly exhilarating.

Their equipment was worth hundreds of thousands of dollars, and everywhere they went they were greeted with curiosity and scrutiny. In India they expected to find it impossible to walk down the street. But the same was to be true in Jerusalem, Lima, Athens, Santorini, London, Tokyo, and even the smaller towns surrounding the caves of Lascaux, the monoliths of Stonehenge, and the ruins of Cuzco.

They worked and ate together and, except for sleep, were never apart. They developed their own lingo, and if at the end of the day they were heard to say, "Six A.M. having had," it meant to meet at six in the morning, having already had breakfast. "One and done at the Acropolis at sunrise," meant a single sunrise shot at the Acropolis, while "crisp and clean" was an alternate to "It's a wrap."

Every minute of every day and night was an adventure. Every free moment was spent visiting the strange cities and exploring additional sites. Downtime consisted of going to spas or just shopping for gifts for family and friends. By the end of the twelve-week shoot they considered themselves not only shared adventurers, but true friends . . . and that was what they were.

Max knew which whiskeys were preferred, what types of chocolate; and with his petty cash assignment and the ubiquity of the duty-free shops, the film team never lacked their favorite beverages and treats. His other unique skill turned out to be his ability to chase down taxis.

Arriving at airports, it was easy to commandeer the cabs needed for crew and equipment, but when going around a city to check on locations, there never seemed to be enough taxis to do the trick. Yet Max, with his easygoing, matter-of-fact approach, seemed able to magically manifest all the cars they needed, even when it was raining or in a location where cabs were in short supply.

In Israel, however, they all knew it was going to be different.

Given the extra precautions that had to be taken for security it was decided that a local production manager would be hired to handle all of the logistics of car rentals, planes, and related production needs. Max was perfectly happy to relinquish these headaches.

In Jerusalem, he would focus on the research and interviews. After twenty-hour work days it would almost seem like a vacation.

The New York office phoned Max at his Athens hotel, even as he prepared to depart for the airport. They told him the production manager who would meet him at the other end was named Yutsky Hasfor.

Max turned white as once again memory struck with utter clarity.

Yutsky Hasfor was the second name on the list of the Twelve.

※　　※　　※

During the three-hour flight, Max pondered what the significance of the Twelve might be.

It had been eight years since his near-death experience, and he had barely thought about the Twelve for most of that time. Now suddenly, within the space of four weeks, he would have met two of the Twelve, yet he still had no idea what this might foreshadow.

To his thinking, there had to be a connection between the film production and the twelve names. Could it have something to do with the extraterrestrials they were seeking? Perhaps they really did exist, and this was their way to prove it.

Based on his experiences at Yale, where even the most educated men had proved themselves unwilling to consider new ideas, Max decided that when they met, he wouldn't reveal to Yutsky the nature of their connection. No, he would watch, observe, and try to find a connection of some sort that might offer an explanation.

❋　❋　❋

Yutsky was all smiles at the airport. He was a bear of a man, short yet powerful, with a moustache and a receding hairline. He wore green fatigues from his military days, and had a ring with countless keys hanging from his belt. He also wore a long, white scarf around his neck.

He laughed easily and loved telling stories, making jokes, and beaming when others smiled. He had been a major in the Israeli Army and was proud of his military achievements.

As far as Max could tell, there was nothing that Yutsky could not accomplish. He was the most organized man Max had ever met and was considered the top production coordinator in all of Israel. He had worked on many feature film productions and knew everyone in the business.

Yutsky made sure that vehicles were always ready as needed and arranged for access to Masada, Jericho, and even the more remote locations. He liked to have fun and was a lover of good food and drink, which endeared him to Russ and Andy. He saw to it that the crew enjoyed the best hotels, restaurants, and scenic and relaxing diversions during their downtime.

He introduced Max to the 1,000-year-old original Turkish baths in Jerusalem, took him to the Wailing Wall, the Dome of the Rock, Bethlehem, and all the sacred locations throughout Jerusalem and Israel. Max only stayed five days with Yutsky, but they bonded in a way that only happens during war—or the intensity of making a film.

At the end of that time, as they drove to the airport where Max would catch a plane to Delhi, India, Yutsky turned and asked him about his Israeli visit.

"So, Max, of all I have shown you these last five days here in Israel, what will you remember the most?"

Max thought a moment before answering.

"It's all been so amazing—I can't choose just one site, but perhaps in some mystical way it is the land itself and the energy of the people. There's so much focus and intensity in the streets, the restaurants, the bars, and everywhere," he said.

"I am so glad you felt this energy," Yutsky responded, and he smiled. "Yes, the true magic of Israel is in the people. Some, like me, come from families that have been here for centuries. But the others, who have come more recently from Europe, Russia, and even your own United States, capture the magic and purpose of this sacred land.

"Now that you have had your first Israeli experience, I am sure you will return—and when you do, I will be here to greet you."

Yutsky beamed as he parked the car in the airport parking lot.

Just before Max entered the elaborate security area at the airport, he turned to his friend.

"You have been like a second father to me here in Israel," he said. "I will never be able to thank you enough or repay your hospitality."

Yutsky just smiled.

"Do not worry. I enjoyed every minute working with you and your crew. You are young. Some day a young person will need *your* help. In that moment, remember me, and I will be well thanked.

"Now go, and make a great film. Travel safely."

While he boarded the plane, Max was certain that he had made a lifelong friend. And yet despite the close bond, he could not discern any mystical connection that might explain Yutsky's presence on the list of the Twelve, so he decided not to share this secret as they parted.

As a soldier, Yutsky didn't seem the type with whom to share a "woo-woo" experience. But it was enough to know that Yutsky had come into his life.

India

JULY 1973

UPON LEAVING DELHI AIR TERMINAL, MAX WAS SURROUNDED BY porters, beggars, taxi drivers, *would-be* taxi cab drivers, pickpockets, and fellow travelers decked in a swarm of brightly colored clothing. He had to fight to keep control of his bag and after some stress was able to get a cab to the Ashoka Palace Hotel, one of the three luxury hotels in Delhi.

After a good night's rest, he was ready to meet with the chief of cultural affairs, Projab Akbar, who was responsible for all foreign film projects shot in India. Upon entering the government center, Max was startled to see forty monkeys dressed in red suits, standing guard outside the main gate. It was just like a scene from the Wicked Witch's castle in the *Wizard of Oz*, and these monkeys were no better than the witch's minions, sweeping down on tourists and grabbing any food or small items they could.

Once past the monkey gauntlet, he made his way into the office of Projab Akbar, a portly man in his fifties. Akbar listened patiently to Max and explained that he would not be able to give permission for the film crew to enter the country unless he had a complete copy of the script—in triplicate—showing all the scenes to be filmed there.

Max tried to explain that there was no script, as they were shooting a documentary film. Projab just laughed.

"Well, then there will be no film," he said. "You must at least give me the overall storyline, a list of locations, and what will be shown and said in each segment. Unless I have this script by 5:00 P.M. today, there is no way I can process the clearances you require."

Undaunted, Max stood up.

"Thank you. I will get you a script and be back by 5:00 P.M."

It was almost noon by the time Max returned to the Ashoka Palace. He knew all the locations and enough of the script to create the document being sought, but he had no typewriter, nor a copier to create the necessary duplicates.

He would have to work fast.

Max explained the nature of the project to the desk clerk, Shiva, who smiled and said that he was a proficient typist with access to one of the hotel's backoffice typewriters.

By 3:00 P.M. Max had a finished script and thought he was home free. But when he explained that he needed three copies, Shiva informed him that at that time there were no copy machines in Delhi or, to his knowledge, in all of India. He did reassure Max, however, that he had a plan.

✳   ✳   ✳

The taxi threaded its way into Old Delhi, past the cacophony of sounds emanating from the rickshaw drivers, the pedi-cycles, the bicycles, the cows, the horse-drawn carts, the tractors, the wooden trucks, the modern automobiles, the diesel-belching buses, and the countless pedestrians, many carrying huge burdens on their heads.

Suddenly, Shiva signaled the driver to stop in front of a nondescript photography store. Max was a little uncertain but followed his guide through the door. Minutes later it was explained that this shop had an old-fashioned, 8" x 10" camera. They would take pictures of each page of his document and then develop them in the chemicals in the darkroom in the back of the shop.

Within forty minutes, Max would have the three perfect copies, ready to present to the government.

❋   ❋   ❋

Max entered Projab's office at precisely 4:59. The official was pleased and yet surprised to see him and was even more surprised when Max presented him with the three copies of the "shooting script."

"I will review this and in two days will contact you to tell you if this will be sufficient for the granting of permission for your crew and equipment to enter India," he said pleasantly. "If you are approved, you will have a film observer assigned to you."

With great relief, Max hurried back to his hotel, collected his belongings, and then took a flight to Pakistan, where he was to set up arrangements for filming in Lahore.

He would have to work fast, for he now had to be back in Delhi the following day and would have to condense the two days he had allocated for Pakastani location scouting into one.

Despite the rush, he was happy to sit back on the aircraft and take a breath. He reflected on the amazing serendipity of meeting Maria and Yutsky, and while he felt deeply connected to both of them, he didn't think it likely he would ever even see either of them again.

It was ironic, really, that he was working on a film entitled *In Search of Ancient Mysteries*, for his own experience seemed to be evolving into an important journey of personal discovery. He had no idea what was around each corner, and the intrigue both excited and stimulated him.

Max felt alive with possibilities of what the future might hold.

Keeper of the Fifteenth Century

JULY 1973

Max QUICKLY ASCERTAINED WHAT THERE WAS TO BE FILMED IN Lahore and spent the rest of the day taking in the exotic city with more donkeys and rickshaws than cars or buses on the main thoroughfares.

However, he was anxious to get back to Delhi as quickly as possible, to make certain that his shooting script had been approved, and the crew and equipment would be cleared for entry. So he took the first available flight back to India and settled into his hotel to await word.

The next day Max was delighted to learn from Projab that the film commission had approved the script and had assigned a government film official to ensure that the local laws were observed during filming. He also learned that it was forbidden to film bridges, beggars, or the railway stations, and if they didn't abide by this law, all film would be confiscated, and the crew would be deported.

One of the locations—the National Museum of India in New Delhi—required permission from the museum director himself, and this letter of authorization had to be presented to Projab the following day.

"To my knowledge he has never granted permission for *any* crew to film in the National Museum, so I doubt that you will be successful," he told Max. Something in the way he said it insinuated that he might be able to override the museum director . . . under the right circumstances.

Max had been aware from his very first dealings that money talked and also opened doors. He was reluctant to go that route, however, and was determined to do everything on the up-and-up. So far, he had been successful and had more or less charmed his way through several potentially difficult situations.

He didn't expect this one to be any different.

Thus armed with his ideas, he set out for the museum. Upon arrival he explained his mission to the guards at the entrance, and they helped guide him past the beggars and street hawkers, taking him to the special entrance reserved for employees and those on official business.

The museum was vast and represented more than twenty centuries of civilization on the great subcontinent of India. Each area was marked by its timeline, and Max was told that the custodians of each period were assigned the title of keeper. He found it amusing that a single human being might be responsible for an entire century of history and civilization.

Everywhere he went he was entranced by the contents of the museum, and as he sat in the anteroom outside the director's office, he nervously contemplated how he might convince the director to grant permission to film.

"You may go in now," the cheerful receptionist told Max as she adjusted her sari. A few seconds later Max was sitting in front of a tall, impressive man in his sixties, with a white beard and glasses.

This was V.S. Naipul. He had been the museum director for more than twenty years, and as they spoke Max could tell that he still had the same intellectual curiosity that had made him a formidable scholar on his path to his much-coveted position. His eyes emanated wisdom and knowledge.

"Our policy is not to allow filming of any kind in this museum," he explained in a matter-of-fact way. "Our antiquities are quite delicate, and we cannot allow any to be moved unnecessarily, as it could create damage that would be impossible to repair.

"Our mission is to preserve our antiquities for the benefit of scholars and the Indian public," he continued. "Why, then, should we allow you to film?"

Max weighed his words carefully.

"I am not sure that you should allow us to film," he said frankly. "As I walked through the museum to meet with you today, I noticed how extraordinary and delicate many of the exhibits are.

"I studied literature and anthropology at Yale University and did much research in the rare book library on campus. Like yours, Yale's policy was not to allow photography of any kind. However, we would on rare occasions make exceptions. I believe that our project, *In Search of Ancient Mysteries*, may merit such an exception for your museum."

"And why, exactly? What is so special about your film?" V.S. Naipul pressed.

"Part of the goal of our film is to show the advanced technologies of ancient civilizations," Max said with total candor and honesty. "Our research indicates that there are ancient Sanskrit texts here in your museum that document the existence of ancient flying machines in India centuries ago. We want to film those texts and interview experts who might be able to confirm that such flying machines actually existed."

A smile brightened Naipul's face.

"I am a Sanskrit scholar, and I have read the texts you describe. The knowledge of flying machines in India goes back more than one thousand years. The only texts we have documenting our ancient flying machines here in our museum are from the fifteenth century, but I have personal knowledge of other ancient texts in which there are many references to the design and capabilities of such devices."

He went on to tell Max that he had studied at Oxford and was always ridiculed by his fellow scholars when he declared that the first flying machines were not developed at Kitty Hawk in the United States, but in India. He confirmed that the museum's texts contained diagrams, but he said that Max would need the approval of the keeper of the fifteenth century to move and open the texts without damaging them. If such permission were gained, he said he would make an exception to his general policy and permit them to film.

Excitement grew in Max, as he realized that he was on the verge of an important breakthrough. But time was of the essence, since the permissions letter had to be filed the very next day.

The keeper of the fifteenth century was summoned, and when he arrived, he was introduced to Max as "B.N."

A man in his mid-twenties but prematurely gray, B.N. was soft-spoken and had a very gentle quality. He had studied at Boston University in the United States and had taken many courses in advanced mathematics and anthropology, while pursuing his advanced degree in archaeology.

Coincidentally, he had studied under professors who had also studied with professors at Yale. Max had, in turn, studied under those same professors.

It seemed like an intellectual family reunion.

The museum was closed, and B.N. was free to show Max the entire hall of fifteenth-century exhibits without interruption. The manuscript to be filmed was in good condition, and it wouldn't be a problem to open the pages that referred to the ancient flying machines in order to reveal the diagrams.

He reassured Max that he would make certain that V.S. would provide the necessary permission letter, which Max would be able to pick up the following afternoon. Then he invited Max to accompany him to his home for dinner.

"I know my family would enjoy meeting you," he said warmly. Then he added, "We will have to take the train."

❋　　❋　　❋

It seemed to Max as if everyone in Delhi was at the station. B.N. navigated through the crowds, found his train, and made his way to a compartment that had eight reserved seats. Six other upper-class Brahmins like B.N. were already seated, and he greeted them all as if he knew them from countless commutes.

The less fortunate commuters sat outside the compartment on the floor of the train, and there were even those clinging to the top of the train, holding on for dear life as it lurched forward, stopping and starting every five to ten minutes.

From the compartment window Max could see fields and workers coming home to the small towns along the way. It was like going back in time a century, or perhaps more.

When they exited the train forty minutes later, they were in a small town with dirt streets. There were scores of children riding bicycles and playing Kick the Can and other games. The children were intrigued by Max and his light skin—many rubbed it to see if he was painted this odd white-pink, and underneath there was the browner color of their own bodies.

B.N. joked with the children, and turned to Max to explain.

"Even though we are just twenty miles outside of New Delhi, you are the first white person these children have ever seen. They think it is some kind of trick and that you cannot really be that white.

"Others wonder if you are ill. Our schools are primitive in this town, and except for my family and the other Brahman families, the children of this village are quite isolated. They have no knowledge of the rest of the world. They've never even heard of America."

After a fifteen-minute walk along the dusty but lilac-lined street, B.N. and Max proceeded through the gate to the family compound. The single-story house was sprawling and boasted a large courtyard. There was a vast outside porch area on three sides, with chairs, tables, and sleeping hammocks. Presently it was occupied by more than twenty men.

An equal, or greater, number of women lived in the compound, B.N. explained, but they were all either in the kitchen helping to prepare the food or relaxing in the large gathering rooms inside the dwelling.

B.N. introduced Max to his entire family—his wife and young daughter, his father, and a multitude of other relatives. Each was clothed in simple, white traditional Indian garments, and all wore contented smiles. As Max was asked question after question, in impeccable English, he came to realize that despite the seeming humility of the surroundings, this was a group of powerful and knowledgeable men. They were all professionals, ranging from architects to professors and engineers with the highest levels of education, and many had traveled abroad for their studies and work.

Toward the end of the evening Max was sitting in the open courtyard being served tea by the women, when he entered a dialogue with B.N.'s Uncle Gupta, a slim, fit, fifty-year-old who had lived in England and studied philosophy at Oxford University. He was a true intellect with an advanced degree in architecture from Cambridge University, as well as a degree in economics from the London School of Economics.

At the relatively young age of thirty-five, he had become the administrative director of the University of Delhi. B.N. deferred to him, as did his five brothers, and they always sought out Uncle Gupta's advice when dealing with matters of career, politics, or economics.

He was the first person with whom Max had enjoyed the opportunity to discuss the intricacies of Spinoza, Whitehead, and his other favorite philosophers since Yale had banned him from studying philosophy.

Max also shared with Uncle Gupta an incident that had happened the previous day, while he was being interviewed by a reporter for the *Hindustan Times*, the largest English-language newspaper in India.

He hadn't sought out the interview, but the concierge at his hotel—upon learning of Max's film project—had considered it newsworthy and called in the reporter. Max had tried to explain to him that he wasn't even in charge of the film, but the concierge had refused to listen.

"You are such a foolish man," he said. "It is clear from your aura that you are the person in charge. This film cannot happen without you." Despite Max's protests, he had continued.

"I deal with the most powerful men in the world, and I can assure you that you are a very special man. In fact, I can see from your aura that you have no karma at all but are here on a special mission for the benefit of others."

Gupta laughed when Max reported the conversation but then startled Max with his next comment.

"I am not sure why he bothered to tell you all this," Gupta said, "but for what it is worth, it is true. I, too, can read your aura, and there is little doubt that you truly were karma-free at birth and are a man of destiny.

"However, do not let this go to your head. Even with a karma-free birth, you are responsible for your actions while here, and no doubt you have created some karma along the way. I am not an expert in these matters and pay little attention to them since I find this present life challenging and exciting on its own merits. I do not think you need to trouble yourself with such philosophies. Just continue to focus on your work, and you will live a long and productive life."

After that, Max felt comfortable enough to share with Gupta his experience with Maria. As they continued to discuss the nature of time and space, Max tried to apply what they were theorizing to what he had experienced.

"Does that moment I experienced still exist? Were Maria and I meant to share a lifetime together? For that matter, are we actually sharing such a lifetime as we speak?"

"In a word, yes," Gupta replied. "Such moments do exist forever, but if you are not with her now, and circumstances do not permit you to be with her in the future, you need not concern yourself with it. The experience you had was a *déjà vu* of what has already transpired. It is not an indication of a future life and need not be pursued."

Max was a bit shocked at Gupta's practical approach but was impressed by his wisdom and sought to ascertain how he felt about other seemingly mystical occurrences.

He considered sharing his near-death experience, and the revelation of the twelve names but instead decided to ask Gupta how he felt about yogis and gurus who were becoming popular in the United States.

"A true yogi can travel anywhere in the universe," Gupta explained. "I have known such yogis, and they are quite remarkable. They do not publicize their abilities, and they do not try to make money by doing tricks."

Max was somewhat surprised at this pronouncement from a man who had seemed quite grounded and skeptical of grandiose claims. So he pressed on.

"You mean a true yogi can go anywhere in the universe in his mind?"

"No," Gupta corrected. "He can do so in his actual body."

At that moment B.N. came up to Max and pointed to his watch.

"There are no more trains tonight, so you will need to return via the bus, and we must get you to the station immediately, or you will miss the last bus back to the city," he warned. "I have a rickshaw waiting." As Max stood and prepared to depart, B.N. continued.

"Perhaps I will see you when you return to film." He handed Max his business card. "Let us stay in touch in any event."

❈　　❈　　❈

So Max soon found himself on a bus headed back to Old Delhi. The bus crowd wasn't as dignified as the train crowd, and in fact seemed somewhat sinister.

When he disembarked it was even worse. There were pickpockets, common thieves, pimps, prostitutes, beggars, and people who were dying, sick, and homeless surrounding him. Only by keeping his face down and pushing toward the rickshaw stand was he able to escape the heavy stench of fear and sickness that enveloped the station itself.

Within minutes Max was back at the Ashoka Palace Hotel and headed to his room. He was a little astonished to encounter the shoeshine man sleeping in the alcove outside his door. He knew it was the custom, passed down from the days when the English ruled India, to have hotel guests leave their shoes outside their door so that they would be polished and ready for wear the following morning. He had never given much thought to when and how the shoes were polished.

He apologized for waking the man, whose only response was to ask Max for his shoes, which he handed over.

Entering the room, Max fell asleep as soon as his head hit the pillow.

Sometime during the night, however, he awoke to find his body floating above the bed. He thought he was dreaming, but then he reached his hand down and felt the mattress below him.

He was hovering in the air with no support whatsoever—levitating above the bed. Without warning, Max felt a presence grab his left hand. It felt like a human hand, but lighter, more fleeting. Then he was aware of a body of light. It had all the features of a human body, but none of the density. A voice spoke to him.

"Do not be afraid," it said. "I am a yogi. Gupta sent me. He enjoyed talking with you this evening and wants me to show you the truth of what he told you.

"We can go anywhere in the universe you wish," the yogi continued. "Where would you like to go?"

Max, who could barely think, spoke on pure instinct.

"The moon," he said.

In an instant, he felt his light-body travel to the moon. It was his physical body, but like the yogi's the denseness was gone. Max retained all his features and sensations and his abilities to think, talk, and observe, but in a dimension without heaviness of any kind.

The moon was gray and lifeless, and had a dusty, yet at the same time almost liquid, quality. It was almost transparent. He had a sensation of weightlessness as he bounced from place to place, sometimes thinking that he might fall into the center of the moon itself. After a while the yogi spoke again.

"Where else?"

He was still somewhat flustered but managed to respond.

"Take me to the planet with the rings."

Instantly, Max was in a place that exhibited the greatest sensation of orange he would ever know. It was a color that Max had never seen on Earth—such a vivid hue that it proved that the experience was real, and not just dreamed or imagined.

He spent what seemed like many hours soaking in the orangeness of the planet when the yogi addressed him again.

"Where else?"

"Oh, this is quite sufficient for one evening," Max replied. "We can go back now. I have a busy day ahead of me."

And just as quickly as they had arrived at the moon and the orange planet, they were back in his hotel room in the aging, once-grand Ashoka Palace.

Max's dense everyday body still was hovering six inches above the bed, and the yogi was still holding his hand as Max felt his light-body once again integrate into his denser form.

He felt the yogi smile at him, and then the yogi departed.

Max felt his body slowly drop back onto the bed, and he looked at the clock.

It was 4:44 in the morning.

He pinched himself to be sure he hadn't been dreaming and then gently fell back to sleep.

When he awoke, just forty minutes later, he looked around the room to be sure he was still in the Ashoka Palace. Getting out of bed, he looked out of the window at the green lawn, smelled the morning air, looked at the flowers and fruit that were sitting on the desk in his room, and smiled as he contemplated his nighttime journey.

He looked at himself in the mirror to see if he was the same Max he had been the day before. For a moment he doubted the entire experience, but then he noticed a glow in his own face and saw for the first time the ethereal body within his body—something he had never perceived before.

*   *   *

Later that afternoon Max returned to the National Museum and was escorted to the director's office. The secretary smiled as she handed Max a letter.

"I have been the director's secretary for more than fifteen years," she said, excitement in her voice. "This is the first time I have ever been asked to type a letter granting anyone permission to film. Your project must be very important. Congratulations."

Max took the letter to Projab Akbar's office that very afternoon, and when the chief of cultural affairs opened the envelope, his expression showed complete disbelief—along with a note of disappointment.

"I am admittedly surprised," he said frankly, "but the director is granting you and your crew permission to film in the museum, and so it shall be. Your film guide has been assigned and will meet you and your crew at your hotel on Thursday at 9:00 A.M."

And with that Max was out of the office, past the red-suited monkeys, and back to researching the rest of his location list—ranging from the ancient astronomy observatory in Delhi to the Ajanta Caves outside Bombay.

These were but a few of the many unsolved mysteries that were the essence of India.

*   *   *

Max knew he would need to be at the airport at 4:00 A.M. the following morning, to assist with customs and get his crew through

the crush to the Ashoka Hotel, so he had an early dinner and prepared to go to bed.

Upon emptying his pockets, he read B.N.'s business card for the
first time.

Keeper of the Fifteenth Century
National Museum of Delhi
Brama Nepal Mahars

For the third time he was stunned by sudden clarity and a startling
revelation.

B.N. was Brama Nepal Mahars, the third of the twelve names.

The Keeper of the Fifteenth Century was connected in a way that
extended far beyond simply granting permission to film in the National Museum.

On to Japan

AUGUST 1973

AFTER THE CHALLENGES HE HAD FACED MAKING A SIMPLE SET OF copies in Delhi, by the time Max reached Japan, he was ready for the high-tech, efficiently organized society that was Tokyo.

An interpreter had already been lined up, cars had been rented, secretaries were available, and communication with the United States was relatively easy. What *wasn't* easy, however, was the fact that it was August, and all of Japan seemed to be on vacation. Max had planned on taking the crew to Hokkaido, the northernmost island of Japan where the Ainu—a white-skinned race—was known to live.

This white-skinned race had no connection with the gene pool of the rest of Japan. There was a great deal of speculation about who they were and where they had come from, and some suggested that they might be descendants of an alien civilization.

Max felt this was a real stretch and not necessary for them to pursue. When he found it impossible to book a flight for the crew, he cancelled the location shoot and told the crew they would be filming at the National Museum instead.

By this time he was convinced that the Von Daniken theory of ancient astronauts was thoroughly unbelievable. He had—as his contract required—searched for ancient mysteries wherever the trail of research led him. In the process he had surveyed more than ten million museum pieces throughout the world and found just six artifacts that could possibly be attributed to ancient astronauts or ancient space ships.

The odds were pretty good of finding six of *anything* out of a pool of ten million. The more he searched, the more frustrated he became that he couldn't refocus the television documentary on the unbelievable mysteries he *had* uncovered.

There were the mysteries of Stonehenge and brain surgery performed six hundred years ago in Peru and proof that ancient civilizations had possessed amazing technologies that somehow had been lost. The people of ancient times were impressive in their architecture, their technology, their social organization, and their art. There seemed to be no limit to what they could achieve, and he saw no need to introduce extraterrestrials in order to develop a compelling storyline.

His own out-of-body experience had elements that were both alien and otherworldly, but strangely enough, he didn't think it was extraterrestrial in nature. It actually didn't seem that unusual to Max—during the excursion he'd felt at peace and retained a sense of belonging.

Did that mean he was from an alien culture? If yogis could leave the planet and return, were they aliens, too?

Max didn't think so. He had certainly met a lot of strange people in his life who, he thought, might have been from another planet— his brother, Louis, chief among them. But as amusing an idea as it was, and while it did seem possible that all kinds of alien beings could exist on planet Earth, he had yet to see proof.

He mused on these ideas while he took a taxi to the museum to prepare for the shoot. He had already secured the permissions, so this was a relatively easy assignment. Using a brochure, he had identified the exhibits he intended to visit.

As he entered the building, he dropped the brochure and reached down to pick it up. When he did so, he heard a loud rip.

He looked down and realized a seam in the seat of his pants had torn and left an eight-inch gap, exposing his underwear. Max was embarrassed and not sure what to do.

He tried to explain to the guard at the museum entrance, saying that he needed needle and thread. Although the guard eventually understood, he couldn't oblige, since sewing implements weren't the tools of his trade.

As Max tried to figure out his next move, a young Japanese woman, who identified herself as Yoko, approached him. She was wearing a bright yellow dress, which perfectly complemented her black hair and flawless complexion, and she spoke in halting English.

"Come with me. I can help you," she said.

Yoko led him to the door of the men's room.

"You go inside and give me pants," she told Max, and though startled, he did as he was told.

She sat on a chair next to the security guard and a few minutes later handed Max flawlessly repaired trousers.

"Thank you so much," he said gratefully. Then he added, "Please join me on my tour of the museum. I am working for American television selecting what to film for a documentary film."

Yoko smiled a shy smile.

"Okay," she said, and they spent the next two hours touring the exhibits while Max made note of the various artifacts for filming.

"Your work is very exciting," Yoko observed. "I greatly enjoyed learning about these Japanese mysteries."

"Well, I greatly enjoyed your company," he replied. "Please join me for dinner."

Yoko smiled shyly again.

"Are you sure?"

"Yes, I am," he replied. "I'm all alone, and have reason to celebrate as this was the final location here in Japan. Please help me celebrate."

"Then I agree," she answered in her limited English. "Will be fun to join you."

Max quickly found a taxi, and they ventured to the Imperial Palace Hotel, where Max was staying. The dining room there was a five-star restaurant, and Max encouraged Yoko to join him in the elaborate, seven-course, set meal.

During dinner some of Yoko's shyness melted away, and she talked about her life. She was a travel agent and a seamstress, the only daughter and youngest child of a middle-class factory worker's family, with five brothers and seven nieces and nephews. She lived alone in a tiny studio apartment in the same building as her aging parents, and it had fallen on her to take care of them.

Yoko explained that she had been a surprise baby, born when her mother was already forty-three. She still remembered the horrors of being a young child during World War II, living in the aftermath of the atomic bomb.

Nevertheless, she enjoyed being a travel agent, and her great luxury in life was taking two weeks every year to go to Hawaii or Paris or to other exotic locations made available to her by her travel agent discounts. She revealed that she didn't think she would ever marry and felt as if with her nieces and nephews she had all the children in her life she would ever need.

As she finished her story, Max ordered champagne to celebrate the end of his grueling twelve weeks of nonstop work. He described some of the more interesting adventures he had experienced, and Yoko laughed as she drank the champagne. She wasn't used to drinking and finally told Max that she didn't feel as if she was in any condition to go home on her own. Although she knew it was scandalous, she asked Max if she could take a nap in his room, and he agreed.

Soon they were resting against each other on the bed, and before long the combination of closeness and champagne were too much to resist.

Max hadn't been with a woman since the beginning of his travels, and he had the sense that Yoko might not have been with a man for several years. What started as gentle caresses soon led to passionate lovemaking, and with Yoko, Max felt a sense of balance in his body, mind, and spirit. He had never felt skin as smooth and delicate as Yoko's, and she was as fragile as a porcelain doll.

※　※　※

When he woke the next morning, Yoko was gone.

On his bedside table he noticed she had left her business card with her full name and address and a note that read:

> *It was wonderful being with you. Have safe return to America and write me if you will ever come to Japan again.*
>
> *XOXOXO*
> *Yoko*

The name on the business card read:

MIYAKO MITSUI

Apparently Yoko was a nickname. And with a sense of clarity that was beginning to be familiar, though no less astonishing, Max realized that Miyako Mitsui was the fourth name on the list of twelve.

Synchronicity was beginning to be the order of the day, he realized, and he wondered at the forces that seemed to be propelling him without his being aware. Whatever they were, their effects seemed to be accelerating.

Yet he was no closer to understanding where those forces might be directing him. What was this mystery of the Twelve? It no longer seemed plausible that it could just be a random assortment of names. But how was it that he was meeting these people?

His trip to Trujillo had only occurred because he was afraid of what might happen if he returned to Bolivia, yet it was in Trujillo that he met Maria.

Yutsky could be explained by the connection of their work, but his meeting with B.N. had depended entirely upon broaching the one topic that V.S. Naipul was willing to discuss.

Even his visit to the museum in Tokyo was due to the fact that he had been unable to get to the Ainu—and no one could have anticipated that Max would tear his pants.

Most indisputable of all was the utter lack of connection between the four.

Life Unfolds

1973–1976

MAX RETURNED TO THE UNITED STATES AND TO A MORE NORMAL lifestyle.

He had always been a dutiful son, and a major reason for working at his father's publishing company had been to help out after his dad's first heart attack. Now that Herbert seemed back to normal health, Max decided to give teaching a whirl.

He returned to Phillips Academy in Andover, Massachusetts, to teach Spanish for a year, trying to instill in his students some of the enthusiasm he had garnered from Señor Iglesias, years before.

But his stint at Andover was a stopgap, and when the year was up, he received a grant from the National Institute of Mental Health to study cultural anthropology at Harvard University. After six months at Harvard, however, Max realized he had made a mistake.

Anthropology, he discovered, was no longer about the study of indigenous people. In truth, there were few indigenous groups left, and mere contact with modern Western civilization seemed to doom any of the few remaining authentic tribes either to slow or immediate destruction.

Max came to the realization that, on a significant level, modern humans were in fact evolving into what he called "nonhuman beings." He wrote an essay on the topic, which his professors failed to appreciate. The essay explained that the essential attributes that made humans "human" were becoming extinct.

His Harvard professors, however, felt he was romanticizing primitive civilizations; yet Max remained firm in his conviction that something fundamental was being lost through the headlong pursuit of technology and material ease and abundance.

He watched early ethnographic films such as *Nanook of the North*, combining what he saw with his own experiences among isolated peoples in the Amazon, India, the Andes, and the other exotic locations Max had visited while making films and doing anthropological research. He concluded that the art of living in harmony with nature was being lost.

Some of these primitive peoples had developed ways of growing gardens that were works of art, as well as sources of nutrition. They had created geometric designs that changed color with the seasons. Often these designs could only be detected when viewed from the hillsides above the fields. It seemed inconceivable to him, though, that so much extra effort would be put into an agricultural pursuit, just to ensure the by-product of an aesthetic experience.

Other cultures, he noted, had developed intimate rituals of dance and music, which actually healed and cultivated human relationships. Max observed patterns among the so-called primitives in which there was an abundance of creativity and joy, even in the smallest of details—the embellishment of a digging stick with special carvings, a piece of clay, cooking pottery that displayed colors and shapes demonstrating gratitude to the soil from which it was made.

Max didn't ignore the benefits of modern society and the abundance he personally enjoyed, but he *did* think that they came with a price, and that price was to sacrifice the essential elements of being purely human. He felt that modern man was evolving into a consumer being whose authentic needs were becoming secondary. The

economic and technological imperatives of the modern world had replaced authentic human needs. It was only by fulfilling one's consumer needs that an individual could gain status, become a person of
power, and maintain psychological integrity.

This psychological integrity came with a steep price—the evolu-
tion into what Max saw as a more automated, less authentic nonhuman being.

Even as he posed these ominous hypotheses, Max felt that he,
too, was somehow becoming a nonhuman being, and he wasn't
happy with the sense of powerlessness he felt. He distrusted the
businesses of "doing" and "having" that seemed to control his life.

He wondered what his life would have been like if he had stayed
in Trujillo with Maria. He had written to her, as he had promised and
she had, as anticipated, married her *novio*. She was already pregnant
with her first child.

He remained certain that he and Maria had been together in another life, but it seemed indisputable that they weren't intended to be
together in *this* lifetime.

During his study at Harvard, Max continued to get calls to do research and location scouting for exotic, documentary film assign-
ments that required travel to countries all over the world. Happy to
have an opportunity to explore even more cultures, he took the as-
signments whenever he could, and before long he was considered the
go-to guy by numerous Hollywood-based film companies. There
were very few people in the business who could navigate the red tape
and handle the logistics for these documentary productions.

So despite his father's contention that it was all nonsense and that
Max should transfer to Harvard Business School, where he might
learn something practical, Max decided to go on the road again with
In Search of the Historical Jesus.

He was pleased to learn that Russ Arnold—the cameraman from
In Search of Ancient Mysteries—was on board for the project, and Max
was looking forward to another good film experience . . . until he met
the line producer.

* * *

Amanda Harding was an impossible boss. She was gorgeous, had started in the business as a model, and then became an actress. She hadn't excelled at either, yet somehow managed to rise to the level of producer—perhaps through her indomitable spirit . . . or perhaps by other means.

She was a tyrant . . . a real ballbuster. No one respected her, and yet she was in charge, at least theoretically.

Nothing pleased Amanda. She worried about *everything*: in particular how she looked, what she ate, how clean her clothes were, and other concerns that had no relevance to a film project that needed to traverse five continents and twelve countries in eight weeks.

She would only eat tuna packed in water and had to have cans of it shipped to her whenever she ran out, no matter how expensive and inconvenient it might be. It drove Max crazy to waste time on such irrelevancies, as he tried to concentrate on the necessary details of the project.

In Search of the Historical Jesus revolved around the ancient Ahmadiyya and other religious sects, who believed that Christ had not died on the Cross but had survived his ordeal and lived for many years in India and elsewhere until he died a peaceful death, as an old man with children and a loving family.

The Ahmadiyya were a Muslim evangelical sect whose most famous adherent was Muhammad Zafrulla Khan who, in the 1960s, had served as undersecretary of the United Nations. He had written a book in which he claimed that his religion possessed proof of their claims. His evidence revolved around the literal meaning of "give up the breath," which was the phrase used to describe what happened to Jesus on the Cross.

Muhammad Zafrulla Khan explained that Jesus had stopped breathing but that this didn't mean that he had actually died. Yogis can control their breath, he argued, and stop breathing for days at a time. Certainly, he theorized, Jesus must have had the powers of a yogi.

There was also the issue of the Issa Ointment, which, according to Mr. Khan, was still used in India and Pakistan to cure cuts and wounds. Issa Ointment was translated from Hindi as "the ointment of Jesus," and was so named because it was this very ointment that was used to resurrect Christ when he was taken down from the Cross.

The Ahmadiyya further pointed to a tomb on which was sculpted a figure displaying holes in the hands and feet exactly where they would have been on Christ's body when he was nailed to the Cross. It was suggested—and believed—that this was the tomb in which Christ had been buried when he died peacefully in his sleep.

The current Ahmadiyya believed that Christ was reincarnated in 1835 in a remote village called Qadian, outside of Amritsar in the Punjab region of India. Amritsar was best known for the golden temple— the most sacred shrine of the Sikhs, who outnumbered Hindus and Muslims in that area.

Max's job on the film included conducting pre-interviews with almost every major spiritual and religious leader on the planet. This list included the Dalai Lama, the major gurus in Rishikesh, the head of the Greek Orthodox monastery of Mar Saba in the biblical no-man's-land outside of Jerusalem, the Rabbi of Jerusalem, the head of the Church of England, several monks in Japan, Muslim holy men in Damascus, and countless less prominent and self-appointed religious and spiritual leaders.

He also interviewed some of the most unusual individuals on Earth, from psychics to geniuses with unusual talents.

For the most part he was unimpressed by those he interviewed. Most seemed to be power-hungry cultists, more interested in preserving their traditions and power bases than in transmitting true spiritual knowledge.

One interview that impressed him was with the Dalai Lama at his home in Dharamsala, in India. The Dalai Lama possessed true charisma and spoke openly about the world situation and his own shortcomings.

"The Chinese are not altogether to blame for the plight of my Tibetan people," he explained. "Tibetan society was corrupt and tyrannical. We had serfs and an unjust society. The Chinese cleaned things up, but they have gone too far. They are destroying Tibetan culture, and we need to work with them to find a better solution for the fate of my people.

"I exist to benefit my people," he further explained. "I am not just their spiritual leader, but their political leader as well. I may be the last of the dalai lamas—there may be no need for dalai lamas in the future. If Tibet can be integrated into Chinese society while retaining its autonomy, my purpose will have come to an end. Buddhism should be allowed to flourish.

"The essence of all religions is the same. It does not have to be Tibetan Buddhism. The teachings of your Christ are similar to the teachings of our Buddha. Light is light, and truth is truth. Compassion and love are the universal laws of all true religions. Beyond that it is merely a matter of what costumes we wear. In our Tibetan traditions, our holiest monks wear the funniest hats. It is to remind us not to take ourselves too seriously."

Max enjoyed this interview immensely, but other than that, the entire trip was full of aggravation and frustrations, dealing with Amanda's neurotic needs and the self-important, power-hungry religious leaders he had to interview.

He was intrigued to note, though, that the negative energy Amanda embodied seemed to fall into alignment with many of those who came forth to be part of the project. He couldn't help but wonder if this was further proof of synchronicity and how negative or positive energies seemed to connect with its own level of vibratory energy.

Max thought often of the Twelve, and of his own spiritual quest. Why had he been chosen to meet all these spiritual and religious teachers? None of them appeared to have any connection with his twelve names. None of them—except for the Dalai Lama—even made for interesting conversation. Far too often the sacred trust of simple peoples had been handed to individuals who lacked basic scruples.

But why was he required to meet them?

Was he supposed to "come to Jesus"?

Max didn't think so. Each exposure just made him more skeptical of the entire human drama of religion and the quest for spiritual bliss. The more he was treated as a spiritual envoy, the less he respected those he met.

❋   ❋   ❋

The culmination came in the little Indian town of Qadian, which had blossomed in the desert, fulfilling one of the twelve prophecies of the reincarnated Christ who—it was claimed—had founded the Ahmadiyya religion.

Max had flown to Lahore, where he interviewed the head of the Ahmadiyya. Though unorthodox, the Ahmadiyya were considered Muslims—or at least their twenty million followers were almost all originally Muslims. Other Muslims considered them heretics and not only shunned them, but attacked them violently when they could.

The head of the Ahmadiyya acted and dressed like a sultan with a large turban on his head. It was evident from the start that he saw the film project as a way to glorify and expand the reach of the Ahmadiyya. He told Max that his crew could film the enormous temple outside of Lahore, filled with tens of thousands of praying Ahmadiyya, and Max quickly realized that it would be good visual theater.

He was told that the small village of Qadian, near Amritsar, was essential to the project, and he was encouraged to go there and meet with the elders and see for himself the birthplace of the religion.

Thus Max flew to Amritsar, and when the plane landed, he was told to wait until all the other passengers had disembarked. When it was his turn to leave the plane, he saw that the stairway was covered with a red carpet, which continued thirty feet out along the tarmac. On either side of the carpet stood dark-skinned men holding huge flower garlands.

As he walked down the stairs and stepped onto the ground, he was draped with these garlands—some of which reached his knees. At the end of the carpet was a table set with tea and cookies, which Max was invited to enjoy.

After being introduced to his hosts—the mayor of the town and various religious leaders—Max drank the requisite two cups of tea, ate two cookies, and was then escorted to an ancient, white Rolls-Royce parked nearby.

He was asked to sit in the backseat with three of his hosts, each of whom wore white suits and robes and rectangular hats in traditional Muslim style.

Even in a Rolls-Royce, four in the backseat was one too many, and Max was overcome by the body odor of his hosts, whom he suspected did not bathe daily in their desert town.

Then as the Rolls turned onto a dirt road, the ride became even less pleasant. Precision engineering notwithstanding, the ruts in the road caused huge bounces, and Max did his level best not to vomit. After forty minutes, the car slowed down at a divide in the road. Situated at the divide was a young man on a motorcycle.

Upon seeing the Rolls, the cyclist took the inner road straight to the center of town, while the car followed a circular route that ran past a cemetery on the outskirts.

The Rolls took about ten minutes to reach the center, and the extra time allowed the village to prepare for their "very important guest." The car lurched to a stop, a band played on the bandstand, and a large banner was displayed on which huge red letters proclaimed, in English:

WELCOME HOLLYWOOD!

Max stepped out of the car, and a speech was recited by the mayor of the town. It reminded Max of the greeting Dorothy had received from the Munchkin mayor when her house killed the Wicked Witch of the West.

The band continued to play, and then Max was escorted down the main street of the town, where on each side of the road all the inhabitants had been assembled in order of spiritual seniority, there to receive Max's blessing. Each and every individual touched Max, and tried to embrace him. There were two thousand inhabitants, Max learned, and he found the experience exhausting.

After he had greeted the entire town, he was taken to a special guest house where a feast had been prepared, featuring the most sacred and delectable dishes the Ahmadiyya could obtain. There were dates, fresh-grated coconut, soft drinks, and special appetizers, followed by a selection of main courses that included many exotic vegetarian entrées as well as meat, fish, and poultry dishes.

It was a meal of enormous variety and quantity, a kind of Thanksgiving feast that seemed endless.

❋　❋　❋

Two hours later, after a very necessary nap, Max was ready for the tour. Only then did he discover why he had been given such a royal welcome.

Of the twelve prophecies that the founder of the town and of the Ahmadiyya religion had made in the nineteenth century, all had now come true.

The first eleven prophecies included such unlikely claims as:

The desert shall bloom.
The founding group of twelve families shall become more than twelve million believers of the Ahmadiyya.
A great temple—which will hold more than one hundred thousand in prayer—shall be constructed.

These and eight other lofty predictions had all come true, but it was with Max's arrival—representing a Hollywood film crew—that the final prophecy was deemed complete.

The world will seek us out.

Having cleared up that mystery, Max set out to examine the sacred sites the town had to offer.

Very quickly he realized that there was nothing visually interesting to film, and there was no need to include any of the details of the Ahmadiyya beliefs. So in the end, as with so many prophecies, their fulfillment rested with the subjective experience of those who believed . . . or chose not to believe.

Louis

1976–1977

WHILE MAX WAS TRAVELING THE WORLD, LOUIS WAS FINISHING UP law school at Duke University in Durham, North Carolina. He was last in his class at Duke, not because he couldn't do the work, but because he did not *want* to work. He felt that he was owed a living by his father, whom he hated even more than he hated Max.

Louis had even confided to Max that the only reason he went to law school was that it was the longest and most expensive graduate school program he could find. He knew that their mother would force Herbert to pay for law school, since to her education was the highest priority.

The summer following Louis's graduation, Herbert arranged for Louis to work in a law firm in New York City. At the same time, Louis began preparing to take the bar exam—the same test for which his father's publishing company published the primary test preparation guide.

Ironically, he failed the test on the first two tries, and it was on his third attempt that Louis finally passed. It had taken him more than a year, and during that time he had worked as a lowly clerk for the prestigious firm of Gottlieb Harris.

Gottlieb was a criminal attorney who handled some of the most notorious Mafia bosses in New York City. Herbert had met Gottlieb at a Jewish Defense charity benefit, and they had become casual friends. Herbert made it clear to Louis that he was doing his son a great service to get him a position with such a prestigious law firm. For his part, Louis felt he was doing his father a tremendous favor by taking a position that paid him anything at all.

Louis hated working for Gottlieb, whom he thought was as crooked as his clients. He would complain to his mother that Herbert must be a criminal, as well, just to be associated with Gottlieb. In the course of his college career, Louis had become a self-proclaimed moralist with rigid ideas about what was ethical and unethical behavior. Thus, he said, he felt that any behavior that generated "easy money" was certain to be unethical.

When confronted with the fact that he'd been financially dependent on his father his whole life, he responded loudly that he didn't consider that "easy money"—that it was an altogether different circumstance and that such was his right as the eldest son.

It was during a Thanksgiving dinner that Louis—pent up with frustration, hatred, and resentment—finally cracked in front of his father. Max was away, so it was just the three of them at the house in Greenwich. He handed Herbert a letter from the IRS that threatened action against Louis for not having paid his income taxes—yet another thing Louis felt was unfair, given the meager income he had earned at Gottlieb Harris.

"It's not right I have to pay taxes," Louis stated angrily. "You have plenty of money—you should pay this for me."

Herbert just laughed as he handed the letter back to Louis.

"That's ridiculous. Everyone pays taxes, and that includes you."

"Well, if that's the case, then I'm going to start billing you and mom for the time I spend here. My special rate for you will be $50 an hour, but I've already been here more than twenty-four hours, so you owe me more than a $1,000."

Herbert laughed even louder, but there was a harshness to his laugh. He rose and left the table to go into the garden room, where he sat in his favorite chair among the plants, next to the fireplace, and began to read the newspaper.

Not long before, Herbert had had a second heart attack, and he knew he should avoid an emotional confrontation with his eldest son.

Undeterred, Louis followed Herbert and continued his rant as to why he should be paid for his "legal services." When his father made it quite clear that he was not going to pay any of Louis's bills—or his taxes—and that he expected his son to get a *real* job now that he had passed the bar, Louis started yelling, calling his father a crook and a cheat.

Finally Herbert rose and made as if to strike Louis—something he had not done since his son was twelve.

This was all the provocation Louis had been waiting for. He seized Herbert by the neck, thrust him to the hard marble floor, and started beating his head against the marble.

He yelled more obscenities at his father, releasing resentment that had built up over his entire life.

"You son of a bitch, you never wanted me! You never loved me!"

The commotion brought Jane racing to the garden room, and she tried to separate them, but she simply wasn't strong enough to pull Louis away.

She ran to the phone and called the police, who arrived within minutes.

They found Herbert, semi-conscious on the marble floor and covered with blood, a distraught Jane holding a towel to his head.

The two officers pulled their guns and carefully searched the house. It didn't take long, and they cornered Louis in the garage, where he was hacking away at Herbert's Rolls-Royce with an axe.

Subduing him, they marched him off to jail as the ambulance arrived to take Herbert to the hospital.

※　　　※　　　※

Herbert had suffered a concussion, and it was several days before he could leave the hospital, but there seemed to be no permanent damage.

For the first time he had experienced directly the rage that had repeatedly been directed at Max, and he now realized that Louis wasn't just lazy and mean, but that he was dangerous.

Nonetheless when it came time for Louis's trial, Herbert couldn't bring himself to testify against his own son. A deal was worked out with the prosecutor, requiring Louis to spend thirty days in a mental treatment facility rather than go to jail. If after that time the doctors at the mental institution felt that he was competent to take care of himself, he would be released.

There was an added provision that, if released, Louis would be subject to a restraining order that covered the entire town of Greenwich, Connecticut, where Herbert and Jane were living. Since prior to this, Louis had never committed violence against anyone other than Max, they had no reason to think that he would cause any harm to others.

As long as there was no contact with them, Jane and Herbert hoped that perhaps Louis would find his way in life.

※　　　※　　　※

To everyone's surprise, Louis was a model patient while incarcerated in the mental institution, and at the end of the thirty days he was released.

It was clear to Jane that he was never going to find traditional work, let alone take advantage of his law degree. She felt tremendous guilt over his mental condition, and despite her son's brutal behavior, she insisted that Herbert set up a small trust fund for him so that he would be able to sustain himself. Jane hoped this would take some financial pressure off her son and perhaps allow him to find a modest career, which might keep him away from the family and out of trouble.

❋ ❋ ❋

When Max returned from his travels and learned of the events, he was openly relieved. Finally his father and mother understood Louis's violent nature and had taken some action to protect the family.

He felt sorry for Louis and actually loved him and wanted to help him, but at the same time he did not want to have any contact with him.

Max was still frightened that Louis might continue to erupt violently against him.

Disillusionment

1978

IT WAS WITH A SENSE OF RELIEF THAT MAX RETURNED TO HARVARD and what he thought would be praise from his professors and colleagues for his use of anthropology in his involvement in the creation of documentary films.

However, he was greatly disappointed to learn that his side-career did not sit well with his colleagues at the university. This popularization of science wasn't, in their eyes, serious scholarship. They felt that the recognition that Max was receiving was almost unseemly and not appropriate for a graduate student.

But just as Max's professors were becoming disenchanted with Max, he was becoming disenchanted with Harvard.

He was bored and in search of greater challenges.

❋ ❋ ❋

It didn't take long for the challenges to find Max. His father called and confided to him that the publishing company needed him. Herbert had backed out of the deal to sell to Perfect Films and had spurned all offers since. Herbert promised that if Max would agree to move to New York and run the editorial department, Herbert would attempt to buy his partner out and turn the company over to Max.

However, Herbert was adamant that Max gain more experience in the New York office before he made his move.

Max accepted and moved to New York City, but he quickly became disenchanted. Despite a new romantic entanglement that quickly became serious, he did not enjoy living in the city and didn't find the position particularly challenging.

Less than a year into his work with the editorial department, Max received a phone call inviting him to go around the world on behalf of yet another documentary feature. It was to be a twelve-week shoot, and he could write his own terms.

Based on the length of the gig, Max arranged to take a leave of absence.

No big deal, he thought. *It will all be here when I get back.*

❋   ❋   ❋

Unknown to Max, Herbert Doff suffered his third heart attack the day Max left for India and points unknown. This was a more serious heart attack than the previous two, and Herbert felt compelled to protect his family and sell the company to the highest bidder. By the time Max returned, the sale was complete.

For the first time in his life Max could choose his own destiny. It was liberating.

He tore up the three-year contract his father had negotiated for Max and moved to Hollywood to act as the associate producer on a major documentary film. After two weeks, he realized that he had made yet another mistake.

He hated his job.

As an associate producer, he was expected to ensure that the creative team remained productive and happy. That meant that if they wanted cocaine, Max was supposed to arrange to acquire the drug for them.

Max resigned on the spot.

He moved *back* to New York, but far from being liberated, he had no job and no direction.

He considered his options and decided that his best immediate alternative was to play poker in a dive bar in Soho on Saturday nights. Louis had taught Max how to play poker when they were quite young, and Max had gained additional poker experience in his travels with the various film crews. Max also had the gift of being able to visualize any card he needed. Somehow he simply willed a card to be the one he needed, and it seemed to appear.

Whether this was luck or something more, Max had always had an affinity for numbers. They'd been alive within him when he was a child and unable to speak. They were his playmates . . . his friends.

So poker was a natural for him.

❋　❋　❋

He would show up on Saturday around midnight for the weekend game. The stakes weren't particularly high, but there were always suburbanites out for the night who proved to be easy marks. They would drink too much and play loose hands.

They were there to have fun.

Max was there to make money.

Very few of the regulars were what could be called legitimate players. Frequently they found ways to team up or cheat in ways that wouldn't cause them to get caught. Thus, Max didn't get involved in hands with the regulars.

And there were enough tourists for Max to make his $200 or $300 every Saturday night, and that was all he needed each week to pay his rent, his gym fees, and food bills.

But none of this was satisfying—nor was it much of a career choice.

Max was at a crossroads.

He had bailed on Harvard, bailed on his father's publishing company, and even bailed on Hollywood. And another romantic relationship had ended badly.

❋   ❋   ❋

He had been engaged to Tina just before heading off for his twelve-week film project. While away, he had bought her a beautiful engagement ring in Damascus and exotic silks so that she could create a custom wedding dress.

There had been no date set nor a formal announcement, but Tina and Max were agreed that upon his return they would let the families know.

Unfortunately for Max, by the time he returned from the project, Tina had changed her mind about marriage altogether. She had started seeing a therapist to explore issues concerning past traumas that related to early childhood sexual molestation.

This, of course, came as a complete surprise to Max.

In the process of the therapy, the therapist had suggested that Tina abstain from sex until she could sort out her deeper feelings. She thought this was a good idea and announced to Max that she also felt that getting engaged—or even continuing the relationship—made no sense.

Max couldn't understand what had happened. They had seemed so happy together. Suddenly his fiancée was distant, and he hardly recognized the person she had become.

The magic in his life was gone, and Max was not certain how to get it back.

Once again he fell into a deep state of depression. He stopped eating, shaving, or even bathing. He slept for days. He was worn out and had lost perspective on who he was and what he wanted to do with his life.

In his eyes, there was little likelihood that he would ever reach the expectations to which he had aspired as a child. He was a disappointment to his father . . . to himself.

In the midst of this funk, he decided to write a novel that would reflect his present state, and he called it *Suicide Plus*. He crafted the opening line:

Sir Winston awoke to the sound of muffled screams . . .
his own.

The novel documented the daily struggle Max encountered with
his own thoughts of suicide. He began to write his feelings in erratic
bursts on an old typewriter his father had given him.

> I have reached the black edge of despair . . . I don't know
> who I am or what I want or what I can do or where I am
> going . . . I'm sick of self . . . no hope . . . must cash in this
> life . . . I want to abdicate.

He knew that death itself wasn't something to fear and longed to
return to the white light and bliss he had experienced in Dr. Gray's
office, back in 1965.

At the same time Max still believed that he had some kind of destiny that required him to remain alive. He decided to turn his fate
over to a higher power and wrote: *THY WILL BE DONE.*

He carried on writing and fighting against his suicidal tendencies.

The day Max finished his novel, a neighbor two floors above his
apartment leaped to his death. It was an act Max had contemplated
many times and had visualized for weeks. The reality of it stunned
him, and he wondered if his novel had been capturing his own destiny or someone else's.

❋　　❋　　❋

Louis reappeared in Max's life.

When he appeared at the front door, Max barely recognized him.
He was smelly, dirty, unshaven, and overweight with a potbelly.

He was grotesque.

Louis babbled incoherently about how everyone was breaking the law—especially his father and the lawyers at Gottlieb
Harris.

"You have no idea how rotten they are . . . and it's not just them. *Everyone's* breaking the law . . . *all* the laws. They're even starting to break the laws of gravity, and when that happens, you know we're all going to go to hell," Louis proclaimed, expecting Max to support his concerns.

But Max could only smile at the combination of intelligence and madness his brother exhibited. And it caused him to shudder, realizing that what his own existence had become wasn't much better.

So Max bought Louis a nice meal—perhaps the first he had had in a very long time. The entire time he hoped that Louis's insanity wouldn't erupt into violence and was very relieved when it did not.

Then he gave his brother a hug and suggested that he find a quiet place outside of New York City, where fewer people would be breaking the laws of gravity, and he would be safe.

Louis left, and Max wondered what would come next.

California

1979–1982

Max's poker playing days abruptly came to an end. It started with the worst toothache he had ever experienced.

The pain was excruciating, and try as he might, he couldn't avoid the fact that he was going to have to do something about it. As he was going into the dentist's office, he bumped into a former high-school classmate Peter Bohr, who was just leaving the office.

"Great to see you Max! How's tricks?" Peter asked as he grabbed Max's hand. "Still working for your old man?"

"Just hanging," Max replied through the pain. "My dad sold his company a few months back. Not sure what I'm going to do next, but I always looked up to you at Hackley. Give me your card, and let's catch up soon." Max grimaced as he spoke.

Indeed, Peter had gone to Hackley with Max but had graduated a year ahead of him. He'd been in charge of Max's first-semester study hall, was president of his class, and valedictorian. He had also been one of the school's top athletes.

"Absolutely—here's my card," Peter said enthusiastically. "I recently took over the business division for CRM Films. Give me a call—we should have lunch and continue to catch up."

❋   ❋   ❋

Max called, and before two weeks had passed, they met at a posh restaurant in Tribeca. Max told Peter about the films with which he had been involved, and before the meal was done, Peter had offered him the position of associate producer in charge of the West Coast offices of CRM Films.

"My father is the CEO, and we've been looking for someone with entrepreneurial instincts who knows the ins and outs of documentary films," he explained. "As improbable as it was, our meeting may turn out to be a break for both of us."

"Well, I do know documentary films," Max admitted, "and this is right up my alley.

"I accept," he said.

❋   ❋   ❋

With few loose ends to tie up, Max was soon living in Del Mar, California, enjoying the almost perfect weather and the complete autonomy he was given to run his division of CRM. Del Mar was a small community north of San Diego that was home to a racetrack made famous by such celebrities as Bing Crosby. Each year during racing season the town more than doubled in size.

Homes there were expensive, but Max's position paid well.

More important was the fact that his new position was enjoyable, and he felt productive for the first time in a long while. His office was manned by a sales manager with whom he shared an executive secretary. Each morning, twenty or thirty fresh film treatments were waiting for him, and it would only take him an hour to go through them, then select the ten or twelve that he thought had creative or commercial potential.

Max would take the treatments he had selected and walk across the hall to the sales manager's office. The atmosphere at CRM was very relaxed—every meeting was unscheduled and started the same.

"Frank, got a minute?"

Max would start describing each treatment that he had selected and ask key questions.

"If this is the best possible film on this topic, how many units would you be able to lay down in the initial distribution?" Though they were involved in a creative field, the sales were still the primary consideration.

In most cases, the answer was "not enough" or "not many," or sometimes "none," and those treatments were never looked at again.

Occasionally—once or twice a week—the answer would be different.

"We could lay down ten thousand or more units if the talent credentials check out."

So in those instances, if the right cast and crew were, indeed, attached to the project, and the concept was the best it could be—or at least within the realm of being made decent through good editing—Max would acquire the rights.

Often the process lasted through midafternoon at most, leaving Max most of the day to explore the beaches and hot tubs and other attractions of Southern California.

He did so, and before long he had met someone who had him utterly entranced. Weeks turned to months, and he pursued her with relish until she agreed to marry him. With that, Max's life was everything he could have envisioned.

He was efficient and successful. He started getting attention from the press, until he was written up in the *San Diego Tribune* and in *San Diego Magazine*, where his photo was spread over two pages.

"Brilliant young producer comes to San Diego," proclaimed the headline. San Diego was considered a sleepy town with military bases and some agriculture, leading many residents to resent its larger neighbor to the north, so they leaped at any opportunity to stand out. However, Max's fame came with a cost.

It didn't take long for his peers to become jealous of the attention he was receiving.

❋   ❋   ❋

CRM maintained several divisions, and the head of the general interest section, Bill Battely, was a competitive man. Max inadvertently poached one of his top experts to create a film on OPEC and the oil crisis, and Battely took particular offense.

Battely was hoping to move up to CEO when old man Bohr—Peter's father—finally retired. This Max kid was getting too much press and having private dinners with "the chairman," as Bohr senior was known.

A story appeared in the press in which Max was incorrectly given credit for CRM's top-grossing film, *Free to Choose*, by famed economist Milton Friedman. The reporter had been hoping to gain favor with Max, yet the only reason the film had been produced by CRM was the personal relationship between old man Bohr and Dr. Friedman.

Battely leapt upon the opportunity and sent the article—along with four or five others about Max—to the chairman, along with a simple note.

> You might want to look into this.

Max was fired. William Bohr had his son Peter make the call and sent along a personal message:

> If we were back in the old country, we would throw you in the brig. But since this is civilian life we can only take away your stripes. We will pay you through the end of the year but have everything packed and gone by the end of business today.

Max was in shock.

He had done nothing wrong and had signed up more than thirty titles in the eighteen months he had worked for the company.

He was advised by industry colleagues that he could sue CRM for wrongful termination, but that wasn't Max's style.

In a bizarre twist of events, the day before he was fired, Max's fiancée ended their engagement, and Max was left crushed on all fronts. He was so devastated by the sudden end of his engagement that he was in too much shock to even analyze what getting fired really meant to him.

When in the next few days he did think it over, he realized that he didn't really want to work for anyone—even with a sweetheart situation such as he had had with CRM.

He wanted to live life on his own terms.

So as far as he was concerned, he was once again free to create his own destiny.

※　　※　　※

Max had no money, so he would need to start small.

He made arrangements to use the local cable television equipment to produce a "how-to" video in the style of the popular Jane Fonda workout videos and thus was born MAXimum Productions. He teamed up with the creator of the *Del Mar Workout* at the local gym and thought it was a catchy name and a good workout—ideal for the Jane Fonda market.

His greatest problem was that he didn't have Jane Fonda—or any celebrity, for that matter—associated with the Del Mar Workout, so when he took the rough cut to a distributor, he was told that they could take five hundred units to test it, but they were pessimistic.

Max needed a minimum order of five thousand units just to break even. At five hundred units he would lose $2.00 on every tape and didn't have any capital to make up the difference. It appeared as if MAXimum productions would never get off the ground.

While pondering his options, Max received a phone call from a neighbor Andy Kay, who had an intriguing new idea.

"Max, I remember from one of our dinners that you said you know test preparation training from the days you worked with your dad's publishing company."

Max didn't know what he was getting at, but he was interested.

"Yes, that's true. What's on your mind?"

"My pet project here at Nonlinear Systems has been to develop a machine I call the 'tutor-computer,' designed to help students improve their vocabularies. I've long been a fan of Johnson O'Connor's work and believe that vocabulary improvement is the most important educational goal for everyone.

"Would you consider helping me out with this project, as an outside part-time consultant?" Andy asked eagerly.

"Absolutely," Max replied and added, "I can start immediately." Once again, synchronicity seemed to present him with an ideal work opportunity, just when he needed it most.

He served as project director and marketing manager, in return for a percentage of future sales. They got to work immediately and moved ahead at a rapid pace.

Two months into the tutor-computer project, one of Andy's engineers developed what became known as the KayPro computer— immediately the second most popular portable computer in the world after the Osborne, which it was soon outselling.

Work continued on the tutor computer, but it was no longer a priority. The KayPro took off, and Andy's little company soared from $2 million in annual sales to $250 million.

Suddenly there were dozens of technical writers and computer consultants on staff. When these writers learned of Max's background and connections, they asked him to help them create "how-to" training films.

Overnight MAXimum Productions had morphed into a thriving training film company, featuring some of the best technical talent in the world. Max was intrigued by the advances in technology and the high-tech world. He wasn't technically oriented himself, but he soon figured out how to determine which films were likely to be popular. And in a training world that didn't know a DOS from a CMP, or Lotus from WordPerfect, Max was considered a technical guru.

Gone were his ambitions to produce "real films," or do anything other than play golf, date beautiful women, and generally enjoy the California lifestyle.

❀ ❀ ❀

The years passed without Max encountering any more of the twelve names. It was almost as if Maria, Yutsky, B.N. Sharma, and Yoko had been part of a dream life.

With the exception of the one improbable name—Running Bear—they would have been easy to discount as an illusion, born of a near-death trauma.

But one by one, they had appeared to him, so that he could no longer shrug them off. Neither could he explain them, though.

And yet . . . *Running Bear?*

As absurd as it seemed, there had to be an explanation.

❀ ❀ ❀

Every few months he would receive word—usually from his parents—of an incident that had resulted in Louis being taken to a mental facility for observation, only to be released within the mandated thirty days.

He knew the routine. His brother would take his medication while incarcerated but would stop as soon as he was released.

One time, after an incident that had led to a short period of institutionalization, Louis actually showed up in California. He was still smelly, dirty, and speaking loudly and only semi-coherently. Max felt sorry for him and arranged for Louis to stay at the Marriott Hotel where he could get a good night's rest and clean up.

They met there for lunch the next day, and Max offered to pay for Louis to stay another night.

"Oh, no—the hotel's much too expensive," Louis protested. "I won't stay there. I can just sleep in my car in the parking lot and save all that money."

Max was appalled.

"But it's my money," he countered, "and I don't mind paying." But before he could continue, Louis interrupted him.

"No! I like to save my money. I'll be fine in the car." With that they parted and agreed to meet at a diner the following day.

The next morning Max went to the Marriott parking lot to look for Louis but couldn't find him. Nor was he in a room.

Several hours later, when they met for dinner, Max asked Louis where he had slept.

"I saw a Motel 6 down the street, so I parked my car and slept in it there instead. The Marriott was much too expensive."

"But the Marriot parking lot would have been free as well," Max asserted. "There's no difference."

"You don't understand anything about money." Louis insisted, and his voice took on a tone Max didn't like. "The Marriott would have been more expensive, and with what I saved, we can afford a good dinner."

Max let it drop, and they enjoyed a quiet meal.

Despite the years of youthful beatings, he couldn't help but feel sorrow. As they ate, Max came up with what he hoped would be a solution, and suggested a psychiatrist to treat Louis. He made a deal that he would provide a monthly stipend, above and beyond what Louis received from their parents, provided the doctor could confirm on a weekly basis that he was taking his medication.

Louis agreed, and the treatments began. At the same time he became an avid gambler and a regular at the famous Del Mar Race Track. He was good at it, too, and winning regularly so that he didn't need to take the extra money from Max.

After two months Louis stopped seeing the psychiatrist and went off his medication. Like all the Doffs, food was one of his primary delights, and his excuse was that the medication upset his stomach, interfered with the taste of the food, and made him feel groggy and less alive.

Max warned him that the payments would stop if he didn't resume taking his medication, but with Louis's newfound income, the threat had little weight.

Louis responded by writing a long letter accusing Max of illegal activities. He said that he was going to report Max to the IRS and the FBI.

Soon thereafter he disappeared altogether, and Max lost track of his whereabouts. Through some discreet inquiries, he heard rumors that Louis had adopted a nomadic lifestyle—living in his car, spending summers in Michigan and winters in Tennessee and Florida.

Louis would rent a room when he felt the need for a shower and a bed but mostly just seemed to live out of his car at campsites, Motel 6 parking lots, and horse racing events.

＊　　＊　　＊

It was shortly after reconnecting with Louis that Max's mother, Jane, was diagnosed with cancer. The tumor was located on the left side of her brain, exactly where the trauma of her car accident had been most severe.

Jane struggled with radiation and chemotherapy treatments for close to two years, but when she lost her ability to speak or move she handed Max—who had flown back to Greenwich for a final visit—a short note.

I am ready to enter the light.

Within two days she was gone.

Max helped his dad organize the funeral and a special memorial service for Jane. Louis was neither invited nor banned, though Herbert did confess that Jane secretly believed the ongoing heartache over her son's erratic behavior had hastened the onset of her illness.

In any event, neither Max nor Herbert had any way of contacting Louis, so they couldn't invite him to the funeral—even if they had wanted to—and they couldn't inform him of his mother's death.

Grace

1979–1984

W HILE HIS FILM CAREER WAS PROVING TO BE A REAL ROLLER-coaster ride, his love life turned out to be similarly dramatic . . . and unpredictable.

Grace Bradley was the first woman Max had met after moving to San Diego. He ran into her at a "residents only" swimming pool in the exclusive Sea Point Village condominiums in Del Mar, where he was living. She was swimming laps, and the moment she got out of the pool, Max knew he was in love. She was blonde and possessed the finest legs he had ever seen. In his eyes, she was his absolute ideal.

He followed her into the hot tub.

Her eyes laughed as if she did not have a care in the world, and her voice was as sweet as any music he had ever heard.

"Well if you aren't the most crooked swimmer I have ever met," Grace said, laughing. "Or were you just trying to bump into me on purpose?"

"I'm just directionally challenged, I guess," Max replied, and he smiled back. "Though I'm awfully glad I bumped into you. You're probably the most beautiful woman I've ever met."

That caused her to smile even more broadly, and he was entranced.

"I don't see a ring on your finger," he said. "I hope that means you're single."

"I am single, but don't get any ideas. I'm just coming out of a divorce, and I promised myself I wouldn't start dating again for at least six months," Grace responded, her blue eyes glittering in the sunlight.

"Well, we don't need to date, but I hope we can become friends," Max said. "I just moved in yesterday and hardly know a soul in Sea Point."

"I have lots of friends, and I'll be glad to be on your informal welcoming committee," she said cheerfully. "My mother back in Iowa raised me to be part of the Junior League, and even though everyone here in California seems so laid-back, I still believe in honoring social obligations.

"I'll introduce you around, and in a week or two you'll realize I'm just one of many beauties living here in Sea Point."

At thirty-three, Max was enjoying the freedom of being single in San Diego at a time when most women in their twenties thought nothing of having sex on the first date. So while he waited for Grace, he could still have all the sex he wanted with the many available and attractive women he was meeting at film festivals and through his new California friends.

❀   ❀   ❀

Yet Grace was wrong, as far as he was concerned. Even after six months, Grace was far more than just one of many beauties—she was the one he was destined to marry.

❀   ❀   ❀

After nine months of dating, Max proposed and Grace accepted.

She was still the woman of his dreams. He would beam with happiness when he was with her, pinching himself to convince himself that it was real—that he would soon have this perfect mate.

Her greatest interest was in *Get Real*, a New Age meditation regimen started in California by a fellow named Harold Henderson. It seemed strange to Max, but he didn't give it much thought as long as it made Grace happy.

And Max had to admire success. Harold didn't seem to have much going for him, yet by teaching meditation he had—in essence—created his own cult.

People would pay good money for the meditation classes, and Harold ended up having as many women to sleep with as he wanted. Though he was in his sixties, he spread rumors that he was over one hundred years old, and that the meditation techniques had given him perpetual youth. To keep his "chi," he claimed, he needed to sleep with younger women.

The majority of his young disciples thought it was an honor to be chosen to help keep him young.

Grace, being from Iowa, was relatively conservative. So despite practicing the meditation, she had never slept with Harold and claimed that she never intended to do so. She believed in sex *within* marriage, she said flatly, yet she also believed in *Get Real* meditation.

Grace was clearly under Harold's spell.

When Harold had learned that Grace was engaged to Max, Harold had suggested that she align herself with a more advanced *Get Real* practitioner.

He introduced Grace to Stephen, who was a "third-level" student. Grace had been meditating for nine years, so she had risen all the way to the "fourth level." There was much she could teach Stephen, Harold explained, and in doing so she herself would rise higher in the ranks.

In addition to being a third, Stephen was a multimillionaire real estate developer. Max at the time was earning an associate producer's salary of $40,000 a year and could not compete.

Grace returned the ring to Max. Within three months she was engaged to Stephen. There was nothing Max could do.

He was devastated.

*   *   *

The day after Grace broke off their engagement, Max was fired from CRM.

He was distraught over losing Grace and for a long time, despite the impracticality of the situation, he refused to give up hope of reuniting with her.

Before long, however, MAXimum productions was formed, and he had no time for anything but work. It was a blessing in disguise, really—intellectual and emotional synchronicity at work, though from his position in the midst of the drama, he didn't realize it.

Indeed, it would be ten years before he began to form the full picture.

A Return to Grace

1994

M AX RECEIVED A CALL FROM MEG PERKINS, ONE OF GRACE'S closest friends.

He hadn't stayed in touch with Grace or any of the *Get Real* groupies, but enough time had passed that he agreed to meet with Meg, who was an actress.

She drove down from Los Angeles to ask Max's advice about films and to pitch him a concept she wanted to develop. He explained politely that the concept she was proposing was good but not the kind of material he handled.

Then an afterthought struck him.

"By the way, whatever happened to Grace?" he asked nonchalantly, though he realized that the old wounds hadn't entirely healed. "I heard she had moved away. Is she still with Stephen?"

"Oh no," Meg replied, shaking her head vehemently. "That marriage lasted only three years. Grace moved up to Portland and is selling real estate. In fact, she's coming down next week to a business conference. I am sure she'd love to see you if you have the time."

Max wasn't sure how he felt about Meg's revelation, but curiosity beat out common sense, and he said that he would like to see her. Meg agreed to set it up.

※　　※　　※

Two days later Max was sitting at his desk looking out at the ocean from his second-floor office in the MAXimum building. He had bought the building for the view and spent most of the day on the phone while watching surfers, dolphins, migrating whales, and other attractions of the beach.

He was shocked out of his reverie by a female presence behind him who placed her hands over his eyes.

It was Grace. He could tell without even hearing her voice.

He could feel her energy. He heard her laugh as she removed her hands, and when he turned around to face her, he was amazed to see a woman now nearly forty who hadn't aged even a day in ten years.

Maybe that Get Real stuff really works after all, he mused, but he didn't say it aloud.

They chatted for a while, and to Max it felt a lot like his near-death experience. He knew it was him doing half of the talking, but it was like watching himself from a distance, as he asked her out to lunch.

※　　※　　※

Within three months Grace and Max were again engaged to be married.

He invited one hundred of his closest friends and associates to Aruba, in the Caribbean Sea, and celebrated a three-day wedding that included golf outings, boat outings, traditional feasts, and tuxedoed guests dancing to big band music at the Brickell Bay Hotel, rented just for the occasion.

Grace had really done her homework and had incorporated many traditional island elements into the activities. She had a great aesthetic sense, and with Max's ability to provide an unlimited budget, the wedding met all expectations . . . but one.

* * *

Even before the ceremony, Max had a feeling he was making a mistake. In fact, he had decided to consult several friends and psychics—as well as the minister who was to marry them—and they all were of the opinion that it would be a mistake for him to marry Grace. Yet once again, Max allowed his heart to supersede his brain.

"If it doesn't work out, we can just get a divorce," he said, trying to sound cavalier. He was caught up in the romanticism of the occasion and the fact that this beautiful woman, who had remained in his heart for ten years, was going to be his wife. He saw her as a deeply spiritual life partner, with high aspirations for mankind and the desire to create a community where the leading spiritual teachers and minds of the century could come together.

This, Max was certain, was to be the marriage that would give his life purpose.

The Tibetan Miracle

1996

I T WAS TWO SUMMERS AFTER THE WEDDING, AND MAX'S MARRIED bliss was already teetering.

Ever since she had returned to California, Grace had made it clear that this wasn't where she wanted to be. Her dream home, she explained, was an estate in Virginia, and she constantly pressured him to move. But this was where MAXimum Productions was based, and it was Max's company that kept her in the lifestyle to which she had become accustomed.

Despite her continued activities as a meditation teacher, Grace was the most self-absorbed person he had ever met. She had little-to-no interest in his career, and the things that fascinated him.

He tried to tell her about the Twelve, and she always started out interested, then feigned the need to do something very important. If he mentioned it again later, she had no idea what he was talking about.

She decided to go to Jackson Hole, Wyoming, for a special retreat at the ashram of the only blue-eyed Tibetan nun in the world. The nun was Agatha Winright, who at age nineteen had gone to Tibet and been ordained. A few years later she realized that the celibate life wasn't for her, found a compatible spiritual partner, married, and had four wonderful children, all while maintaining her Tibetan Buddhist practices.

She eventually raised enough money to purchase a four-hundred-acre tract of land outside Jackson Hole and founded Mandala Mandala as a retreat center for spiritual students. Agatha had announced that a famous Tibetan monk would be giving a special class at the end of August. This monk was six foot two inches tall—almost a foot taller than the average Tibetan. It was rumored that he had magical powers and could put his hand through boulders.

This was the kind of spiritual teacher Grace longed to meet, so she signed up immediately. She encouraged Max to participate, as well, but he was resistant.

She told him that she didn't want to nag him into attending the retreat, but instead handed him a little blue book with the title *Dzogchen Meditation*. Max opened it up and read the first sentence.

The goal of meditation is not to meditate.

"Well, that's a nice change," he said wryly. "I might actually read this book."

But Grace was undeterred.

"I think you'll have a totally different take on meditation if you join me on the retreat," she said.

Max wasn't convinced, but he wanted to keep his wife happy and to show her that he was open-minded—if not eager—to learn a new discipline.

So, he paid the registration fee and soon he was headed to Jackson Hole with Grace to learn this meditation that would guide him toward not meditating. She tried to explain that the goal of not meditating was in essence to be meditating all the time, in every conscious and unconscious moment—what the Buddhists called mindfulness.

Eventually she gave up, but still Grace was ecstatic.

"I'm so glad you decided to come," she cooed. "You're going to love this retreat."

Landing in Wyoming, they picked up a rental car at the airport and drove to the retreat center. It was hot and dusty, and the final three miles of road were unpaved, rutted, and challenging, even in their luxury car.

Max hadn't been paying much attention to the accommodations, which he assumed would be rustic, and as they arrived, he saw signs that pointed toward campsites, and realization set in.

Max wasn't the camping type—he had never set up a tent in his life. It was almost seven in the evening by the time they arrived and getting dark. Except for the flashlight that Grace had brought, there was no light.

Apparently the entire site was electricity-free.

Grace remained undaunted as she selected a campsite and directed Max in the proper way to erect a tent.

❊   ❊   ❊

An hour later, frustrated and irritable, he and Grace joined the rest of the group in the main building, where the meditation classes were to be held. A warm-up meditation was about to begin, and Max and Grace were given pillows and told to follow along.

Fortunately for Max, it was a short, fifteen-minute sampler. Everyone else in the room had been meditating for five years or more, and after the session, everyone was asked to introduce themselves and express their goals for the retreat.

Most of the meditators were hoping to elevate their practices to the next level. Many felt they were close to reaching nirvana, or at least a state in which they had no attachment to their bodies or their senses or any thoughts related to normal human activity—something they called "Samadhi."

Max was last, and when it came his turn to reveal his goals, he spoke frankly.

"I'm really just here to accompany my wife, Grace," he admitted. "I know nothing about meditation, but she has been meditating for twenty years, and this is important to her. So here I am."

This didn't seem to sit too well with his new classmates, and from what he could gather, the retreat was only for advanced students. Many of them felt as if Max had slipped in as the spouse of an advanced student—it was rare that an advanced practitioner would be married to anyone who wasn't similarly advanced or at least highly motivated.

Max resented the fact that he was being judged in this way. He saw it in the faces of the people around him—these so-called advanced students. It reminded him of the spiritual leaders he had met on his travels who refused to accept those who were different.

It was okay if you agreed with the doctrine they were practicing, he noted, but if not, your value as an individual was diminished. He hated the hypocrisy of it all and realized that was why he had never embraced any particular religious belief system. Max was on his own path of discovery and didn't want to be distracted from the truth of who he was and the discovery of his true purpose.

The next person to speak was Agatha herself, the organizer and founder of the retreat center. She looked from one person to the next, engaging each with the kind of calmness that came from thirty years of meditating, and started speaking.

"We've had a change of instructors for the week," she admitted. "I realize most of you came specifically for the opportunity to meet and meditate with Tulku Hanka. Unfortunately, the Chinese government has denied him the visa he needed to leave China, and he is unable to join us."

A murmur rippled through the crowd, and she waited for it to subside, then continued.

"Tulku Rinpoche Chiba, founder of the Turquoise Convent in Nepal, will be taking his place. Tulku Chiba was coming anyway, since he was scheduled to perform the ceremonies to dedicate the new stupa, which will be finished this week. Tulku Chiba is the foremost authority on stupa ceremonies in the world."

While he understood "Turquoise Convent," he still couldn't quite make out the names of the persons who seemed so very important to the crowd. Since there was no difference among them, as far as he was concerned, he just shrugged it off.

"He is also a great teacher," Agatha continued, "so I hope you will find the retreat just as rewarding as if Tulku Hanka had been able to attend."

Max had learned about stupa ceremonies when he was working on *In Search of the Historical Jesus*. A stupa was a round structure filled with sacred articles, such as pictures of the Buddha and relics made by monks, around which devoted Buddhists would circumambulate while making their prayers.

It was believed that a stupa was the physical representation of the Buddha on Earth, and actually drew Buddha's energy to itself, then passed it along to those who financed, built, maintained, and paid homage to it, as well as to those who prayed around it.

Despite her entreaties, the news that Tulku Hanka was unable to attend did not go over well with the attendees. They had paid good money and flown from all over the country specifically to meet with the tall monk of miracles.

This Tulku Chiba was no miracle monk.

Grace was the most vocal in expressing her disappointment.

"This really isn't right," she said loudly. "I came in part to interview Tulku Hanka for a book I intend to write. You should have let us know before we arrived.

"We'll stay," she continued, "but it's more than disappointing."

A rumble of agreement spread throughout the crowd, but before Agatha could respond, her husband walked into the retreat room and drew everyone's attention.

"Who owns a car with license plate 4G 18VR?" he asked, speaking over the hubbub. "It's parked on the campsite, and all cars must be

parked in the special parking area only. This is sacred land and eco-
logically delicate. We must all honor it, so whoever owns that car,
please move it immediately."

The car belonged to Grace and Max, so off they went, and she
was able to fume all the way back to the campsite, then from the
campsite to the parking area, and then back to the tent.

It was past eleven by the time they returned and complaints or
not, there was nothing left to do but go to sleep.

❄   ❄   ❄

The next morning the teacher, or Rinpoche, as he was called throughout the retreat, arrived at the camp. He was a well-built man with a
buzz cut and sharp Tibetan features and was dressed in a purple robe.

Rinpoche spoke only Tibetan—not a word of English—so he
came with his own translator.

The sessions did not run on time, but once Max got used to the
delays, the classes were more or less like any other college class.
Much to his surprise, he found it amazingly interesting—at least on
par with the best classes he had attended at Harvard and Yale. It was
the first time since he had been banned from taking philosophy
courses at Yale that he was genuinely stimulated by a professor.

Rinpoche, however, was better than the Yale professors. He didn't
merely ask questions such as: What is the shape of the universe? Or,
what color is the universe? He also had the answers. But rather than
simply reciting his own opinions, he seemed intensely curious to
hear what people in the group thought.

Most of the attendees wouldn't even volunteer an answer, but
Max was used to participating . . . and being right. For some reason
he said, he thought the universe was blue.

When he gave this answer, he was told that he was wrong and
that he should go outside into the surrounding forest and meditate
on the correct answer. He was told that Rinpoche would send for
him when enough time had passed.

Max ended up spending more time in the forest than all the rest of the meditators combined.

He envisioned the universe shaped as a double helix. According to Rinpoche he was wrong.

Out to the forest he went.

He began to feel as if going to the forest was like wearing the dunce cap back in second grade and sitting on the stool in the corner of Miss Montaldo's second-grade classroom where the other children would snicker.

But these meditators didn't snicker, though some couldn't help but smile at the frequency of his trips.

Nonetheless, this was serious business for the participants, and they *did* seem to appreciate that Max was engaged. Grace never went to the forest because she never volunteered any answers to Rinpoche's questions, nor did most of the group. The nature of the teaching didn't require being called upon, and no grades were being given out—other than the grade each participant might give himself or herself on the road to enlightenment.

✳ ✳ ✳

Max learned many things, including the fact that their teacher had a wonderful sense of humor.

At the age of three, Rinpoche had been annointed as the lineage carrier of a great monastery in Tibet. At the age of six he was recognized as a tulku—or high priest—of a neighboring monastery. This was most unusual, since such appointments meant being discovered as the reincarnation of a past tulku, much as the dalai lamas are selected. It was rare indeed to be selected twice, as the reincarnation of two different enlightened souls, but apparently the Buddhist path allowed for such exceptional occurrences.

Even rarer, from Rinpoche's perspective, was that both lineages he represented had enjoyed more than five hundred years of uninterrupted autonomy, then came crumbling down during his reign.

He was only fifteen when the Chinese—who had already invaded Tibet—decided to imprison all lamas and put them in the highest security prisons, in essence work camps situated in deep forested regions, where the prisoners were compelled to cut timber all day and then be tortured at night. The only other prisoners in the camps were murderers and others who had been condemned to death.

The guards came in the middle of the night and chose a lama or murderer, and more often than not the individual would never appear again. In the few cases when they *were* returned, they had been brutally beaten. Yet it would only be a matter of time before these tortured prisoners would be taken out again for questioning, and after every second questioning, they never returned.

"I actually was grateful to the Chinese for my incarceration," Rinpoche explained through his translator. "It was like being in the highest lama university in the world. The Chinese had gathered up the wisest lamas from all over Tibet, and I learned from all of them. I was young and strong, and one of the best workers. So I remained low on the list of those to be tortured and executed.

"But of course, nothing was certain," he continued. "When I meditated, I was able to meditate on the nature of impermanence in a way that I might never have experienced without the very real awareness that I might be killed in any instant."

After fourteen years of hard labor, Rinpoche said, he had been released and made his way to Nepal, where he created a monastery for female nuns—mostly refugees from Tibet, many of whom had been beaten and raped by the Chinese conquerors. It was there that he had met Agatha and was invited to perform his sacred rituals for the dedication of the stupa.

He was from a lineage of Dzogchen Buddhists, who had combined the teachings of the Bon people—a shamanic tribe that existed in the mountains—with the teachings of Padmasambhava, the great Tibetan Buddhist master and founder of the religion. The Bon people had existed centuries before the Buddha, and were believed to have magical powers. The goal of Dzogchen Meditation was to be able to take "rainbow-body"—a designation used when a soul fulfilled the all-knowing, and could take any form at any time.

This was much like reaching a state of nirvana, but more colorful in that the subject was able to reincarnate at will as any entity or substance the soul might choose, whether as a bird, a mountain, a stream, a stone, an animal, another human, or the rainbow itself.

✳   ✳   ✳

On the fifth day of classes it was time for the stupa dedication itself. The interpreter asked everyone to gather round and told the students that while everyone would participate in the chants, Rinpoche was going to need an assistant to help him with the ceremonies. This would be a great honor.

Max was the only one there who had no attachment to being chosen. Whether Rinpoche knew this or not, he ended up choosing Max.

While he still didn't feel Rinpoche was enlightened, Max had come to like and respect Rinpoche. He had a disciplined work ethic that had him up at 4:00 A.M., giving private consultations, then teaching from 8:00 A.M. until 6:00 P.M., Most evenings he performed rituals in meditation huts, sheds, and cottages spread across the four-hundred-acre retreat center.

Max also liked the fact that Rinpoche was a confirmed meat-eater. He had mutton at almost every meal—usually in a nice curry with rice and vegetables—but always meat and a lot of it. This was refreshing for Max and somewhat amusing since Grace and most of her fellow vegetarian friends thought meat-eaters were automatically condemned to one of the inner circles of hell.

For two full days, Max served as a kind of sorcerer's apprentice. He would hold the tray upon which the sacred rice was placed, and hand sacred objects to Rinpoche, who would toss them among the gathering of students as he dedicated the objects to different sacred gods and goddesses.

When it came time for the lengthy recitation of precise rituals, it was Max who would turn the pages on the ancient scrolls, and many times a single ritual encompassed twenty or more pages, taking an hour or more to recite.

After each break, Max assumed that his time was done, but each and every time Rinpoche sought Max out. Before long he was caught up in the pageantry of the ceremonies. Time seemed to stand still during these rituals, and strange cloud formations would appear in the sky.

The attendees were convinced that the clouds were in the shape of the Buddha and were a sign that he was present. Max was less certain, but he *did* find a sense of familiarity in assisting Rinpoche, and even without words, he had a sense that they had formed a bond for life.

He still couldn't meditate for more than twenty minutes without becoming seriously bored though.

※　※　※

When the ceremonies were completed, there was a great feast in which every kind of food—sweet and sour—was presented to the group, along with wines and other beverages. The theme of the feast was "one taste," reflecting the concept that all is equal and that they shouldn't prefer one food over another.

They weren't supposed to look at the food on the plate, which servers kept refilling. There were no utensils, so each person would simply grab whatever he or she first touched. Max might find a sweet cookie in his hand along with a vegetable concoction of some kind or other unidentifiable delicacy. It was an adventure of sorts, and he enjoyed every minute of it.

Toward the end of the feast Agatha Winright came over to Max and asked him if he had scheduled his private consult with Rinpoche. When he said that he hadn't, she was surprised.

"No? Well, you really should," she said, smiling broadly. "Everyone else has already had their private consult. You were an excellent assistant, and I don't want you to miss out."

※　※　※

The next morning at 8:00, everyone gathered in the great hall for the final wrap-up session. Before the meditation chants began, the interpreter asked on behalf of Rinpoche if there was anyone in the room who had not already "taken refuge." This referred to the act of accepting a special Tibetan name that would allow the recipient access to Padmasambhava during meditation and a chance— infinitesimal though it might be—of achieving enlightenment and rainbow-body.

Except for Max, everyone in the room had already "taken refuge," so he was called to the front of the room. In a quick fifteen-minute ceremony he was given refuge, and Rinpoche slipped him a piece of paper on which was written his new Tibetan name.

Max immediately lost the paper and never learned to pronounce his Tibetan name. However, he was told that it meant "diamond" and signified a pure thinker of strength and brilliance.

Then there was one more order of business before the meditation could begin: Rinpoche had brought with him from Tibet a special black herb, which he passed around the room. His interpreter told everyone that the herb had been planted by ancient Tibetan lamas in gardens tended for centuries by monks. The special energy and blessing the monks and lamas had placed in the herb enhanced the spiritual journeys of all who consumed the herb.

Each person took a tiny portion of no more than a gram and chewed or swallowed it. Since everyone else seemed to find this business as usual, Max followed suit and swallowed the herb.

He didn't notice anything particularly strange, but he *was* surprised to discover that for the first time he was able to endure a two-hour meditation without becoming completely bored or preoccupied with work and other more practical issues.

When the meditation ended, and everyone else was saying their goodbyes, Max headed down to Rinpoche's private campsite for his private consultation. Both the teacher and his interpreter were already waiting.

The interpreter started the session.

"Rinpoche wants to know what you seek and if he can be of help to you," she said.

"I actually seek nothing," Max replied honestly. "But I do wonder why the world is full of so much violence and hatred and why so many people suffer."

When his comment was translated, Rinpoche thought a moment and then replied.

"Just love everyone as if they were all your children," the translator instructed. "In this way you will begin to understand that what you see as violence and hatred is simply hurt children acting out. There is no permanence to such behavior."

Rinpoche then gave Max a picture of himself and a business card, so that Max could write to him if he had future questions. He thanked Max for assisting him and then went back into his tent to pack for his departure.

On the way back to his own campsite, Max found a strange sense of awareness creeping over him. He started to feel that the trees and plants were alive in a more vivid way than he had ever felt before. Next he began to feel a sense of communion with the rocks and even the ground upon which he was walking.

It all seemed very strange but pleasant—almost as if all boundaries between Max and all other matter had begun to fade away.

Could this be Samadhi, he wondered abstractly.

When he arrived, he found that Grace had already taken down the tent.

"I've got everything packed and ready to go," she said. "All you have to do is bring the car around. We have forty-five minutes to get to the airport, so let's get moving." Her crisp instructions broke into Max's moment of acute awareness, and he did as she asked.

It wasn't until Max was sitting on the plane from Wyoming to California that he actually looked at Rinpoche's business card. The top of the card displayed simple yet elegant letters.

Turquoise Monastery Xan Nepal

Below that appeared a name.

Rinpoche Gyuatma Chiba

Max had not really been paying much attention the first night of the retreat, when Agatha had announced that Tulku Chiba was replacing Tulku Hanka.

Now, as Max looked at the name "Gyuatma Chiba," he knew with startling clarity that Rinpoche was one of the Twelve.

He leaned back in his seat and let it sink in. Finally, he turned to his wife and spoke.

"My God, Grace . . . " he murmured. "Rinpoche is one of the Twelve."

"The Twelve?" she responded. "The Twelve? What are you talking about?"

"The twelve names revealed to me during my near-death experience, when I was fifteen," Max said, irritation rising up in him.

"Oh, that old story," she replied dismissively. "I thought you'd given up on that years ago. You said that after meeting the first four, it was just a dead end, and no rhyme or reason or connection between the four you did find."

"That's true, but this changes everything—Rinpoche is one of the Twelve!" he said, excitement brushing aside his irritability. "Maybe I abandoned the quest too soon."

To his chagrin, Grace just adjusted her special neck brace and the pillows she took on every flight.

"Well, that's very nice, Max," she said. "Now, I didn't get much sleep last night, and I need to take a nap. You can tell me all about it when we get home."

Max just stared at her, then gave up and tried to read a newspaper.

But he couldn't stop thinking about Rinpoche and the unbidden return of the Twelve to his life. Without any distractions, he drifted back into the altered state he had experienced earlier in the day.

His senses seemed to expand again, and he could see the connections that linked everything around him, whether animate or inanimate. Everything seemed alive, seemed to have consciousness—even the ink on the newspaper he was reading.

The negative feelings he had been experiencing melted away, and Max felt nothing but love and compassion. There was a story in the newspaper about a young girl who had been raped, and his feelings extended, not only to the girl, but also to the ink that was trapped forever in this story about rape.

To him, it seemed as if the ink itself was experiencing the horror contained in the words it formed, and that the consciousness of the ink would never be released from that horror until the paper itself disintegrated.

It was in this state that Max recognized his life purpose. He was, indeed, destined to pursue the Twelve. He didn't know why, and he didn't know how. He had no idea how the Twelve were actually connected.

But he did know that he had to find them.

The Chinese Sun

1996–2001

MAXimum Productions continued to flourish, to the point that Max didn't need to be on hand to make all of the decisions. So soon he found himself living outside of Charlottesville, Virginia, on Grace's dream estate.

Summit Farms had been built in 1908 by the Du Pont family at the same time they had purchased and renovated James Madison's birthplace of Montpelier. Summit was even grander than Montpelier, having been built in the traditional southern style with large columns supporting the entrance to the three-story, twelve-thousand-square-foot mansion.

At the time it was built it was among the most beautiful homes in the United States and certainly the most fortified. The walls were three-feet thick and built to last. There was a three thousand foot, two-story library that Max converted to his office. Grace had her own wing, as well, and there were five guest bedrooms and a converted servants quarter on the third floor.

The basement boasted a billiard room, wine cellar, washing area, and an ancient kitchen harking back to the original custom of using a dumbwaiter and pulley system to deliver the food to the upstairs dining rooms.

There was a full, three-story high ballroom that allowed up to two hundred couples to dance without being crowded, with balconies built above the dance floor to house the musicians.

Max liked the house, but Grace loved it. To guarantee her future there, he put the property in her name. And she took to it with relish.

She went to auctions at Sotheby's and Christie's and found chandeliers from the original period, along with antiques and rugs and dining tables and knickknacks and statues that she thought would accent the home's natural beauty.

Max's friends commented that the house seemed too large for just two people, but Max explained that he liked to entertain and that their home gave Grace an outlet for her aesthetic creativity. Her plan was to turn the two-hundred-acre horse farm into a winery. She would convert the original carriage house to a fully functioning office building, fortify the bridge that crossed the creek on the mile-long driveway that led to the main home, refurbish some of the barns and other outbuildings, add a modern indoor horse training ring, and install a three-acre lake to replace the corn field that lay between the back woods and the main house.

It would be good "feng shui," she told Max.

He had almost nothing to do except pay the bills. Grace hired housekeepers, farm managers, and building managers. The house was always teeming with people, and all in all it was quite a circus. Max would just retreat to his library and focus on business opportunities.

Occasionally he would slip out to nearby Keswick for a round or two of golf. Keswick was a unique private club that also housed a luxury inn and Charlottesville's highest-rated gourmet restaurant. Max wasn't much for the high style and slow service of the restaurant, but the bar and grill at the golf club served the same food without any of the fuss.

Max had come to like doing things quickly, and for that reason Keswick was perfect. There were relatively few members, so that when he arrived late in the afternoon after work, he could get in a round in two hours or less.

As much as he enjoyed golfing, however, he found himself disliking the materialism his wife had embraced and wondered if being a member of an exclusive golf club fed her desires more than his.

He hardly recognized the man he had become.

Once again he began to question his life's purpose. Was this it? Did he exist merely to create wealth and provide Grace with a lavish lifestyle?

More and more he longed for answers, and he was always looking for new challenges.

※　※　※

One such challenge came in the form of a business opportunity through a referral to Mike Gallaway.

Gallaway was the man who in 1999 created the Easyread Book— the first electronic reading device that could hold dozens of novels, newspapers, and magazines, and would allow readers to take their reading materials with them wherever they went. There was tremendous hype that this device might change the nature of book publishing and generate billions of dollars for early investors.

Consequently, Max became an early investor and developed a friendship with Mike, who was a technical genius and had many exciting hobbies—including racing high-speed cars.

Max began to fly out to Palo Alto, California, to race cars with Mike. On one of these outings he was approached by a young Chinese investor named Simpak, who had flown in from Vancouver, Canada, specifically to meet with them. Simpak joined them as they headed out to the track. On the drive, he explained that his company was launching new publishing and film ventures in China, and they wanted to secure the rights to produce the Easyread Book there.

Mike turned and asked Max what he thought.

"China's a big market," Max said frankly. "We should explore it."

＊　　＊　　＊

The next thing Max and Mike knew, they were on their way to Beijing.

Simpak's company—Quinoot—was hosting a major conference on the future of publishing, and they had invited both men to be speakers—Mike, because he was the technological genius behind the Easyread Book, and Max, to discuss the business applications. The Chinese government was partnering with Quinoot and the major television, radio, and newspapers would be covering the event.

Mike and Max explained that the device would enable all Chinese texts to be stored on a simple electronic device, thus saving millions of trees and billions of dollars spent in producing, warehousing, and shipping physical books. Their presentations caused quite a stir, and afterward there was a major banquet at which the founder of Quinoot publicly announced that both men would serve as advisers for the new electronic initiative.

At the banquet, Max sat next to Quinoot's chief technology officer, who was introduced to Max simply as Sun. He was in his early forties, tall, intellectual, reserved, and meticulous. He wore heavy spectacles and a conservative suit with a gold tie.

Sun spoke excellent English, yet thought carefully before he spoke. Over the course of the meal, however, Max learned that he had an unusual history.

He had been a teenager during Mao Zedong's Cultural Revolution, and had demonstrated an extraordinary talent as an ice hockey player. He'd represented China in the 1980 Winter Olympics and was the star of the team.

Sun was offered a full scholarship to study neurology at China's leading medical school, and as China began to open up to capitalism, he was chosen to be the spokesperson and to serve on the boards of several medical care companies. As his prominence grew, he was sent to Wharton Business School in the United States and received a masters in business administration. He had homes in Vancouver, Chicago, and Beijing. Though business occupied much of his time, he exercised to remain fit and studied numerology as a hobby.

His involvement with Quinoot was significant, but represented only about 20 percent of his work time, since he had important roles with several other leading Chinese companies and was sought after by major American venture capitalists interested in exploring investment opportunities in the growing China marketplace.

Yet none of these things interested Max as much as one pivotal piece of information—Sun's full name. It was Dr. Cho Sun Pak, and the moment he heard it, Max knew Sun was one of the Twelve.

Number six, to be precise.

Somehow, a chance meeting in Palo Alto, California, had sent Max thousands of miles to Beijing and the latest in a series of impossible encounters.

Yet as startling as it was to be struck by that familiar feeling of sudden recognition, Max remained calm.

"Sun, let's have lunch tomorrow," he proposed cautiously. "I want to learn more about Quinoot, and I think there are other opportunities we might be able to discuss, as well."

❉   ❉   ❉

The next day, over a delicious lunch at one of Sun's favorite restaurants, Max slowly guided the conversation away from business, carefully observing Sun's reactions. When it became clear that the man was open to new and esoteric ideas, he described to Sun his near-death experience and the unfolding mystery of the twelve names.

Sun listened patiently. As a man of science he was skeptical—although equally curious—about Max's story.

"From what you have said, there is no proof that you actually were dead," he said, speaking as if he was analyzing a business model. "You could have been hallucinating. When oxygen is cut off from the brain, the mind can do strange things."

Max appreciated his frankness, but as always, he remained undeterred.

"That may have been true at the time," he countered, "but if that was the case, how is it that I have now met six of the twelve persons? How would you explain the ways in which they have reacted as well?"

Sun considered his question seriously before responding.

"It is a true mystery. I have read that the new physics is positing that all space and time coexist in a single zero point where all matter, all energy, and all events coexist. Perhaps there is some truth to this theory, and somehow you entered that space during your out-of-body experience.

"While there," he continued, "perhaps you encountered my name. Or perhaps something in that event stayed with you and caused you to *think* mine was a name you saw." He shook his head. "In any event, we must stay in touch, not only to pursue our business interests, but to see if either of us can learn more about these mysterious twelve names."

With that—and, Max realized, with more questions and still no answers—they parted.

❋　　❋　　❋

Over the next two years, Sun and Max formed a steadfast friendship, and in the course of many philosophical discussions, Sun was drawn further into the mystery of the twelve names through his use of numerology. Sun noticed that the numerology of the letters in both his name and Maria's were "nines," but none of the other names had identical numerological vibrations—so that analysis, too, seemed to be a dead end.

The Chinese market for Easyread Books proved to be a disappointment as well. It was much harder to penetrate than had been anticipated, and after an investment of tens of millions of dollars by venture capitalists, Quinoot was shut down—written off as a good idea that was ahead of its time.

While it was a financial disappointment for Max, he nonetheless felt as if his friendship with Sun outweighed the downside.

Before long, however, that viewpoint would change.

Financial Collapse

2000–2004

M AX FELT THE BUBBLE BURSTING.

By the year 2000, he had taken positions in a number of Internet startups.

In 2001, by the time vesting was completed and he was able to exit these companies, he saw $30 million in paper options shrink to $30,000.

That amount didn't even cover one month of living expenses at Summit Farms, and Grace wasn't pleased when Max informed her that there would be no restaurant, vineyard, or horse training facility and that they would have to sell the house, move back to California, and start again.

"That will never happen," she said calmly but forcefully. "The big earthquake is coming, and it's not safe to live in California. I'm not moving, and we are not selling Summit Farms.

"You put the home in my name," she continued, "and I'm not going to sell."

Max tried to reason with her.

"You know that was just to protect you in case something happened to me," he said, trying to damp down the panic he was feeling. "We need to sell, and we need to do it now. I need your help," he said earnestly.

"No," she said, and she turned away from him. "I'm late for my riding lesson. Figure something out. This is not my problem."

With that, she walked out the door.

✳   ✳   ✳

Max went to see his attorney, who confirmed that, with the house in Grace's name, Max could not in fact sell the house. However, he suggested that Max discontinue mortgage payments on the property.

"Won't that ruin my credit rating and put the home into foreclosure?"

"Probably, but it's also likely to get Grace to sell or at least work something out."

So, Max did as his attorney had suggested. Then he moved back to the townhouse he maintained in Dana Point, north of San Diego.

It took several months before Grace became aware that the mortgage payments weren't being made. Her response was swift and final. She filed for divorce, asking for $75,000 a month in alimony payments.

An extremely messy divorce ensued, which ended up costing Max hundreds of thousands of dollars in legal fees. Grace found a way to sell Summit Farms, pocketing 100 percent of the monies.

Max was stretched too thin. He was concentrating on finding ways to generate more money through MAXimum Productions and didn't realize what Grace was doing until it was too late.

But MAXimum was suffering. Since the attacks of 9/11, the demand for technical training films had diminished. The company's financial reversals were causing real pain for Max, a pain that lodged in his back.

✳   ✳   ✳

Max had been working with Jeff Charno, founder of the Relaxation Company, a small audio publisher that specialized in exotic music and spoken-word audio books. They attended the Book and Film Exhibitors Association meetings in Los Angeles, and Jeff noticed that Max looked terribly uncomfortable.

"I don't think I ever told you," Jeff said over dinner, "but before I started the Relaxation Company, I was a chiropractor. It looks to me as if your back is out of alignment, and if you'd like, I can recommend a former classmate of mine in Dana Point, who I think you should see. He'll get you straightened out in no time," Jeff told Max. "I'll e-mail you his information."

Thus, when Max returned to his office he found an e-mail waiting for him. When he opened it, he was surprised to see that the address for Jeff's friend was just two blocks away from his office.

More startling was the name of Jeff's friend.

Dr. Alan Taylor.

Max had been so preoccupied with the divorce and trying to recover from the dotcom downturn that he had forgotten all else. Yet it seemed as if fate had not forgotten.

Dr. Alan Taylor was one of the Twelve.

Max made an appointment and decided he would observe Dr. Taylor before broaching the topic of the twelve names.

A week later, he entered a turquoise-painted office and met the doctor, who was over six feet tall, with thick sandy brown curly hair, a sympathetic smile, good humor, and a mild disposition. A very patient man, Dr. Taylor seemed rarely to get excited. He exhibited an intellectual and analytical side, and seemed skeptical of most people and most ideas.

Though a practitioner in Southern California, he did not appear to believe in New Age jargon and fads, which surprised and delighted Max.

Alan explained how he worked, had Max fill out some paperwork, and within five minutes Max was on the treatment table having his limbs manipulated.

"With a few treatments your back pain should be gone," Alan reassured him.

Much to Max's amazement, this proved to be true. Alan had a unique technique. Once Max was on the treatment table, the entire realignment technique took less than two minutes, and already he felt much better.

❋   ❋   ❋

After a few weeks of treatment, Max decided to share the story of the Twelve.

"Dr. Taylor, do you believe in near-death experiences?" Max asked one day, after an adjustment.

"Call me Dr. Alan—everyone else does," the doctor responded. "But to answer your question, no, not really. I've had other patients tell me about these types of experiences, but I am sure there's a logical explanation. Either you are dead or you're not dead. Near-death makes no sense. Why do you ask?"

Max decided to press on.

"Because I had such an experience when I was only fifteen, and your name was one of twelve I saw in my near-death state," he explained.

Dr. Alan thought about that for a moment, and when he spoke, there was no sign of condescension in his voice.

"Seems unbelievable to me," he said. "But from what I know of you, you're a pretty practical and grounded guy. So tell me more."

Max went into a detailed description of what he had seen and felt, and the mystery of the Twelve became the topic of conversation on every subsequent visit—although neither of them could identify any prior connection they might have had, and Alan had no connection with any of the other names. But caught up in the excitement of the Twelve, he offered to help Max find the other five, if he decided to seriously pursue the search.

"Thanks," Max responded, "I may take you up on that. Let's see how things develop."

That ended their exploration of the Twelve, at least for the moment, and their conversation returned to topics of golf and women, surfing, and keeping Max's back and spine in alignment.

❉ ❉ ❉

Although Max's physical pain was gone, the financial chaos had not abated. The marital settlement into which he had entered was based on the high income he had enjoyed prior to his divorce. Currently, however, the alimony he gave to Grace was more than his income, and the settlement ate up all of Max's property and savings, as well.

All he had left was his film house, MAXimum Productions.

He was able to stop the financial hemorrhaging within his film company, but the large alimony payments prevented him from maintaining the carefree lifestyle he had once enjoyed. Strangely, though, Max didn't overly concern himself with his financial losses.

With his trademark adaptability, he had already started to change his focus from technical films to business and lifestyle films, and he began representing motivational speakers outside of the technical film area.

Among these luminaries was Dr. Ivan Varne. Ivan was the first scholar Max had met with whom he could discuss the details of Whitehead's philosophy. He was delighted to find that Ivan had a similar appreciation for Whitehead's complex metaphysics.

Over time they became more than colleagues, and were true friends.

Ivan was almost twenty years older than Max, so the relationship had a father-son feeling to it. Herbert Doff had passed away just as MAXimum Productions had started to soar, and Max was relieved that his father only lived to see his success and not his more recent financial reversals.

He missed terribly the frequent phone calls he had shared with his father, who was always both pleased and amazed by Max's numerous training film hits. With Ivan, he shared enthusiasms for art, music, and philosophy, rather than business issues, but increasingly

Ivan became the person Max called when something wonderful occurred in his life.

Ivan Varne was the founder of the Club of Miracles, a philanthropic think tank dedicated to uniting humanity into a single, cohesive planetary civilization, and he invited Max to join the board of trustees as the U.S. representative for the club. Max agreed and began attending stimulating meetings throughout Europe, alongside prominent scientists as well as prime ministers and presidents.

And yet, despite the best of intentions, there never seemed to be enough funding to trigger their audacious plans. Nevertheless, the group would have a serious impact on the planet, albeit inadvertently.

Istanbul,
the City of Hope

2004

AS THE CLUB OF MIRACLES ATTEMPTED TO EXPAND ITS ACTIVITIES, IT sought an alliance with a man named Erol Resu, who lived in Istanbul.

Erol was the eighth name of the Twelve, and he was a remarkable man. Max met him in Istanbul and, upon doing so, experienced a mixture of excitement and urgency.

Erol wore a suit of sky blue, was short and stocky, with sharp, dark eyes, a wry sense of humor, and a generally happy disposition. And he was a man who could not stand still—he was addicted to deal making.

Since he was so successful, however, he was simply admired as an eccentric workaholic who had an almost magical ability to make money. He enjoyed juggling several major deals at a time and refused to accept defeat. The greater the challenge, the more pleasure he got out of it.

His mother was Muslim, and his father was Jewish. He had been born in Istanbul, the youngest of five brothers. His father had worked as a fruit vendor selling produce in the market, and Erol started selling lemons at the age of six.

Immediately he stood out as a consummate closer.

He had intelligence and drive, and of the five brothers he was the one chosen to attend school, where he excelled. He earned a scholarship to go to university and decided to pursue a career in government.

Following his graduation he chose to serve as an assistant to a member of parliament, and within two years his employer had been elected prime minister. Erol was only twenty-three and yet was positioned as a person of influence and power.

His superior started grooming him to be a future cabinet member or perhaps even prime minister. The training lasted for six years, at which time the prime minister came to Erol with a proposition.

"Forget about becoming prime minister, or any such position," he said earnestly. "That would be a terrible waste of your talent. No, with your business acumen, I have an even more important job in mind for you.

"I want you to run the oil import and export business for the government," he announced.

Erol accepted and swiftly proved that the prime minister had chosen wisely. He thrived in this new position and generated tremendous wealth for the government. But three years later, his political party lost in the election, and Erol was removed from his position.

Nothing could have been more fortuitous. With his contacts and knowledge, Erol immediately found financial backing that enabled him to set up a private oil import-export company, and within three years he was one of the wealthiest men in all of Turkey.

Erol brought a level of contagious enthusiasm to everything he did. He had a generous heart and a sincere desire to help others. He had become one of the major philanthropists backing the Walk of Abraham, an intercultural organization encouraging Jews and Muslims to retrace the steps of Abraham on his journey through the desert to Jerusalem.

Abraham was honored in both religions as the founding father. Such a trek would require cooperation between Israel and the neighboring Arab states, with the hope that this joint venture would contribute to better understanding and mutual cooperation between peoples too often locked in conflict and violence.

During their meeting in Istanbul, the directors of the Club of Miracles were well entertained by Erol, who enjoyed life fully. He filled their every free minute with trips to museums and architectural wonders and boat trips on the Marmara Sea, the Golden Horn, the Black Sea, and the Bosphorus. He introduced everyone to wonderful Turkish cuisine, and there was always high-spirited drinking and entertainment.

When he saw how open Erol was to everything in life, Max decided to confide in him. So toward the end of the second evening, he shared with Erol the revelation of the twelve names.

To his delight, Erol not only accepted what he said, he did so with his usual gusto.

"I am certain this is important," he said to Max. "My intuition tells me that we will not be able to unravel this mystery, however, until all twelve of the names have been identified, and all twelve of the individuals have been found."

"Very true," Max agreed, "and there is nothing I can do but wait for them to appear. Until then, the only name I have is Running Bear, and as elusive as he has been, I might as well have none at all."

"It is a puzzle, and I will do all I can to help you piece it together," Erol added. "Anything you need, just ask."

"Why do you think this is important?" Max asked him. "Why were you so able to accept what I said, as outrageous as it sounds?"

Erol was clear in his reply.

"I have known from birth that my destiny requires me to act in certain ways. I have never questioned the opportunities that have come to me, and I will not question now.

"But I can assure you that both our destinies are linked to the unraveling of this mystery."

Colliding Forces

MAY 2012

*C*RASH!

The sound of metal against metal was inescapable.

Max had been talking on his hands-free cell phone, closing a film deal and hadn't been paying attention. He was actually stopped at a traffic light at the corner of La Brea and Citrus avenues in Los Angeles, waiting to make a left-hand turn, so technically the accident wasn't his fault.

The car in front of him had pulled out to make its own left turn, and realizing she was caught in a no-man's-zone as the light changed, the driver backed up without realizing that Max had pulled up to the edge of the intersection.

Max closed the deal on the phone and got out of his BMW to check on the damage. There were a few scratches on his front fender and a broken front light, but he was relieved it wasn't worse.

The SUV that had backed into him did not have a scratch. The woman who had been driving it got out of her vehicle to assess the damage and saw that her car was fine. She turned to Max, who just waved her off.

"Doesn't seem like much damage, and it's hardly worth reporting to the insurance company," he said amicably. "Your car seems fine, so from my perspective it's 'no harm, no foul.'"

Realizing she was off the hook, the woman didn't hesitate, jumped into her SUV, and drove off. Max was able to make his next meeting, and it wasn't until he was back in Dana Point that he realized he had a large dent in the front of the car that he hadn't noticed before, and he could no longer operate the hood release to gain access to the engine.

This wasn't his first fender bender, and he had discovered a company called Dents R Us, which would send out a fully equipped truck to fix the car on the spot. Max made the call, and they scheduled a repair for the next day, which happened to be a Saturday.

Around 11:00 the next morning the Dents R Us repair truck pulled up. The driver, whose name was Juan, assessed the damage, quoted $800 to make the car look like new, and as soon as Max agreed he got to work. By 2:00 in the afternoon he rang the bell and showed Max a totally repaired BMW.

They chatted while Max examined his handiwork. Juan was from Mexico, and since Max spoke Spanish, they were able to converse casually. Max had to explain that he didn't keep cash on hand, and the bank was closed, so he would have to pay with a company check. Juan said he would have to get permission to accept a check, but couldn't call it in until Monday.

"*No es problema. Yo vuelvo el lunes por la manana y lo podemos arreglar entonces. Aquí tiene mi tarjeta si tienes que cambiar la hora el lunes,*" Juan said, and he handed Max his card.

There, below the Dents R Us logo, was his name.

JUAN GONZALO ACOSTA

Max looked at the dark-haired, slender man standing in front of him and realized that Juan was wearing an indigo shirt. That was the color Max had seen around Juan's name during his near-death experience. Eight years since the last such encounter—a time that had seemed like forever—Max had finally found the owner of the ninth name on the list.

He immediately invited Juan into the house for a beer. He asked where he had been born, if he was married, how he came to be in the United States, and dozens of other questions.

Juan was delighted to accept the beer, and after a few moments of trepidation at all of the questions, he seemed comfortable, though curious, at why Max had taken such a sudden interest in him.

Juan was from a small town called Izapa, in southern Mexico just eighty kilometers north of the border with Guatemala, on the Gulf Coast. He was the youngest of seven children. His father had a small farm and was also a daykeeper—a sacred spiritual shaman in the ancient Mayan tradition. He was married and had two small children.

He had been in the United States for only two years but had been able to secure a green card and was proud that he was able to make enough money repairing dents, not only to take care of his growing family, but to send money back every month to support his father and brothers. His mother had died a few months before he had come to the United States, and he knew how hard his father and brothers had to work to support themselves.

"My father is poor, but he is an important man in Izapa," Juan explained. "He is not only a daykeeper, but also the custodian of the ancient ceremonial ballpark in Izapa. It is believed that this ancient ballpark is the oldest in all of Mexico. It has fallen into disrepair, but it still has several statues with carved messages, which archeologists from all over the world have come to study.

"Many believe that this ancient ballpark is the place where the long count Mayan calendar was first conceived."

Max had heard about the Mayan calendar but never explored it in detail.

"Is the Mayan calendar the one that has the world ending in 2012?" he asked.

"That is the common misinterpretation of the calendar," Juan acknowledged. "We believe the world will change when the calendar ends, but the world itself will not end.

"December 21, 2012, will mark the end of a twenty-six-thousand-year-long cycle. The ancients did not predict that this would necessarily be the end of the world. Our ancient beliefs are that human beings have free will, and there is the opportunity for a change that could create a better world yet to come.

"Such are the teachings I have learned from my father."

Max was intrigued. Finally, one of the Twelve was expressing knowledge that might be linked to a higher concept that might lead to an explanation of their purpose.

Of *his* purpose.

Things began to fit together. Max had been born on December 12, or 12/12, and his father on November 11, or 11/11.

Was his life's purpose somehow linked to the 2012 prophecy?

Based in part on what he had learned from Dr. Cho Sun Pak, he started to calculate the numerology of his father's birthday, keeping in mind some of the dates he had just learned from Juan, pertaining to the Mayan calendar. Juan said he had heard about something called a "harmonic convergence," which had occurred on August 16 and 17, 1987, introducing the final twenty-five years of the Mayan calendar, and for the first time Max started to see a pattern emerging.

Recognizing that Juan's background would cause him to accept what others might see as fantastic, Max described his near-death experience and revealed to Juan that he was one of the twelve names.

Sure enough, Juan just raised his beer bottle and nodded.

"This does not surprise me," he said. "My father told me our family had an important role to play in the fulfillment of the ancient prophecies. He would always say, 'The world is vast and strange and full of mysteries. Do not doubt, even in our humble circumstances, that you have an important role to play in this mystery called life.'"

Once again, the words of Jane Doff echoed in Max's head. He was intrigued by this latest connection and wanted to meet Juan's father.

"Let me know when you will next be returning to Izapa," he said earnestly. "I want to meet your father and learn more about the prophesied end-times."

"Thus it shall be, my friend," Juan replied. "I am glad you crashed your car. This has been a most auspicious meeting."

Into the Sunset

MAY 2012

Max stood on the eighteenth tee at La Costa. The sun was setting as he powered his drive toward the left-hand side of the fairway, and at the last moment he noticed that there was a golfer in the left rough, just off the fairway about two hundred and thirty yards out.

Max's normal drive only went about two hundred yards, so the golfer wouldn't have normally been in jeopardy. But this was one of the best drives of Max's life—it traveled two hundred and twenty yards on a fly, hit, and rolled another twenty yards, passing the golfer in the rough.

"Wow," exclaimed his golfing partner Kim. "That came close."

"We'd better apologize," Max said.

As Max approached in his golf cart, with apology written all over his face, a tall African-American man wearing emerald green trousers, turned and smiled.

"Didn't even come close," he said. "No worries. My motto is 'chill,' and that's also my name. I'm Chill Campister."

"Well, Chill, thanks for being so gracious," Max said gratefully. "I really should have looked more carefully before teeing off. And if you're not too busy, let me buy you a drink in the clubhouse after this hole."

"Done deal. Make your par."

✳   ✳   ✳

Later at the bar, after Max introduced himself, he learned that Chill Campister had become somewhat well known because he had, along with his wife Rachel, won *The Amazing Race*, a popular television reality show. With the million-dollar prize money, he had decided to take early retirement and go back to school to study filmmaking. Chill told Max that he had been an actor in his youth and had played the young Cassius Clay in *I Am the Greatest*, the documentary film about Mohammed Ali.

Max was bowled over, not because of what Chill was telling him, but because Max realized that Chill Campister was the tenth of the twelve names.

Whatever's going on, he mused, *it's accelerating.*

In just two days, Max had met numbers nine and ten of the Twelve, when it had taken *years* for him to meet the others. He wasn't sure how to react, but because there were other golfers close by, he didn't feel comfortable revealing the story of the Twelve.

So he kept his cool.

He also learned that Chill had written a treatment for a motivational film, based on what he and his wife Rachel had experienced in winning *The Amazing Race*. When Max revealed that he owned a film company and said that he would be willing to review the project, Chill was thrilled.

But Max had an ulterior motive. Once he had read the treatment, he felt he could continue his discussion with Chill in private and uncover more of the secrets of the Twelve.

✳   ✳   ✳

Max liked the treatment and felt he would be able to sell it based on the recognition Rachel and Chill had received as very popular winners of the television show. They were the first African-American couple to win the contest, and at the time they had competed, they were also the oldest.

One of the qualities that came through in the treatment was their strong faith in Jesus. Even on the air, they had never quarreled the way other teams did during the stress of competition, and in their motivational film they wanted to emphasize that faith had been their secret weapon.

Since the show, they had embarked on speaking tours and become popular motivational speakers putting forth the theme of using faith and teamwork to accomplish miracles.

Everything they were doing, Max knew, would provide them with a solid platform for a film, a book, and many other materials they might want to develop. So he set up a meeting with both Chill and Rachel in his office and was impressed with their positive and upbeat approach to life. They genuinely exuded love and kindness. They told him even more of their story, and Max learned that at the time they won *The Amazing Race*, they were on the verge of bankruptcy. Money had been embezzled from a software company Chill had formed years earlier, and if they hadn't won the television contest, they would have lost their home and all their possessions.

Max felt as if he had never met a nicer couple, and he invited them both to dinner. They ate at the Chart House Restaurant, looking out over the sea at sunset, and as the evening progressed, Max revealed the story of the twelve names and told Chill that he was the tenth name on the list.

"I still have no idea what the names are all about, but something is heating up," he said. "I know it must sound fairly strange to you, but believe me, I'm not crazy. There's got to be a reason for all of this. I only wish I knew what it was."

Chill smiled as he responded to what Max had told him.

"The Lord works in mysterious ways," he replied. "As a born-again Christian, I am certain Jesus has brought us together. I see His work in this. Why else would you happen to hit one of the longest drives of your life—right at me?" They all laughed at that.

"But I was born Jewish," Max countered. "I'm not sure I even *believe* in Jesus." He talked about all of the superficial people he had met when working on the film *In Search of the Historical Jesus,* and both Chill and Rachel nodded.

"Jesus is the savior for all peoples," Rachel said, "not just those who believe in Him."

"Absolutely," Chill agreed. Then he pointed the conversation back in a more analytical direction. "But let's focus on what *you* experienced and how these names might be connected. Maybe Jesus has something to do with it and maybe he doesn't, but the bottom line is that there are no coincidences—it's all part of a plan.

"So if there is a list of twelve names, as you say—and I have no reason to doubt you—then I want to know why I am on it."

Chill went on to tell Max that in addition to their winnings, he and Rachel had recently been awarded a judgment against their former partner who had embezzled the funds from their software company.

"As a result," he said, "I have the time and means to assist you in solving this mystery. Just tell me how I can help."

Max was relieved to hear that Chill was open to an explanation that might not include Jesus. He was also grateful for the offer of assistance.

"I have to go to New York for the documentary and training film trade show next week," he said. "But when I return, let's get together and focus on solving the puzzle of the Twelve. Perhaps we can organize a trip with Juan to Izapa, Mexico.

"I don't know why, but I think Izapa may be one of the keys to this mystery."

Vietnamese Melody

MAY 2012

THE FLIGHT TO NEW YORK WAS QUICK AND PAINLESS. MAX'S MIND was racing for the full five hours. All thoughts of normal business had vanished.

He had now encountered ten of the people on his list of twelve. Every name seemed to represent a different geographic area, a different religion.

Chill and Rachel had pointed out that there were twelve apostles and suggested that perhaps that was the reason Max had been given twelve names. Perhaps these were the twelve *new* apostles, waiting for the return of Jesus.

Max felt such conjecture fanciful, but he now knew that he had to pursue this mystery with all his energy—and all his focus.

❉   ❉   ❉

Max always stayed at the Yale Club when he visited New York. It was conveniently located near Grand Central Station and was a relative bargain compared to the Grand Hyatt and the other midtown hotels. Max's company was celebrating its thirtieth anniversary, and he had rented out the Yale Library on the fourth floor, where he was serving French champagne and desserts to celebrate the accomplishment.

Not many independent film companies had survived for so many years, and it was good business to celebrate the event. MAXimum's foreign rights manager was especially eager to invite the foreign agents who were so important to the international network.

Their Vietnamese agent had requested to bring a guest, and Max assumed the guest would be a girlfriend or wife. So he had approved the request.

The party was a huge success, with more than two hundred guests. Toward the end of the event a short Asian man with a tall, slender, Asian girl as his companion introduced himself.

"I am Do Van from Vietnam," he said. "This is my niece, Melody Jones. Melody lives here in New York and is studying to be a ballerina. I am so grateful that you invited us to this wonderful event."

But Max found it impossible to concentrate on what the man was saying, as the now-familiar sensation assaulted his senses.

Melody was the eleventh name from the list of Twelve.

In the space of less than a week, he had met the owners of three of the final four names. Yet with the festivities still winding down, he didn't want to show his excitement, so he replied calmly.

"No, it is I who am grateful that you have joined us," he said, shaking Do Van's hand. "I am quite pleased with the wonderful work you've been doing with our rights in Vietnam."

Turning to Melody, he continued.

"You are simply beautiful," he said. "Thank you for accompanying your uncle and favoring us with your presence." He wanted to say much more but did not.

Melody was wearing an orange dress and moved with the grace of the dancer she was. She was confident and assured and clearly comfortable with social situations such as this one.

He wasn't certain how to reveal to Melody that she was one of the Twelve. Yet he knew he had to find a way.

"Would you be willing to join me for dinner tomorrow night?" he said, addressing both of them.

"Thank you, but that isn't necessary," Do Van responded.

"It would be my pleasure," Max insisted. "You do such excellent work on behalf of the company, I won't take no for an answer."

Do Van accepted, but Melody explained that she had arranged to meet her boyfriend and wouldn't be able to make it.

"Nonsense," Max said quickly. "I'd be thrilled if he could join us, too."

She agreed, and they arranged to meet.

* * *

The next day Max found himself uncharacteristically anxious, uncertain as to whether or not Melody would show up as she had promised. After years of starting and stopping, with revelations followed by long periods of nothing, the mystery of the Twelve was moving forward at a headlong pace.

And Melody was a pivotal part of finding the answer that had eluded him for so long—ever since that moment, years ago, when the names had first slipped through his fingers. He couldn't allow anything of that sort to happen again.

However, when he arrived at the restaurant, he was thrilled that Melody was there with her uncle and her boyfriend, Matthew Jordan. It seemed that Matthew had been an award-winning competitive surfer and had done a lot of hallucinogenic drugs in his day.

During dinner Max chatted with Do Van and found him both refined and intelligent. Yet it was all he could do to keep his mind on any given topic.

Then Max turned to Melody and asked her about her life. She told him that her grandmother and her mother—who was only seventeen at the time—had been boat people who had escaped from Vietnam in 1971, as the Vietnam War was coming to an end. They were brutalized by pirates and raped.

After great suffering they had arrived in New York and were able to rebuild their lives, though it took Melody's mother many years to deal with the trauma she had experienced. She had worked at many jobs and finally found her calling, working in set design for various theaters around town.

She met a choreographer, Anton Jones, and after a year of courtship, they had married. Melody was their youngest child and the only one who had sought to pursue a life associated with dance and the theater.

"My grandmother feels it was a real miracle they were not murdered at sea," Melody said. "She told me many times that there's a story that our family was destined to 'create heaven on earth,' and says that is why they were spared.

"Whenever I misbehave, she tells me that I was born to fulfill a destiny and that I must behave better, or the miracle of their escape will have been in vain." She smiled at the memory.

Do Van remained silent and listened to her story. He simply nodded his head in agreement—and with some sense of sorrow.

He excused himself so that he could make a phone call and Max—thoroughly taken with Melody's story and family prophecy—decided to reveal the story of the Twelve.

After he had recounted the details of his near-death experience, he named the twelve names, ending with "Running Bear." He expected Melody to be skeptical, but to his relief she listened intently and was very curious.

The entire time, Matthew just sat at her side, looking from Melody to Max and back again, listening intently.

"Please write down all twelve names," she asked Max. "Let me see if I can find a connection."

Though her request surprised him, Max wrote the names on a napkin, and Melody studied them for a long while. Finally, after several minutes, she looked up.

"I'm afraid I recognize none of these names," she said. "I can't see any connection—there's nothing I can do to help you."

Then Matthew asked to look at the list.

"This last name—Running Bear," he said after a moment. "Have you met him yet?"

"No," Max admitted. "That's now the last name on the list. Why do you ask? Do you know such a person?"

"No," Matthew replied, much to Max's disappointment. "But my dad, Toby, is part Native American. This must be a Native American name. If anyone knows a Running Bear it would be my dad.

"He lives in San Clemente, not far from where you said you live. Let me borrow your cell phone for a minute, and I'll check this out."

Max handed Matthew the phone, and within minutes Toby was on the line.

He confirmed that he knew a tour guide in Sedona, Arizona, who went by the name Running Bear.

Max could hardly believe his ears. He and Toby talked and agreed to meet the following weekend in Sedona, where they would try to find Running Bear.

Max's hands trembled with excitement as he hung up, and the reality of it all set in. He realized that, within days, he might finally meet the last of the Twelve.

But what then?

Red Rocks

JUNE 2012

TOBY JORDAN WAS A SURFING LEGEND.

He had won many tournaments in his youth but was even better known for surfing photography. This had led him to surf films and later a career as an artist creating montages that used actual surfboards as well as paint and other materials in the creation of unique sculptures.

In addition, Toby had founded a business for designing surfboards and selling surfing accessories. Because of his artistic temperament, he was friends with many major artists whose works he featured.

Toby's two sons had also been champion surfers, and his eldest son, Matthew, was known for acrobatic jumps and similar exploits that other surfers hadn't even imagined.

Toby had fought drinking problems as a youth. He always blamed it on his Native American heritage that he had no resistance to alcohol, and so, as a young adult, he decided never to drink alcohol again. Combined with his commitment to surfing, this contributed to a healthy lifestyle, and he added extensive hiking to his repertoire, thus opening himself up to an entire new world for his photography.

One of his favorite areas for hiking and photography was Sedona, Arizona, a small city in the high, southwestern desert, famed for its stunning red rock formations. He made a pilgrimage there at least once a year, so it didn't take much coaxing to get him to agree to make a quick trip with Max.

They made the drive in a single day, and along the way Max shared the story of the Twelve. Toby, in turn, filled Max in on everything he knew about Running Bear, who he said was the best tour guide in Sedona. Running Bear knew all the secret caves and sacred Indian sites.

"He was named Joel Sheets at birth," Toby explained. "I got to know him more than twenty years ago when I first began to photograph Sedona's beauty. When I shared my own heritage with him, that's when he told me his Indian name. Not many people even know him as Running Bear, so it really surprised me when Matthew called.

"I'm not sure you would have been able to find him any other way, not even with Google."

"Of course, when all of this began, Google didn't exist," Max noted. "In fact, the Internet itself didn't yet exist.

"It's been a remarkable journey," he continued, "although the people to whom the names belong seem always to have found me. Some of the Twelve believe that we're all connected by some profound destiny, and I tend to agree. I just hope Running Bear has some insights for us—it would be terrible to find that this was just a colossal coincidence, without any real purpose or meaning behind it."

Toby nodded his agreement.

"If anyone will have the answer to your mystery, it will be Running Bear," he said confidently. "He's a bit of a shaman, as well as a guide, and he's knowledgeable about ancient Hopi beliefs and customs."

He paused, then continued.

"Running Bear uses hallucinogens in his rituals and is an expert on sweat lodges as well."

*　*　*

Toby and Max arrived late and checked into the Best Western motel. Despite his excitement, Max quickly fell into slumber, and when he awoke he was surprised to find that he had had a good night's sleep.

Running Bear joined them for breakfast at a nearby diner. He was in his seventies, tall, with long, braided hair that was speckled with gray and wore a red vest with beautiful, turquoise jewelry.

He had a magnificent presence.

Max discovered that he was a direct descendant of a line of powerful Lakota and Hopi Indian shamans, and as a tour guide to the sacred sites of Sedona, he passed along a true love of the earth and the heritage of his native peoples.

Without hesitation, Max told Running Bear all the details of the twelve names. Running Bear listened carefully and simply smiled. When Max was done, he spoke, and his voice was deep.

"We have been expecting you."

"How can that possibly be?" asked Max incredulously. "It's been forty-seven years since I first saw your name, and the entire time I've not known where I was going, or why. How could you have known?"

"It was not you specifically," Running Bear explained, "but Native Americans have known about the twelve names for centuries.

"The great transformation is upon us, and the knowledge has been passed down from generation to generation that in these times the true humans—those with strong, integrated spirits—would reappear, and the ancient spirit guides of our people would lead us to a world of peace and harmony." Despite the weight of his words, Running Bear spoke calmly.

When he replied, Max was less calm.

"But what do I have to do with this legend?" he asked, confusion in his voice. "I have no Native American blood. My grandparents are Hungarian on my father's side and Russian on my mother's side."

"I do not know your specific role, but if nothing else you have served to reunite the Twelve. Each name represents one of the modern tribes of color, reincarnated now for the end-times of this Earth as we know it."

Seeing concern etched on Max's face, he continued.

"Our ancient peoples realized that in the end-times, it would be necessary that we Native Americans return as people of *all* colors. There could not be a world of red against white, black against yellow. There can only be one world in the new times, and only those who are ethical and aligned with true spirit shall appear on Earth to heal the wounds caused so long ago by the greed and violence of so many.

"My brothers knew then that our defeats were only of a single time and not permanent. That is why we created the ghost dances and other rituals—we always knew that the real people could never die and would return in other bodies representing the twelve colors and the twelve tribes of humanity."

As his words sank in, Max found himself accepting what Running Bear was saying . . . yet there were still so many questions to be answered.

"Based on my own experiences, I think you must be right," he said, staring out the window across the dusty, desert landscape. "I think somehow your ancient legend is indeed true."

He turned to look at his host again.

"But even so, what does it all mean?"

"The answer can only come from the Great Spirit," Running Bear replied. "We must organize a sweat lodge for sunrise tomorrow morning."

He rose from the table and pointed to the mountains on his left.

"Do you see those red rocks, far beyond the road?"

Max saw them, and nodded.

"There is a path that leads three miles into the deepest crevices of the red rocks. Few people know of this crevice. There is an ancient cave next to the crevice. In this cave I will prepare the sweat lodge. Toby has been to this sacred site with me before. He will guide you in the morning, and I will have everything prepared.

"I will go this evening and make offerings to the Great Spirit and my ancestors, while preparing the fire and the rocks."

※   ※   ※

The sun wasn't yet up when Toby and Max reached the crevice and the cave. Running Bear was already there when they entered the clearing, magnificently dressed in ceremonial costume that included a sacred eagle feather. He was reciting ancient Hopi chants and was in a meditative state that did not break upon their arrival.

The fire already had the cave tremendously hot, and Max and Toby began sweating as they sat outside the cave. They sat silently and observed Running Bear. After ten minutes of chanting, he stopped and turned to them.

"It was a good night. The spirits are rejoicing. They are eager to guide us.

"Come," he said. "You must smoke some of this tobacco, and then we will enter the cave and start our prayers." He handed them a pipe, and Max suspected there was some type of hallucinogenic mixed in with the tobacco, but he did not ask.

Running Bear went through a series of chants in both Hopi and English. He turned to the four corners of the chamber and asked each direction for a blessing. He asked both Toby and Max to repeat the English phrases, and they did.

"Please purify our entreaties and our bodies and reveal to us our destinies," he said, invoking the Great Spirit. He then asked both the Mother Spirit and the Father Spirit for guidance.

The heat was intense. At times Max felt as if he would pass out, and he was sweating as he had never sweated before. But his desire to uncover his destiny overrode all, and he remained still—transfixed, hanging onto Running Bear's every word and gesture.

Finally, the chanting and supplications ended, and there was silence. Nothing of an otherworldly nature occurred, and Max wondered if Running Bear's ritual had been effective.

The shaman had a dazed look on his face as if he were possessed. He did not move. It didn't even appear as if he was breathing, and Max dared not move.

Toby, having experienced rituals with Running Bear before, nodded to reassure him that there was no need to worry.

After what seemed like twenty minutes or more of silence and utter stillness, Running Bear started speaking in a low, calm voice. His words were in ancient Hopi that Max could not understand.

He then stood and exited the sweat lodge. Toby and Max followed.

Outside, the sun was now shining. It was midmorning, and the red rocks reflected the light in a brilliant tapestry of red and yellow, orange and green. There were bottles of water, which Running Bear had placed there, and they all drank deeply, while appreciating the still, cool morning air.

Running Bear finished an entire bottle of water, came close to Max and looked him directly in the eye as he spoke.

"Your quest begins today. Great Spirit has told me what you must do, what you volunteered to do many centuries ago when you agreed to be incarnated on this Earth."

While he didn't understand, Max was gripped with excitement. At last, he was certain, he would learn the purpose of his near-death experience and understand his connection to the Twelve.

"And what is this quest?" he asked, trying—and failing somewhat— to remain calm. "What have I agreed to do?"

"You are the human whose duty it is to bring the Twelve together," Running Bear revealed. "They must unite outside of Izapa, Mexico, and they must gather there on August 11 at sunrise in this, the year of prophecy.

"This gives you only two months to gather the Twelve," he warned. "Great Spirit has revealed to me that on that sacred day, the mission of the Twelve will be revealed, but *only* if all twelve are present."

Doubt began to creep over Max.

"But some of the Twelve I have not spoken to for more than twenty years," he said. "What if not all will come?"

Running Bear shook his head.

"I know only what Great Spirit has told me. I do not know how you will achieve this goal. As one of the Twelve, I will be at the mountain in Izapa, and I will do all I can to help you reunite us, but Great Spirit has told me that this is your mission, and your mission alone."

Max gulped, and doubts flooded his mind.

What if this was all illusion? He had told Running Bear about Juan and Juan's connection to Izapa through his father. Perhaps Running Bear had simply picked up on that and created a story he knew Max wanted to hear?

After all there were still no concrete details explaining why the Twelve were the Twelve or why Izapa was where they needed to go. He needed more information.

"How can you be sure that we must meet at Izapa, and only at that time, and only on that day?"

"That is what Great Spirit has revealed."

"And you know what we will accomplish?" Max pressed.

Running Bear shook his head patiently.

"Great Spirit revealed nothing more," he said. But Max found it unbearable to accept.

"But you, as a shaman, don't you have any ideas of your own, about why this place and time," Max persisted, "and what may occur?"

"As an individual I have my own thoughts, but they are of no importance," Running Bear said calmly, as if to a child. "Only what Great Spirit reveals is worth discussing." With that, he turned to go down the path, through the red rocks, and back to the road.

With Toby in tow, Max caught up with him and, with desperation clear in his voice, continued to plead.

"But you must have some clue," he said. "Please, give me *something* that is logical, or at least possible to help explain this request from Great Spirit."

Running Bear spoke as they walked.

"August 11 is a sacred day in the long count Mayan calendar. I am sure Juan's father, the daykeeper, will be able to give you more details than I, but based on all that I know, I can only tell you that this will be a sacred meeting, and that if you fail to bring the Twelve together at this time, there will be much suffering."

He fell silent and hiked on ahead, his long legs lending him speed, leaving Max and Toby to contemplate all they had heard.

And Max was left to wonder how and why he had been chosen—if indeed he could believe in the vision at all.

Even the Dead
Are Waiting

JUNE 2012

ONE OF THE FIRST CALLS MAX MADE UPON RETURNING TO California was to Erol in Istanbul. He used his computer so they could teleconference with full video contact.

"It's happening, Erol," he said.

But even as he said it, he found it hard to believe his own words. "I have found the rest of the Twelve. Running Bear, the one name I had all those years, is a Lakota shaman, and according to him, you are right. He claims it's my destiny to reunite the Twelve and take you all to Izapa, the home of the ancient Mayan calendar."

"That is amazing, my friend," Erol said. "I have known for years that our destinies remained intertwined, and this proves it. When are we to travel to Izapa?"

"You must all be there on August 11," Max revealed. "Will you be able to make it?"

"You would not be able to stop me," Erol replied. "And if there are any who do not have the funds to travel, I will cover their expenses. Money should not get in the way of destiny.

"I have always believed that your story hinted at a deeper purpose," he continued, "and have believed that my own destiny was linked to something larger than my love for Istanbul and my homeland of Turkey."

Max was delighted but told Erol that he might also need to fly to the various countries to meet with some of the Twelve.

"That will not be a problem," Erol insisted. "Just let me know what financial assistance you might need for your own trips."

"It is good to know your support is there if I need it," Max replied, greatly relieved.

The next three calls were easy. Dr. Alan Taylor and Chill Campister were delighted to commit, and for Juan it was a chance to see his father, so there was no question.

Melody Jones was the first to require financial assistance, but once that was dealt with, she said that she would join the Twelve on August 11 in Izapa.

He reached Yoko via the Internet, and she replied that she would be delighted. August was her vacation month, and she had not yet booked her annual holiday.

Sun Pak had to rearrange a business trip but was able to do so. That left Yutsky, Maria, Rinpoche, and B.N. Mahars.

Max hadn't spoken to Rinpoche in almost ten years, and to the others in more than twenty. Still, he was able to track down the Buddhist—who had been living in Toronto, Canada, for the last eight years. He now spoke broken but adequate English, had married the daughter of one of his students, and together they had two small children.

When Max explained the situation, Rinpoche said he would be delighted to attend the momentous gathering.

The call to Maria was surprisingly difficult, he discovered. Despite the years, he had never entirely let go of the regret he had felt when she walked out of that park. Nor had he forgotten the intensity of the love they had expressed for each other.

He forced himself to call and discovered that she was still living in Trujillo, Peru. She sounded pleased to hear from him, and they spent the first part of the call catching up. Maria was the mother of four grown children, and the grandmother of seven. She had never regretted marrying her engineer husband, she said, and he had died a year earlier.

With mixed emotions Max said that he was sorry, but she told him that she was happy, living a tranquil life in Trujillo. She accepted his offer—this would be her first major outing after observing the traditional year of mourning. She had modest resources, though, and appreciated Max's offer to cover her expenses.

She would begin making plans immediately, she said.

They hung up, and Max realized that he was exhausted. Whatever it was that he had felt when he met Maria, some of it was still with him. He needed to take a break before continuing his calls.

✳   ✳   ✳

Yutsky was harder to track down because he had retired from the film business.

However, Max used his knowledge of Yutsky's military service to find him. He was living in old Jerusalem and working as a security strategist for top-level dignitaries who visited Israel. When Max finally got him on the phone, it was as if the years just melted away.

"So good to hear your voice, my boy." Yutsky barked. "How have you been?"

"I am so glad I found you," Max replied. "I need your help."

"Anything, my boy," the Israeli said enthusiastically, and Max wondered if he was going stir-crazy, staying in one place. "Not much excitement for me these days. . . . So what do you have? A film crew on its way? Permissions to secure? Just let me know," Yutsky volunteered, "and what you need will be accomplished."

"It's nothing like that," Max explained. "I need you to come and meet with me and eleven others in Izapa, Mexico, on August 11.

We'll cover all your expenses. I will explain the details when I see you, but it's essential that you join us."

There was a long silence, and Max could envision the man's face as he considered the strange request, coming out of the blue after so many years.

Then he heard a long exhale, and Yutsky spoke again.

"Who am I to turn down a free trip to the Americas at this stage in life," he said cheerfully. "You can count on me. Just send me the ticket and the details, and I'll be at your service."

That left only B.N. Mahars to contact.

※　　※　　※

Max punched the numbers into the phone, and soon he had made it through to the National Museum in Delhi.

"Can you connect me to B.N. Mahars, please?" he asked the museum phone operator.

"B.N. Mahars is no longer with the museum," she said, "but let me connect you to the present keeper of the fifteenth century, who will perhaps be able to tell you where you might find him."

Max was startled that B.N. would have retired so relatively young.

After a few minutes, a male voice came on the line.

"I am so sorry to let you know that B.N. passed away eighteen years ago. He was a good friend to me; I served as his assistant for almost twenty years. I still miss him.

"Are you a family friend from the States?" he then asked.

At first Max was speechless, and he asked for a moment to recover.

How can this be? he wondered silently. *And what happens when there aren't twelve?*

When he was able to speak again, he explained that he had met B.N. back in 1972, when he had made a film at the museum.

"He was instrumental in getting us permission to do so," Max said, "and I was able to spend a wonderful day together with B.N. and his family."

His family, Max thought, and a glimmer of hope appeared.

"Do you know how I might be able to get in touch with them?" he asked. "It is very important that I speak with his brother or another of his relatives."

The keeper was silent for a moment, then spoke.

"I do not know which brothers or family members are still alive, but B.N. had two daughters and several grandchildren, all of whom I believe still live in his home village. I can give you their telephone number, if you wish."

Max took the number and immediately put through the call. He didn't recall the name of B.N.'s daughter, but as soon as she spoke, he remembered Shilpa's gentle, almost laughing voice.

"Oh, we still talk about you," she said brightly. "I was only six years old that night you dined with us, and you were the first entirely white person I ever saw.

"My father used to talk about you often and always fondly," she continued. "In fact, on his deathbed he gave me something that he said you might someday ask for."

That took Max by surprise.

"What did he leave for me?" he asked curiously.

"It is a book, but he said that you must come and fetch it personally," she explained. "He said that if you ever called, that I should tell you he is sorry that he could not wait for you any longer in human form. He told me much else as well, and there are some unexpected complications in giving you the book. But as he asked, I will explain it all to you when you come, if you choose to do so."

Mystery piled upon mysteries, he mused. But as long as there was hope, he had to pursue it.

"Of course I will come as soon as I can," he said. "It will be wonderful to spend some time with you and the rest of your family. Is your uncle who taught at the university still alive?" he asked.

"Uncle Gupta is alive and well," she answered. "He is almost ninety, but his mind is still as sharp as ever. He was with me when my father died, and he may have more information to share with you."

"I will fly over within the week and come and meet with you," he said. "We can discuss the details of your father's message to me then." With that, he said goodbye and hung up.

As he put down the phone, though, Max wondered how he was going to reunite the Twelve, when only eleven were alive.

C.D. Mahars

JUNE 2012

Max arrived in Delhi just four days later.

The airport was twice the size it had been on his visit forty years before, and although the road was still jammed with bicycles, rickshaws, donkeys, cows, and pedestrians with huge bundles on their heads, there were primarily cars, trucks, and buses along the almost modern, four-lane highway from the airport to Delhi.

He spent his first night at the Taj Mahal Hotel, as modern and luxurious a hotel as any at which he had ever stayed. He arranged for a car to take him to B.N.'s village, just twenty miles outside of the city, where he would spend the rest of the time with B.N.'s daughter and extended family.

Max didn't remember the road, having only driven it once at night so many years back, yet he was astonished at how he seemed to go back in time with each mile driven. By the time he arrived at the town itself, he was able to recognize the streets, which were still filled with vendors and small shops where everything from water to fruit and candies, old pieces of metal, and modern, electronic toys were being sold.

Small boys played Kick the Can, and girls carried large water jars on their heads, filled from the town well, just as he remembered.

So much was still the same.

When Max entered the Mahars's compound, he noticed that the walls had received new coats of paint, and some of the chairs and benches that populated the outside dining area had been replaced.

Inside the house, however, the furniture was the same—the kitchen hadn't changed, and the many books on the shelves in what had been B.N.'s office were exactly as they were.

As he stood looking at the titles of the books, Shilpa—B.N.'s daughter—entered the room and greeted him warmly.

"We have organized a luncheon for you," she announced. "All the relatives will be here shortly. It is most auspicious that you have come on this day, for today is a holiday and a day of great spiritual meaning. My uncle is certain that the timing is no accident."

Soon the entire clan had arrived, and they moved into the dining area.

During lunch Max was captivated by Shilpa's son C.D. He was seventeen years old and had been born with a rare mental defect much like Down syndrome, so that his mental capacity was that of a three-year-old and would never improve. He could follow directions and make sounds, but he could not speak in sentences or even full phrases.

When he did make sounds, they were usually loud—he did not seem to have much control over the volume or to be able to judge the impact of what he might be trying to communicate. C.D. was very strong, so he was given tasks in the fields, such as picking vegetables. As a result his chest and arms were overdeveloped for his five-foot-six body, giving him the physical strength of a much larger man.

He had enormous brown, almost black eyes that shone with a brilliance and a light that was captivating. He was always smiling, and upon greeting Max, C.D. hugged him so hard that Max thought his ribs would be crushed.

Shilpa gently pulled her son away.

"C.D. is very strong," she said reassuringly, "but he is very gentle. He will not hurt you. He loves everyone and animals most of all. He hugs every living creature he meets. He is more of a joy than burden to us, but of course we must be vigilant at all times, since he really cannot take care of himself."

When she spoke, Max expected to see sadness in her eyes, but all he saw there was love.

As much as Max was taken with C.D., the young man seemed utterly enthralled with Max. He kept offering Max food and looking him directly in the eyes, coming within inches of his face. His intensity and attention were somewhat disconcerting, but at the same time Max felt a connection that was almost overwhelming.

He would look into C.D.'s large, dark eyes and see unconditional love and trust reflected back to him. He couldn't help but stare back, transfixed.

❋ ❋ ❋

After lunch Shilpa and Uncle Gupta took Max into B.N.'s study, which he had always shared with the other scholars in the family. The shelves were full of books and maps, and drawings lined the tables. Some of the manuscripts were very old, and many contained exquisite hand drawings. These were the prize possessions of the Mahars, a family renowned for its scholars.

Gupta, who had just turned eighty-nine, was the first to speak.

"We have been waiting for you for many years," he revealed. "It is almost eighteen years since my nephew B.N. died from cancer, and he was not even fifty years old. He spent the last several months of his life lying on a cot we placed for him in this very room.

"As you know he loved his books and spent the last years of his life studying the ancient texts of the Upanishads, in which the sacred traditions and beliefs of our Hindu religion reside."

Gupta handed Max a small, slim, pink notebook. Its cover had a beautiful picture of mountains and trees and a stream.

"This is the notebook B.N. kept during that time and where he recorded his final thoughts. On the day he died, he summoned me and Shilpa to him and handed it to us. He told us that we must guard this book, that someday someone might come and ask for him, and he instructed that if they did, we were to give it to that person.

"I can only believe that the unknown person is you. B.N. never said so, but no one else has come seeking him in the last seventeen years, and I have no reason to think that there is anyone else out there who is waiting to appear."

Max held the notebook but did not know whether to open it or not.

As he hesitated, Shilpa spoke.

"I was with my father every day and attended to him every hour during his final illness. We grew closer even than we had been, since my mother was no longer living, and I was his closest female relative. I was pregnant with my first child, and this gave us both joy.

"On the last day of his life, when he gave Gupta the notebook, he told us both that whoever came for the book must not take it from us unless my unborn child was to accompany the recipient, as well. The book could travel anywhere in the world, he said, but one day it must be returned to this room, and it must always be kept close to his grandchild."

Gupta stepped in.

"This seemed a strange request, but as you know from our conversation forty years ago, we Mahars are full of surprises and strange knowledge."

At that, Max remembered the yogi and his trip to the moon and beyond. Gupta's voice brought him back to the present day.

"We did not question B.N.'s request then, and we do not question it now. You are free to read this book here, and you are free to take it with you if you need to, but if you do, C.D. must accompany you, for he was the unborn child in Shilpa's womb."

Max was both excited and confused. B.N. had been many things, but he had not seemed given to hocus-pocus, nor to whimsical fantasies. Why would he put such strange conditions on this "gift"?

What was in this notebook?

"Neither Shilpa nor I—nor anyone else—has ever opened the notebook," Gupta explained. "B.N. told us that the contents were for the one who would come seeking him, yet would have no meaning for anyone else."

Max thought about that for a moment—and no matter how he looked at it, what Gupta had said seemed to make no sense.

"We will leave you to read the notebook, and then you can let us know if you will need to have us prepare C.D. to travel with you or not," the old man continued. "If you do, Shilpa will, of course, accompany him.

"C.D. has traveled before, and he even has a passport. He obeys Shilpa, and anyone can see that he has already taken a liking to you."

Gupta and Shilpa turned to depart, and then the old man turned to speak one last time.

"When we return, we will ask for your decision."

* * *

After they had gone, Max opened the notebook.

It was full of numbers.

There were almost forty pages of calculations, and on the final page Max found the final formula, and final notation.

21122012

This number appeared twelve times at various places in the notebook, as the answer to twelve different calculations based on twelve different sets of initial axioms that B.N. had formulated.

There was very little text in the book, explaining that each calculation was based on a different set of beliefs relating to the beginning of different eras of the Hindu calendar and other ancient systems, as well. B.N. had spent the last months of his life—right up until the end, it appeared—analyzing and comparing ancient calendars from cultures throughout the world.

On the last page B.N. had written a personal note:

The energy of my soul and essence is contained within these pages. As I transition and leave this body, I shall direct my essence into the body of Shilpa's unborn child. My essence shall survive within my grandchild and shall be available in that child's form, which, when in the presence of this book, shall embody the ancient vibrations and knowledge that the world shall seek.

In so doing I have fulfilled my destiny and my life's purpose, and I now pass along the task of planetary transformation to you who read these words.

—B.N. Mahars

Max knew instantly that the book and C.D. would have to accompany him to Izapa. Somehow B.N. had known that his essence would be required at some future event, at the same time he knew he was dying.

Max would study the numbers later, in an attempt to discern what they might mean, but it was clear to him that through the book and his grandson, B.N. would be present—and that Max would thus fulfill his purpose of reuniting the Twelve, as the Great Spirit had requested.

He took a moment to catch his breath and then emerged into the sunlight on the veranda where Gupta was napping and Shilpa was cleaning up.

"I will be taking you up on your offer," he announced. "Can you arrange for both of you to fly to Mexico City on the ninth or tenth of August? We'll make arrangements to pick you up and fly or drive you to Izapa, the site of the ancient Mayan who created the Mayan calendar."

He paused for a moment, sat in a chair, and gestured for her to do the same. When she did, he continued.

"I have been told to bring twelve special people to this site on August 11, and B.N. was to have been one of them. After reading his notebook, it is clear to me that C.D. is now one of the Twelve, for his grandfather's energy now resides in him." He paused to see how she would react to this revelation.

Shilpa just smiled.

"My father never told me in words that I would go on such a journey, but in those final days he alluded to the fact that some day I might be called upon to assist with a great event and that I should be prepared, should I ever be called upon.

"I will prepare C.D. for the trip, and I am honored to be part of your gathering," she said. "I am sure much good will come from this."

❊   ❊   ❊

Max spent the rest of the evening playing a local version of Pick-up sticks with C.D. and his younger sister. C.D. had excellent control of his physical movements and won almost every time. He would laugh whenever Max moved a stick and press a finger strongly into Max's stomach, letting him know he had lost his turn.

After every game he would hand over the sticks for Max to count, and although C.D. could not count himself, he could tell just by looking at his big bundle of sticks, compared to Max's smaller bundle, that he had won.

This, too, made C.D. laugh.

When it came time to go to bed, he gave Max a hug and kiss that was as intense as any Max had ever experienced. The energy of his unconditional love reminded Max of the feelings he had experienced in his original near-death experience in Dr. Gray's office in Tarrytown, New York, almost fifty years earlier.

As he fell into a pleasant and satisfying sleep, Max could not help but think, *Finally I'm going to learn the purpose of my life. C.D. is the missing member of the Twelve.*

And somehow, I think he is the one who has the most to teach us.

Izapa

JULY 2012

T HE ANCIENT TOWN OF IZAPA WAS LOCATED JUST NINE KILOMETERS from the modern city of Tapachula, a commercial hub for the south-ernmost Chiapas district of Mexico, north of Guatemala.

Juan Acosta's father, Manuel, actually lived just outside of Tapachula, three kilometers from the ancient ballpark, which was Izapa's best-known archaeological ruin. Coffee was the dominant crop throughout the area, but in Izapa itself cacao was the principal source of cash.

Max could smell both when he visited.

He decided to go down on his own to meet with Manuel and to prepare for the coming together of the Twelve. He had checked with Running Bear, who had told him that Great Spirit would want the meeting to begin on August 11 at sunrise.

Before then, Max would have to find a hotel in Tapachula where everyone could stay the night before the gathering.

The only upscale hotel in Tapachula was relatively modern. Max made reservations as soon as he arrived and then arranged to rent two vans with local drivers.

✻   ✻   ✻

The next day he sought out Manuel, who was almost eighty years old but had the energy of a much younger man. He still cultivated cacao trees on his small plot of land and hiked daily to the ancient site of Izapa—as his fathers and grandfathers had done before him—to open and close the entrance to the ancient ball field and the sacred monuments and other artifacts that tourists visited.

Manuel accepted small tips from tourists, but otherwise was an unpaid daykeeper, following the traditions of his ancestors. He prayed to his ancient Mayan gods, but only when in Izapa and only when opening and closing the site. In his everyday life he attended Catholic Mass and explained that he saw no conflict between believing in his ancient gods and in Jesus Christ.

Since Manuel spoke only broken English, Max addressed him in Spanish, explained the nature of his visit and his intentions to return on August 11 for a special ceremony with the Twelve.

"*Es bueno,*" Manuel replied. "*Yo arreglo todo. Sé que es una reunion muy importante.*"

Manuel explained to Max that August 11 was a sacred date that year and was the beginning of the final one hundred and thirty days of "love-energy" that would terminate on December 21, 2012—the same day on which the entire Long Count calendar would terminate.

This wasn't just an ordinary ending, but the end of a collection of calendars that had covered a period of twenty-six thousand years, Max realized even more than he had before.

As Manuel took him on a tour of the ancient site, he revealed that archeologists had recently confirmed that Izapa had been a thriving town thousands of years ago, with a population of as many as ten thousand people. The monuments showed evidence that it was in this place that the Long Count calendar had been conceived, then shared with other towns throughout Chiapas—and eventually throughout much of Central, North, and South America.

As Max listened in rapt silence, Manuel explained that the ritual ballgames that had been played in this very ballpark were ultimately connected to the calendar itself. According to Mayan belief, on the pivotal date of December 21, a shift of consciousness would have to occur if man were to survive beyond the "end of time."

Despite the enormity of what he was saying, he spoke calmly, as if to any individual or tour group. And as he did, Max suddenly made a connection that had been eluding him ever since his trip to India.

He saw in his mind's eye the key string of numbers that had appeared repeatedly in B.N. Mahars's notebook—21122012. Because he was an American, he hadn't made the immediate connection. But elsewhere in the world, those numbers would reflect a specific date—21/12/2012.

December 21, 2012.

This couldn't be a coincidence.

Somehow, the meeting had to occur on the eleventh of August to begin a sequence that would end with 21122012. And all of the Twelve had to be present.

Max glanced around the sacred site to see if there was a suitable place for everyone to meet. He thought about the ball field itself but knew that they wouldn't be able to rope it off from the tourists who might come, and he had no idea how long the meeting of the Twelve might last. But he *did* know that it would best be held with some degree of privacy.

He peered into the distance, at the volcanoes to the east—Volcán Tacaná and the even higher Volcán Tajumulco—and asked Manuel if there might be a place to meet at the base of either of those.

Manuel smiled.

"Of course there is," he replied, still in his Mexican tongue. "Follow me. There is even a cave where my ancient people used to perform powerful ceremonies. We no longer remember the rituals, or even what they were for, but our legends tell us that the ball field itself is oriented so the light of the sun will be directly over the Volcán Tajumulco at the moment of the winter solstice."

After a twenty-minute ride in the rented jeep and a further twenty minutes of hiking, Max and Manuel arrived at a clearing on the hill. It was next to a cave, and from it they could see not only the ball field and the ancient statues, but even the Pacific Ocean off to the west, fifteen miles away.

"Yes, this is perfect," Max confirmed, even as the vista filled his senses. "Is there any way we can make certain that no one will bother us when we meet in August?"

"Do not worry," Manuel replied. "I will stand at the base of the trail and not let anyone pass. No one lives higher up on the volcano, so you will not have to worry about being bothered."

Max offered to compensate Manuel for his time and effort, but the old man just smiled and shook his head.

"It is enough that I will be seeing my son Juan," he said. "Besides, I feel in my heart that your ceremony is linked to my own purpose. We are both serving our destinies, and there is no need for money to compensate me for doing what I do with love and gratitude to my Creator."

Max smiled back at the man who stood before him.

"I am truly grateful to you," he said. "I'm not as certain as you that this ceremony will truly reveal our destinies, but it will certainly provide some kind of marker to my own odyssey and explain the synchronicities and coincidences that have directed my life." At that, he embraced Manuel.

※　　※　　※

That night Max was too excited to sleep.

He couldn't bring himself to believe that the world would end on December 21, yet he couldn't deny that something important had to be tied to that date. Too many unexplained things had happened, and the closer he got to that date, the faster they came.

What if they continue to accelerate? he mused as he lay in bed, staring at the ceiling. *What could still be in store?*

Synchronicity upon synchronicity. From his tumultuous meeting with Maria to the mystery of B.N. Mahars's final calculation, the many and seemingly impossible set of coincidences had led Max here to Izapa as inexorably as the the tides move.

The beginning of the final count, leading up to the end of the Mayan calendar, had Max frantically calculating numbers in his head.

He had been exchanging e-mails with Sun, an expert in numerology, ever since the final of the twelve names had been revealed. Sun's initial calculations were astonishing. Not only were all of the first nine key numbers represented, but somehow harmony remained even with the absence of B.N.

There were only three duplicate numbers. One was shared by Chill Campister and B.N., both of whom were fours. Of course, with B.N. having died, that was no longer a duplication.

Both Maria and Sun were nines, but they were *different* nines, with Maria's name totaling 189, and Sun's amounting to the sacred Hindu number of 108. The only other duplication involved Dr. Alan and Melody, both of whom were twos. Melody was a triple two, and represented "two energy" more aligned and integrated with the group energy than Dr. Alan, who was the lone nonbeliever among the Twelve.

It was apparent that this grouping of numbers according to numerology had somehow been carefully designed, if not predestined.

And Max kept coming back to 21122012 and the inescapable progression from twenty-one to twenty, still connected with the mysterious number twelve. Somehow the Twelve, the Mayan calendar, and B.N.'s calculations were all related.

As sleep continued to elude him, Max knew that he would never rest until he explained the connections—energetic and numeric—between the people, the dates, and his mission to convene the Twelve in Izapa.

The Thirteenth Apostle

AUGUST 2012

M AX WAS A NERVOUS WRECK.

He flew to Mexico City the evening of August 9 to greet C.D. and Shilpa and had then flown with them to Tapachula on a tiny plane that vibrated so loudly he and Shilpa could barely talk.

C.D. found the entire adventure pure fun. He was as excited as could be, jumping up and down and shouting loudly, pointing at every site from the window of the plane. Max hadn't been around such energy for a while and found it exhausting.

More than ever, he was grateful Shilpa had been able to supervise the journey.

When they arrived at the hotel in Tapachula, all the others were already settled in. Erol had decided that it made no sense to make such a long journey without including a day or two to visit other sacred sites in the land of ancient Mayan pyramids. So he had arrived on the seventh and was already completely at home with his new friends Juan and Manuel.

He had also bonded with Sun Pak, with whom he was discussing business deals. And even though he was twice her age, Erol could not take his eyes off Melody.

"She moves like water and shines like a gem," he confided to Max.

Yoko and Maria had become traveling companions on the trip to San Lorenzo de Chiapas. Juan and Manuel had connected with Running Bear and Yutsky, sharing photos and stories of their families. Manuel took Running Bear to the meeting site to show him the cave and ask him if all was suitable.

Running Bear spoke enough Spanish to communicate, and Juan accompanied them to serve as interpreter, just in case. Running Bear approved of the site, purchased several cases of water, and asked Juan to order sandwiches that could be taken with them on the morning of the eleventh.

"We must meet at sunrise, but I have no idea how long we will be there or what is going to happen. It is best to be prepared," he said.

More and more, Chill Campister was expressing his certainty that the meeting of the Twelve would result in the second coming of Christ and that was all he could talk about. With Juan serving as interpreter, Rinpoche enjoyed several long conversations with Manuel and Running Bear on the nature of their shamanistic practices and rituals.

Alan Taylor remained skeptical of the entire group, since he did not believe in God and admitted that he doubted very much that Running Bear knew what he was talking about. He confessed to Max that he had been reluctant to attend the event until he discovered that Izapa was close to some excellent surfing and that Erol would pay the travel expenses. So he had built in some time to hit the waves.

"Besides," he said amiably, "I like you Max, and there's nothing wrong with an adventure. At the very least it's going to be interesting!"

✻   ✻   ✻

The evening of the tenth, Max hosted a dinner at the hotel. He repeated the entire story of his near-death experience and recounted the new details he had unearthed in India and from B.N. Mahars's notebook. Shilpa was there, caring for her son, and she beamed as Max spoke of her father's brilliance.

It was also during this dinner that Max reconnected with Maria. It was just a glance, but for a moment Max was once again lost in the depths of her still-vibrant beauty. He was again captivated by the music of her voice and calm demeanor.

Maria returned Max's glance, but he fought his urge to make a personal connection as he continued to explain the circumstances that brought C.D. there to represent B.N., since Running Bear had been quite clear that all twelve must be present for Great Spirit to bless the ceremony. Though he was not one of the Twelve, Max would join in the ceremony as the caretaker of B.N.'s book.

"At least in the beginning you should join us," Running Bear confirmed. "It seems clear that B.N. Mahars feels that C.D. will represent him but that the book is also important, and when not in India, it seems to belong to you.

"If the energy does not flow, you can always leave," the shaman concluded.

No others could attend, for according to Running Bear, it was the energy of the Twelve—and *only* the Twelve—that was necessary for whatever was to occur.

Max realized with some trepidation that he would have to attend to C.D.

＊　　＊　　＊

The group was at the base of Volcán Tajumulco by 4:55 the next morning. Manuel met them there with a flashlight in his hand and with sure steps guided them to the hillside clearing next to the cave.

Then he departed to stand guard at the base of the trail, as he had promised.

Running Bear had also been there early and called everyone to-gether around a fire that he had prepared.

"We must sit in a circle around the fire. It is thirty minutes until sunrise, and during this time I would like each of you to pray silently in your own way.

"If your custom is to chant, you may do so, but as quietly as you can. It is my belief that each of us represents one of the twelve tribes of color and that we are here to receive instruction. I do not know in what form that instruction will come, and I do not know how long we are meant to be here.

"We may not be here more than an hour or two, but we may be here all day. Regardless of the time it will take, having come so far it would be foolish for us to leave before our prayers are answered."

He paused and looked from one member of the group to the next, until he had gone full circle. "We are all from different traditions, come from different lands, and hold different beliefs, but in the short time I have spent with each of you, it is clear to me that all of you are souls of destiny. We are living in a time of great promise and great sorrow, so I suggest that we pray—not for ourselves or our own indi-vidual peoples—but for all people and all creatures.

"I do not believe that we have been chosen randomly, but that we are here for a specific purpose . . . so let us pray to our Creator."

Max had never prayed in his life, and he knew Dr. Alan wasn't big on praying either, nor was Erol, so the three of them just stared into space.

C.D. had no idea what Running Bear had been talking about, but he took his cue from Max to be quiet and found some twigs he could bend and use to make marks in the dirt. So the young man spent his time quietly drawing, then erasing, and then drawing stick figures.

❋   ❋   ❋

After what seemed like a very long time, the sun came up and shone in their faces.

Max looked around, and still nothing out of the ordinary was happening. Rinpoche was chanting softly, and so was Running Bear.

Sun Pak had a bored look on his face, but Maria and Yoko seemed lost in some meditative trance. Juan, Melody, Yutsky, and Chill seemed perfectly content to sit and do nothing, and he envied them their calm.

After what seemed like at least an hour, Running Bear stood up and asked if anyone was hungry or thirsty. Since no one had taken time for breakfast, everyone was happy for the sandwiches and corn-wrapped tamales that came from Running Bear's knapsack.

They remained in the circle while they ate.

Another hour went by, and still there was no sign of any kind. Dr. Alan looked longingly at the Pacific, Max noticed, no doubt thinking of the good surf he was missing. After a while, he turned to Running Bear and spoke.

"How long do we need to sit here?" he asked. "I don't get a sense that anything is going to happen."

The Native American's face remained impassive as he replied.

"I do not know how long, but it is evident that we need to give it more time. You may not be aware of any change, but I can assure you that the energies of this place are shifting. The twelve of us must simply sit, so that our own energies arrive at balance.

"We have all come from a single source and have been reunited to bring back those forces that created us. Please be patient—we have only been here two hours. On a vision quest, it is sometimes necessary to spend an entire day."

When he saw the looks of alarm that appeared on some of the faces, he added, "Perhaps we will not need an entire day, but we may need several more hours."

Having said that, he returned to his meditation.

C.D. had been amazingly quiet, but now he was tickling Max and coming up with games that required Max's full attention. Far from being an irritation, this was a relief for Max, as he had little capacity to sit and do nothing. So C.D. afforded him a pleasant distraction.

After a while, Erol, and then Sun Pak, and then Dr. Alan, and then others wandered off to stretch their legs and look around. No one was ever gone for more than twenty minutes, however, and there were never less than nine of the Twelve present at any given time.

Max hoped that would be enough.

✳   ✳   ✳

Just before noon, he noticed a strange wind blowing.

First he saw the branches of the trees moving, and then suddenly there was a mini-whirlwind spinning above the embers of the fire, which glowed and then were extinguished.

Running Bear was transfixed.

Then he looked at Rinpoche, and then Juan, and then Erol. Sun Pak, Maria, Yoko, Melody, Yutsky, and Chill, and finally Alan and C.D.—each and every one of them was transfixed.

They were silent, even C.D., and their eyes were glued to where the fire had been. A calm entered the clearing and time seemed to stand still.

Max blinked but he saw nothing. The wind had died down again, and the silence was complete. He thought he should feel anxious excitement at whatever was transpiring—this culmination of everything he had done—yet the calm gripped him, as well, endowing him with a sense of curiosity and wonder.

Then he glanced again at the Twelve and saw tears streaming down their cheeks. The silence was broken, and soft sobs were coming from each of them.

They seemed to be tears of joy.

Finally, after what seemed like hours, Max felt a presence enter the clearing.

Could this be the one we've been waiting for? he thought. *Is this it, at last?*

"Yes, I am the one," said a deep, calm voice that echoed around them. "The legends refer to me as the Thirteenth Apostle, though you will see me as your God—as Jesus, as Mohammad, Krishna, and Padmasambhava, even as the Buddha. I may appear as pure energy or perhaps even as an extraterrestrial.

"Each of you sees me as the fulfillment of your destiny . . . as the savior or the messiah, and I am indeed the fulfillment of all of these beliefs.

"The twelve of you, by your presence, have created the vortex of energy that allows me to enter your world, and I have come to tell each of you what you must do to save that world. You are part of an ancient pact made tens of thousands of years ago to ensure the survival of this planet and of the human species.

"Each of you will walk to the cave that sits next to this clearing and learn what you must do to fulfill the ancient prophecies and ensure that these end-times do not end your world."

Then only silence.

*　　*　　*

The first to enter the cave was Erol. Minutes later he came out with a transcendent—yet somewhat grave—expression of determination on his face.

Next was Yutsky, and then Sun Pak, followed by Dr. Alan, Chill, Maria, Yoko, and Melody, each only for a few minutes.

Rinpoche remained in the cave for a full hour, and it was dusk when Juan emerged and dark when Running Bear returned.

Only C.D. was left.

Max escorted him to the entrance and meant to stay outside, but the young Indian pulled him in.

He entered and felt a glow and sense of peace. C.D. started laughing as the voice spoke to him and Max.

"You are a child of love," it said. "You have much to teach this world. Your grandfather calculated with his numbers that the end of the universe would occur one hundred and thirty days from today. This in fact is true, but what your grandfather could *not* know is that the end of one universe may mark the beginning of another.

"Human beings have squandered their precious gifts, and the world will indeed end if they do not change their ways and transform their consciousness.

"You see me as Krishna and do not understand the import of my words. But that is why you have a guide. And even if you did not, I can reach your heart. There is an entity that has incarnated on your planet during these times—an entity that is greater even than me, an entity that in fact created me and all that exists. This being is the One.

"This One has made the supreme sacrifice of incarnating as a human being, and in so doing has risked all by forgetting all and by becoming truly and completely human.

"Your task—as is that of the other eleven—is to go back to your home and search out this One. Retrace your steps to the most sacred places you have traveled or lived in this human life. Max will go with you—although he is not one of the Twelve, it is through his connection that you have come together with the rest. It will be easier to convince the One of the importance of your mission if Max is with you. So search diligently.

"Then you must reunite again, just before sundown on December 21. The Twelve and the One must be present, and that is all that will be necessary to ensure that mankind does, in fact, fulfill the destiny promised of heaven on Earth. Together, we will greet the One and learn then what we must do to ensure the promised age.

"Now go and rejoice in the knowledge that you have fulfilled the first part of your promise. You are a special servant of goodness, C.D., and I bless you for all eternity."

Then silence, and Max knew they were once again alone. The Thirteenth Apostle was no longer present.

Max took C.D. by the hand and led him out to the clearing where the others were sitting quietly, still absorbing what, for each of them, had been a miraculous encounter.

They compared notes, and each had seen the spiritual being of their belief. They had been given the same message as C.D., and each felt blessed to be part of the journey.

Each was hoping to be the one who would find and bring back the One. They had entered the clearing that morning as twelve separate individuals, with only their acquaintance with Max to bind them. Now they were united, sharing a common purpose and a mission.

Together they hiked back down the mountain in the dark until they saw the light of a torch. Manuel greeted them without questions, and it was a silent group that returned to Tapachula.

*   *   *

Over dinner, Max told Shilpa of C.D.'s experience, and what he had heard in the cave. He also explained that it would be necessary for them to return to Izapa in December.

Whereas there had been doubters, everyone was now eager for the return trip—even Dr. Alan. Shilpa was concerned that C.D. wouldn't really be able to search for the One, but Max reassured her.

"I will come and help, but I doubt that any real searching will be necessary. I think the One has already decided who will find him—or her—and if C.D. is meant to succeed, the One will come to him."

Retracing Steps

AUGUST 2012

AFTER A DAY OF CONTEMPLATING WHAT HAD OCCURRED, ONCE again they gathered for dinner—this time to compare notes and plan for the future.

There was one common element to the instructions given to each of the Twelve by the Thirteenth Apostle.

"Retrace your steps to the most sacred places you have traveled or lived in this human life. Max will go with you—although he is not one of the Twelve, it is through his connection that you have come together with the rest."

As soon as they had finished eating, Erol sat down with Max and worked out a schedule so that he would spend at least ten days with each of the Twelve.

"We have exactly one hundred and thirty days, including today," Erol noted. "If you spend ten or eleven days with each of us, you will have just enough time. We must book your travel immediately and we must share the itinerary that each will choose to retrace their steps to those places where there is the greatest chance of finding the One." He then offered to pay for the travel expenses.

"You are more than generous, Erol," Max said, relieved to be free of the burden of the cost. "I do not know how we would have managed without you."

"There is no price to put on our mission," Erol said, and his voice was somber. "The message the Thirteenth Apostle delivered to me was perhaps the most dire. He said that if we failed to return with the One, the world would not enter the shift that has been predestined. We will not perish immediately if we fail, but the chaos—the environmental degradation, the violence and the wars, the poverty, greed, and fear which have dominated so much of the twentieth and twenty-first centuries—will continue until the planet itself will enter a dormant period during which humans will eventually destroy themselves.

"This will create a twenty-six-thousand-year period of blackness before humans emerge again to repair the damage that will have been done."

"The Apostle didn't share such dire consequences of failure with C.D.," Max interjected.

"Why would he?" Erol offered. "C.D. alone among us is the true innocent. If he is meant to find the One, it will be by the pure magic of his personality. More likely, the One will find him.

"So C.D. does not need any added motivation. Thus, I suggest that we arrange your travel so C.D. is at the final stop on your journey. You should start with Juan, I think, whose sacred places should be close at hand here in Chiapas and perhaps other sites in Mexico and Guatemala. Then make plans to travel with Alan and Chill, right in your backyard in California.

"Let me talk with the others to see which sites they will choose, so I can make the necessary arrangements for you."

※　　※　　※

As it turned out, Max did not need the full eleven days to travel with Juan.

Juan had been to Chichen Itza, to most of the sacred pyramids throughout Chiapas and the Yucatan, and to some magical hidden oases in the volcanoes that surrounded Izapa. Often they journeyed on foot with Juan's father, Manuel, who accompanied them throughout their journey.

Since they didn't exactly know what they were looking for, the entire time they were alert for any sign—an unexplainable energy, or an individual who said something or did something out of the ordinary.

They bonded, but they did not find the One. Max experienced the magic of the volcanos and felt the presence of ancient spirits at the pyramids, but no person came forth who even seemed a likely candidate.

Max returned to Dana Point and learned that Dr. Alan had spent his youth in Ohio, near many ancient Native American burial mounds. Dr. Alan had also been a mountain climber, and together with Max he visited several peaks outside of Aspen, Colorado, where he had spent winters and then some summers as a boy. But despite spending their full allotment of eleven days in Colorado, Ohio, and other parts of the Midwest, they found no trace of the One.

Since Dr. Alan confided to Max that he had actually seen a UFO many years before in his home state of Ohio, he even thought the One might be an alien. But that didn't help—they still didn't really know what they were searching for.

Max arranged to meet with Chill at the Grand Canyon in Arizona. Chill had felt great joy when visiting natural parks such as this when he was a young boy, and thus he thought the One might return to him in such a place of natural beauty.

From the Grand Canyon, they went next to Yellowstone and then back to California's remote coasts along Big Sur—among the redwoods—and finally Yosemite.

It was their last day together, and they were walking through their campsite when Chill saw a strange-looking, bearded man, grilling hot dogs far apart from the other campers. He had disheveled, white hair, sported a grizzly long, white beard, and wore jeans and a flannel work shirt. He was talking to himself in a loud erratic way.

Their first impression was that the man might be more crazy than enlightened. However, given that they'd already spent eleven days looking for the One without even a glimmer of hope and prompted by Chill's own strong belief that the One would actually be Jesus, they approached the man.

As they approached, something about the man did seem familiar, and, with the shock of realization, Max could hardly believe his eyes.

This was Louis.

Max hadn't seen his brother for more than twenty years and had been left with no idea if he was even still alive.

Louis looked up from his rambling and spoke.

"Well, it's about time you showed up."

For a brief second Max thought that—against all odds—perhaps Louis was actually the One. But then he remembered how violent Louis had been for most of his life, and he fervently believed that the One would never have taken such a form.

Chill, however, had no such baggage, and even after Max introduced his brother, he persisted. The fact that Louis *was* Max's brother actually made Chill think it more probable that Louis could be the person they were seeking. So they sat down at the picnic table next to the grill and shared the hot dogs, chips, and beer that Louis had brought.

During dinner, while Max sat quietly and watched, Chill described the adventure in Izapa and their mission to find the One. Louis showed no surprise at the story, but he peered at Max with a kind of jealousy and inner hatred he had always shown when confronted with any of his brother's accomplishments.

Max became increasingly uncomfortable and suggested to Chill that they had to leave and that he had to meet with Running Bear later that evening to continue his search.

Hearing this, Louis looked at Max and spoke.

"You will never find the One unless you take me with you," he said. "I'll pack up my things and be ready to go shortly."

Max was instantly flustered.

"But there's no time to make the arrangements," he said quickly, "and we don't have the money to make them."

"*Money!*" Louis shouted. "That's all you ever cared about and all our father ever cared about." Suddenly it was as if fifty years had melted away.

Louis lunged at Max and started choking him with all the manic force he had possessed in his youth. But he was only three weeks short of celebrating his sixty-fifth birthday, and although the sudden burst of adrenaline had given him the upper hand, the energy rush didn't last more than a minute.

Chill, at six foot two and in excellent physical condition, was able to pull Louis off Max and hold him down. Other campers heard the commotion and ran to assist as well.

A park ranger was summoned, and Louis was taken off by the local police to be held for assault. Even though his neck was sore, Max was otherwise unharmed. He thanked Chill for saving him, and they departed.

Soon they went their separate ways, and Max continued with his plan to meet with Running Bear that evening.

❋   ❋   ❋

Running Bear joined Max at a lodge in Yosemite, and they began a journey that took Max to ancient Indian sites spread throughout Montana and Canada. Yet despite the ability Running Bear had to enter into communion with the Great Spirit, there was no sign of the One.

Sun Pak was the next person with whom Max was scheduled to travel, and they met in Vancouver. Traveling along the northern coast of British Columbia, they visited places of beauty, but Sun Pak confessed that if he were to find the One, it would most likely be in China, because that was his true home—and the true home of his most sacred memories.

So they crossed the Pacific, landing in Beijing. But despite visits to the Great Wall and the small remote village where Sun Pak had been born, there was no sign of their quarry.

From China, Max flew directly to Japan to meet with Yoko.

Together they traveled to Hokkaido, Niko, and many other sacred sites where Max had also been while making *In Search of Ancient Mysteries*, and yet they found no trace.

Then Max went to Vietnam. Melody had brought her grandmother along in case they located the One in the sacred land of her ancestors. Melody's grandmother had been told the story of the Twelve, and she seemed nonplussed, though proud, that her granddaughter should be part of something so very important.

Yet she cried as she toured the beautiful countryside of her youth. Despite the fact that they visited more than twenty sacred sites and villages throughout the country, their trip proved fruitless.

Melody was very disappointed, but not so her grandmother.

"It is enough that we have sought the One in our sacred land," she said. "Intent is sometimes just as important as results. Our intent has been pure, and have no doubt that it will assist the others in their search for the One."

Max realized then that this woman believed wholeheartedly in their mission, and it gave him new hope as well.

"I am confident," she continued, "that the One will appear as prophesized. The existence of the One is similar to a belief that has been in our family for centuries, along with predictions of the coming of end-times.

"Our role in bringing about heaven on Earth shall soon be realized," she assured Melody and Max, with a wisdom and certainty that comforted them both.

Earthly Love

NOVEMBER 2012

FROM VIETNAM, MAX FLEW TO LIMA, PERU, AND THEN ON TO Trujillo where he was met by Maria and her two eldest sons at the Trujillo airport.

Maria gave Max a warm hug, and he remembered fleetingly how intoxicatingly beautiful Maria had been when they first met almost forty years before.

Stepping back and looking at her as he was introduced to her sons Andreas and Sebastian, Max saw again a woman still beautiful, with a softness and knowingness that only added to her allure.

"You have arrived on a very special day," she explained with a glow of pride. "Sebastian's oldest daughter Renata is observing her fifteenth birthday today. The entire family will be celebrating with her at my home, so you will get to meet all the Tucanos at once.

"I know you must be tired from your flight," she added. "Andreas will take you to your hotel, while Sebastian and I prepare for the festivities. Andreas will come back and pick you up at your hotel at six this evening. No doubt we will party all night, so get some rest." She laughed as she gave Max a kiss on the cheek and another quick embrace.

In the car, Max found it easy to converse with Andreas, who was curious to hear how Max and his mother had met, long before his birth. His mother had never spoken of it, and until Max called and invited her to join him in Izapa, Andreas had had no idea of his existence.

Enjoying the young man's easygoing demeanor, Max decided to open up to him and told him the whole story.

Why not, he thought. *The worst that will happen is that he'll think of me as his mother's crazy American friend.*

But Andreas didn't act surprised when told what had occurred in Izapa, nor even by the appearance of the Thirteenth Apostle.

"My mother described her encounter and explained that you would be coming to help her search for the One. She is a wonderful mother, and I believe every word she says.

"I do not know if she will be the one to find this One," he added, glancing over at Max and smiling, "but I am glad that you have come and brought this adventure into her life. She was very much in love with my father, and when he died so suddenly, she went into deep mourning. It is only now that she is starting to laugh and smile again. It will be wonderful for her to travel with you and revisit places from her youth."

At the mention of Maria's husband, Max was curious.

"Well, your mother is a very special woman," he said, "and I am sure your father must have been a very special man. I am sorry that he died so young."

"Yes, dad was wonderful," Andreas offered. "He was a wonderful provider and such a fun-loving man. He made my mother very happy and was always joking with me and my brothers. The grandchildren miss him so much as well, but we are so happy to have had him in our lives.

"You will see at the party tonight how lively the Tucano clan is," he explained. "My father was from a very large family, and his brothers and my cousins will be joining us. Altogether, there will be more than one hundred people, and almost all of them are family."

At that moment he pulled the car into the parking lot of the same Sheraton Hotel where Max had first met Maria, so many years before. He couldn't help but glance across at the park.

"I will pick you up at 6:00 P.M. Here is my number," he said, handing Max a card. "If you need anything, just call. Sebastian and my mother are handling all the party details, so I really am available to help you should the need arise."

Max exited the car, and the bellman took his suitcase.

"No, I'll be fine," Max insisted. "We have about four hours before you pick me up, and I can certainly use a good nap." He walked around the car, hugged Andreas, and thanked him for his hospitality.

❃   ❃   ❃

Max was asleep within minutes of hitting the bed.

His last thought before sleep was of Maria as the young woman he had met so many years before, kissing him in the park outside the window of his hotel room and telling him that she would love him forever—just as he loved her—but that their destinies would not allow them to be together in this lifetime.

But Max realized, just seeing her at the airport, that part of him was still in love with her and still longing for the peaceful domestic life she had had with her husband.

And not with him.

❃   ❃   ❃

Max had been to many parties in his life, but the love, laughter, music, and festivities at the *quinceañera* for Renata truly amazed him.

There were grandchildren ranging from three years old and up and even a newborn from one of the cousins. There were Renata's closest girlfriends, dressed in colorful gowns, and young suitors dressed in their best suits. There were aunts and uncles and great-aunts and great-uncles, and flowers and decorations, and colored lights, and above all, love.

Everyone danced and everyone sang—it seemed as if half the family could have been professional musicians. They sang folk songs, they sang classic love songs, they played special songs they had written themselves, some of them romantic and some of them full of jokes about Renata and her friends.

As Maria had predicted, the party really did go on all night. They roasted an entire lamb on a spit and had every kind of delicacy imaginable, including a beautiful cake almost five-feet high.

Max was introduced to everyone, and they all hugged him and made him feel part of the family. It was the first time since Izapa that Max actually forgot about his search for the One and just had fun. He danced, and ate, and drank. He flirted with the girls old and young, joked with the grandchildren, and found himself playing word games and number games with the children.

He delighted them with his stories of India and far-off lands, but no matter what he found himself doing throughout the evening, Max could not take his eyes off Maria.

She was dressed modestly in a black dress and spent most of her time playing with the children. A smile stayed on her face almost the entire evening, and she was so animated during the games with the youngest of her grandchildren that one might have mistaken her for one of the grandchildren and not the grandmother she was.

Toward the end of the evening—or the beginning of the morning— after Max had helped Maria put several of the grandchildren to bed, she turned to Max and thanked him.

"Tomorrow, well, I guess, actually today, given how late it is, we will sleep in late, and then I will pick you up at your hotel, and we will fly to Arequipa," she said. "From there we will go to Cuzco, Machu Picchu, Puno, Copacabana, and Lake Titicaca. Those were the most sacred trips of my youth and the most likely places we might find what we are looking for."

"I have been to those places as well, thanks to the work I did on the films," he said. "For now, however, I want to thank you again for tonight. It has been more than a relaxing break from my search. I have never felt so much love in a single home. To see you with your grandchildren and entire family was so special."

"No, it is I who must thank you," Maria insisted. "Your call could not have come at a better time in my life. In Izapa I reconnected with my sense of higher purpose. I have had a wonderful life, and yet somehow I feel my life is just beginning again."

Then she shooed him out toward the front door of the house.

"There is a taxi waiting to take you back to your hotel. We have a 1:00 P.M. flight, and we will have many chances to catch up as we travel. In Izapa, with so many people, I did not get a chance to ask you about your life and family. I look forward to getting to know you on this trip."

* * *

Max and Maria searched for the One for the next ten days but without success.

Max had arranged for separate rooms in each hotel, as was appropriate, but they discovered that the deep love that had first united them so many years ago had never died. Alone, and without others to distract them, they could not help but fall in love again.

They fell into a natural rhythm together that made traveling effortless and fun. They laughed at the stories they told each other, the observations they made, and the people they met. On the train trip to Puno from Arequipa they played cards, and Max was shocked to see how competitive Maria was and how though she never seemed to be paying attention, more often than not she beat him at gin.

On the hike to Machu Picchu, Max gently took Maria's hand to help her cross some of the difficult parts of the trail. He could hardly believe the electricity he felt in so casual a touching and once again desire was alive and pulsing throughout his body and his mind.

By the time they were in Copacabana, Max was holding her hand whenever there seemed a likely excuse. He literally could not keep his hands off her, nor his eyes.

But Maria kept them focused . . . and searching. Finally, on the last day of their travels on a small island in Lake Titicaca, Maria admitted that she, too, had once again fallen in love with Max.

"I am disappointed that we have not found the One," she confessed. "I truly thought that today, on this island, we would succeed. One of our legends is that the era of feminine spirituality will be starting, based right here on Lake Titicaca, just at this time. My Incan ancestors believed that Virachocha had come from this lake and had gone back into it.

"I am sure that, for most of my ancestors, Virachocha himself would be considered the One," she explained, "and it seemed hopeful that he might appear to us today."

She smiled and looked into Max's eyes and then continued.

"But in reality, I am not disappointed at all. When I first met you I knew that on some mystical level you would be the love of my life. That magical moment we shared in the park in Trujillo never ended for me. I loved my husband and the wonderful family we created together, but part of me never stopped loving you.

"I love you now, and unlike the circumstances when we met, I see no reason we cannot pursue our hearts."

Maria held both of Max's hands and kissed him full on the lips in a kiss that he reciprocated with a passion and gentleness that transported them both, back and forth in time, to places they had been or were destined to travel, in their current and future incarnations. The kiss seemed never-ending, but ever so delicately Maria drew back just as tears from Max's eyes touched her cheeks.

"These are tears of joy, my love," he said. "I have dreamed of this moment throughout my life. I can hardly believe after all these years, I have finally found true earthly love.

"Somehow I have always felt drawn to you, and safe—knowing that I could be my true self. Seeing you with your children and grand-children and how giving and generous and nurturing you are with all of them has only confirmed my inner knowing that being with you for all eternity would be the greatest reward of my life."

She smiled at him.

"Max, to know you is to love you. I cannot resist you, and believe that we will be together the rest of our lives. But in this moment you must ready yourself for the boat that will take you back to Puno, and then the train and the flights that will lead you to the remaining members of the Twelve, with whom you must resume the search for the One."

Max started to laugh with a combination of relief and pleasure.

"Yes, but now I have an even greater reason to find the One and to ensure that this planet does not self-destruct in chaos and anarchy.

"I will see you in Izapa in a little more than a month," he added, "and on December 22, once the One has been found, we will make plans on how we shall live the rest of our lives in bliss and love."

Max smiled as he kissed Maria one last time and prepared to continue his search.

Obstacles

NOVEMBER–DECEMBER 2012

Hᴵˢ ꜰᴜᴛᴜʀᴇ ᴡɪᴛʜ Mᴀʀɪᴀ ʟᴇɴᴛ Mᴀx ɴᴇᴡ ɪᴍᴘᴇᴛᴜs. Tʜᴇʏ *ʜᴀᴅ* ᴛᴏ succeed, or all of their dreams would amount to nothing.

Thus spurred on, he landed in London, where he was met by Yutsky.

The Israeli had spent some of the best years of his youth in England, making films at Stonehenge, Glastonbury, the Isle of Iona, Glendalough in the Wicklow Hills just south of Dublin, and many of the same sacred sites Max had visited while scouting sites for *In Search of Ancient Mysteries*. Their tour of these locations, coordinated by the concierge at the Claridges Hotel, was a whirlwind of activity but yielded nothing.

Finding no trace of the One in the British Isles, Yutsky and Max proceeded to Germany, where they explored the Black Forest and several ancient German castles.

Still nothing, and Max was beginning to worry. What had seemed to be a sure thing was beginning to feel like a fool's quest.

I can't let myself think like that, he thought grimly. *We will succeed.*

From Germany they traveled across France, stopping in Lourdes, at ancient sites in Provence, and then into northern Spain, where they had each had powerful experiences in their youth filming at the pre-historic caves in Santillana del Mar outside of Santander.

In a little more than a week of traveling, they visited more than twenty sacred sites, yet there was no sign of the One.

So Yutsky returned with Max to his birthplace of Jerusalem, where they explored the old city, Jericho, Masada, Bethlehem, the Dead Sea, and Galilee.

Still nothing. Almost one hundred days had passed when he arrived in Istanbul to meet Erol.

"Max, you must remain calm—it's always possible that the One will save the best for last," Erol reassured him. "Yet we must move forward as if he may appear at any moment. First we will make a quick visit to Greece, where I visited as a boy, and then I will show you the true beauty of the world, which is my homeland of Turkey.

"Turkey is the most sacred of all countries. If the One has chosen to enjoy life he will have come back as a Turk. I will show you sites you never dreamed of and beauty beyond all imagining—including the site where Noah's Ark was found. I know every inch of this land, and I have made arrangements for us to visit it all within the allotted time."

Despite his friend's unquenchable enthusiasm, however, and the beauty of his Turkish homeland, their search proved fruitless.

❋   ❋   ❋

From Istanbul, Max flew to Nepal to meet with Rinpoche and retrace Rinpoche's flight from the monasteries, where the Buddhist himself was believed to be a sacred reincarnation of their ancient masters.

They continued to the forests in which Rinpoche had toiled while imprisoned in the work camp, but despite the magical mists and the stillness in which they hiked for many days, there was no sign of the One.

When Max said goodbye to Rinpoche, both of them knew that they would reunite in just twelve days in Izapa. Max's anxiety was beginning to show, and Rinpoche tried to reassure him.

"Do not worry," he said. "I am certain the energy of the One is with us even now—I can feel it. I know we have not yet found him, not in incarnated form, but surely the One is waiting for you in India with C.D.

"Travel safely, and we will reunite soon."

✳   ✳   ✳

Max flew directly from Tibet to Delhi, where he learned that Shilpa and C.D. had planned their internal travels throughout India beginning with Leh, high in the Himalayas and back in the direction of Tibet.

From Leh, they visited an ancient monastery where Shilpa had studied as a child and where she had taken a long summer vacation when C.D. had just been born. This monastery was the most sacred in all of India, and there were even rumors that Jesus Christ himself had visited it.

Shilpa thought it would be a likely place for the One to reside. But she was wrong.

From Leh they trekked by car back to Srinagar. It was now almost mid-December, and they narrowly overcame the snows in the passes, which were treacherous to maneuver. Nevertheless, they came no closer to finding the One in Srinagar, so they flew to Rishikesh on the Ganges, where as a boy C.D. had spent summers with one of his uncles.

Rishikesh proved to be a dead end, as had all of the rest, and it was December 18—time to board the flight to Mexico City and then to Izapa.

✳   ✳   ✳

Having begun the quest with so much optimism and enthusiasm, Max was surprised by his apparent failure. C.D. had been his greatest hope, yet the One had not revealed himself to the young Indian or to any of them.

Yet he refused to give up. There were still two days remaining, and until the twenty-first arrived, there was hope.

There has to be! he thought passionately.

With that, he sought out a computer. During his trek in Tibet and the Himalayas, he had been without access to the Internet, and his cell phone had been useless.

Perhaps the One had appeared to another member of the Twelve.

※　　※　　※

Such was not the case.

It was time to return to Izapa—with or without the One—and to meet again with the Thirteenth Apostle.

Then they would learn what was destined to happen on that fateful day when the Mayan calendar—and so many other ancient calendars—ran out.

With the search at an end, Max spent countless hours poring over B.N.'s book of numbers, beginning with his stay in India and continuing with most of the flight from New Delhi to Mexico City.

It was clear to him that 21122012 was the answer. It was an eleven and a two and represented both a beginning and an end. The value fluctuated, based on the number system in which it was considered. The number indicated both light and dark and held almost infinite variations of prime and non-prime numbers within it.

Max's own extraordinary mathematical talents were tested as never before. The number 21122012 seemed to beg for a human interpretation that would vary, based upon the human who did the calculations.

Yet try as he might, he could not find that interpretation.

※　　※　　※

When Max, Shilpa, and C.D. arrived at the hotel in Tapachula, it was late in the evening of the twentieth, and all the other members of the Twelve had gathered expectantly, hoping to greet the One. Maria was the first to greet Max, but as soon as she saw his expression, she held back to give him time to speak.

When he told them that he and C.D. had come alone, they all were crestfallen.

"How can this be?" Melody said plaintively. "We were certain you and C.D. would find him—or her. What's going to happen to us and what will become of the world when the calendar ends tomorrow at sunset?"

Max could tell that several of the others shared her desperation, too. This mysterious mission had demanded complete faith and trust in the process of discovery.

Each one of the Twelve had entered into what might be their final adventure on Earth with enthusiasm and a certainty that they would prevail.

Now that the time was drawing near and the One had not surfaced, fears were creeping in.

"We must not doubt our destinies," Erol reassured her—and the entire group. "We have searched with open hearts and done all that is possible to serve the request of the Thirteenth Apostle. Surely we shall be rewarded.

"Tomorrow will be an eventful day, perhaps the last day on this planet as we know it," he continued. "Let us all be well rested for the challenges. Running Bear, Juan, and Manuel have again secured our meeting place near the cave. We will meet there at 4:00, and the sun is to set at exactly 5:02. That is the minute when the solstice will occur, and the Mayan calendar will end.

"So, tonight, sleep well, and let no one worry. We must trust in the wisdom of a universe that has brought us all together for this special moment in this special place."

※　　※　　※

Exhausted from his travels and his unsuccessful attempts to decipher the equations in B.N.'s book of numbers, Max slept until almost noon.

When he awoke he saw it was a bright, sunny day and decided— just in case this was to be his last day on Earth—to take a swim in the nearby Pacific Ocean. He found Dr. Alan finishing a late breakfast and suggested they take one of the vans to the beach.

Alan had brought his surfboards and had an extra one for Max to try.

"I've never surfed before," Max confessed. "It seems strange to have my first lesson on the day that might be our last here on Earth."

"Well, when I'm surfing, I feel as if I'm most in touch with whatever the rest of you think of as God," Dr. Alan replied. "If today is to be the end of time—which I seriously doubt—then there's nothing I would rather be doing.

"So let's go!" he said.

They loaded the boards into a van. On the way to the beach, Alan confessed that he still had his doubts about the prophecy, despite his encounter with the Thirteenth Apostle and had never entirely believed that the One would be found.

Yet the experience had been too profound to ignore entirely.

During the drive Max noticed that a beat-up, old, brown Chevy seemed to be following their van, but after a time he lost sight of it and gave it no further thought. By the time they reached the beach, there was nothing but blue sky and sunshine.

Dr. Alan handed him a surfboard, and soon Max was crouching and falling, then straddling and falling again.

Finally, he managed to get into a squatting position on the board, and before he knew it he was catching a ride on a small wave. It was a euphoric victory, and he managed to hold on for a yard or two before losing his balance and crashing into the gentle waves.

Dr. Alan was enthusiastic in his praise.

"You have a natural talent, Max," he said. "I can't believe you wasted so many years not surfing."

"I can't believe it either," Max agreed. "My one commitment, if the world is still here tomorrow, is that I'm going to spend more time learning how to surf."

"That's the best idea you have had in a long time," Dr. Alan shouted over his shoulder as he headed back into the surf. While Max followed, he caught a big wave and took it all the way to the shore.

Max lay on his board, admiring Dr. Alan's ability to ride the wave, reaching the beach with a gentle dismount, maintaining his balance all the while. Once on the beach, Dr. Alan pointed to the sun, and then to the van as he started walking away from the water.

The sun was high in the sky, and Max realized that it was time to go. But he wanted to catch one full wave, so he signaled Alan to start packing up the gear and, with hand signals, indicated that he would be there in five or ten minutes. Then he crouched on his board, looking behind him to see when the next good-sized wave might start to break.

Suddenly and without warning, Max felt a hand grab his ankle and pull him off the board. Then a second hand grabbed him around the neck and started to pull him down to the bottom of the ocean. The water was only about eight-feet deep, but Max was instantly disoriented and had no idea even where the bottom was or what direction the shore was.

He tried to fight off the attacker, but he had been caught off guard and was already choking, entirely unable to breathe. He fought desperately and managed to get to the surface for a brief second—just enough to catch a breath, but then he was overpowered and forced under again.

He started to lose consciousness.

He felt weak and unable to resist.

Before blacking out, Max remembered all the times Louis had tried to choke him, and in a blur he thought he could make out the face of his attacker. It was a man with long, gray hair and vicious eyes that had haunted Max throughout his childhood.

But it did not matter. Max was already leaving his body.

He was returning to the peace and bliss of another dimension, of white light, love, and contentment. He looked down and saw his body being grappled and held under the surface.

He experienced again the twelve names and the twelve colors, and this time a message of forgiveness.

It's okay . . . you did your best.

The end of the world is not your fault.

❈   ❈   ❈

Louis had been placed in a mental institution for thirty days after the incident in Yosemite National Park. When Max failed to appear at the legal hearing, he was released.

He had remembered what Chill had said about the meeting in Izapa, on December 21, and as soon as he had been released, he had driven down to Mexico and staked out Tapachula's only modern hotel.

Finally his patience had been rewarded. He had followed Max and another man to the beach, and once the other left, he had struck.

Louis wanted to ensure that, whatever else might happen in his life, Max would not be able to achieve his final goal. He gloated to himself as he held Max down. He was also gasping for breath but did not care.

He was willing to die himself, if it would prevent Max from triumphing.

❈   ❈   ❈

Max resigned himself to the fact that he had failed in his mission, and made ready to enter the white tunnel. Suddenly he saw what looked like Dr. Alan swimming toward the two struggling figures. He turned away from the light.

❈   ❈   ❈

A powerful swimmer, Dr. Alan took only moments before he was on top of Max's attacker who, weakened from holding his own breath so long, was unable to defend himself.

Alan pulled Max from the man's grip and began to make his way back to shore, kicking out at their pursuer whenever he attempted to approach.

The man must have realized that he was beaten, and he swam away while Dr. Alan got Max to the beach. Immediately he started mouth-to-mouth resuscitation, and after several minutes, Max coughed and vomited the large quantity of saltwater that he had swallowed while pinned under the waves.

After a few more moments, he sat up, groggy but alive.

"Who was that maniac, and why was he trying to drown you?" Alan asked. "I've encountered surf Nazis in my time, but I've never witnessed anything like that. Maybe I can find a policeman and have him arrested. He nearly killed you."

Max motioned for him to forget about it and explained.

"That man who tried to drown me was my brother," he said, and Alan was incredulous. "He was just doing what he always does—it's not important.

"The important thing is that we get back to the hotel. The others will be waiting and wondering where we are. We still have time to get to Izapa before the sun sets."

He stood and looked gratefully at his rescuer.

"You saved my life. Hopefully the Twelve can still save the world. We need to get going."

Dr. Alan agreed and drove as quickly as he could back to the hotel in Tapachula. During the drive he glanced over at his friend to make certain he was alright and was happy to see the color return to Max's face. Finally, after a few more moments of coughing, Max spoke up.

"I am not certain why my brother followed us and tried to kill me, but I do know that your intervention has prevented a catastrophe. Even though we haven't found the One, we have to assume that he will somehow yet appear.

"Please don't let the others know about this attack, though. They're worried enough already, and I don't want them to see this as a negative omen or to become concerned about me, while they should be focusing on praying that the One will appear."

Dr. Alan agreed.

"Whatever you think is best," he said. "Frankly I still just find it all preposterous. The Mayan calendar is just another myth, no greater or lesser than any other myth. I never believed the Bible story that said the world was created in seven days, and I'm not inclined to believe this story of the end-times either.

"Don't get me wrong—I *do* hope something miraculous occurs today. But dollars to doughnuts, I'll be surfing tomorrow—and if that lunatic of a brother of yours shows up, he'll be the one to drown, not you."

The End of Time

DECEMBER 21, 2012

THE AIR GREW HEAVIER AND COLDER AS THE VANS MADE THEIR WAY to Izapa.

By the time Manuel met the Twelve at the base of the mountain to start the hike to the clearing by the cave, it had started to rain, cold and hard. Before they reached the clearing, the rain had turned to hail.

It never hailed in Izapa, Juan claimed. It truly did seem as if this might be the end of the world.

The mood was one of apprehension. Even C.D. was wincing as the hail bounced off his dark hair and skin. By the time they reached the gathering place, it was close to 4:30—just thirty minutes before the solstice.

And there was still no sign of the One.

Everyone was cold, so they all went to the cave to get away from the stinging mixture of rain and ice. Running Bear, again dressed in his ceremonial garb, including the single eagle feather in his head-band, built a fire. They huddled close together and were able to dry off. But the calmness and euphoria they had felt when they had last been in the cave were only distant memories.

Suddenly the rain and hail stopped, and the last rays of the sun pierced the trees, and there was utter stillness.

As one, the group left the shelter of the cave and returned to the clearing. The Thirteenth Apostle had reappeared.

The Thirteenth Apostle spoke with calmness and clarity.

"You have returned at the designated hour, yet there is no new face among you—the face of the One. What of your quest?"

No one spoke, and though it was only a minute of silence, it seemed to last forever.

The sun was now sinking quickly.

The end of time was at hand, and the group had failed.

High in the sky, a condor appeared and swooped down, almost landing on the shoulder of Running Bear. Running Bear was startled, but he quickly regained his composure and spoke.

"It has long been said in the Lakota and the Hopi secret ceremonies that the signal for the beginning of the time of peace and harmony would be at hand when the condor and the eagle came together." He gestured to the feather he wore. "Surely this is a sign that we have not failed and that somehow the One is in fact with us now."

After a moment, the Thirteenth Apostle's voice was heard again.

"Running Bear is correct. This condor's appearance is a sign that in this very moment the One must be present. One of you must in fact be the person for whom you searched."

The news surprised them all, and they glanced quickly at one another. Before anyone could speak, the voice came again.

"Whoever you are, you must step forward now. The sun will set, and unless the One is identified and redeems the world and His creation, undesired prophecies will be fulfilled.

"An age of darkness, rather than light, shall be mankind's fate."

All eyes turned to C.D. Among the Twelve, only he seemed to be without ego. Only he seemed likely to without knowing be the One.

But C.D. simply turned to Max and looked at him with eyes of adoration and love.

Max looked back at C.D., and in that moment Max remembered his own birth and the love he had received from his mother.

He realized that, despite all the numbers he had been calculating, he had never calculated the exact numerology of his *own* birth.

In that instant he realized that his birthday—December 12, 1949—possessed the exact numerical value and vibration of 12/21/2012.

He reexperienced his birth and the birth of all humanity, and for the first time, he remembered who he actually was.

He remembered being born as Max. He remembered agreeing to forget all he knew, so he could experience human life.

And as he stepped forward into the center of the clearing, he felt himself a part of all that is and felt his consciousness reestablish connections with all who had ever lived.

For the first time he saw the Thirteenth Apostle in physical form—the form of faithful messenger and accomplice in the grand scheme they had initiated to redeem mankind, many eons ago when first they had observed the unfortunate choices humans had made in creating civilizations of violence.

There was absolute silence as Max and the Thirteenth Apostle looked calmly into each other's eyes. As they shared an endless look of gratitude and recognition, they seemed to mirror each other and become each other.

Then they morphed into thousands of different humans—men and women, young and old of every race and type who had ever lived on planet Earth.

A is and is not equal to A.

Max was and was not Max. Max was and was not the Thirteenth Apostle. Max was and was not every human being who had ever lived.

The Twelve—Melody, Maria, Yutsky, Chill, Dr. Alan, Rinpoche, Erol, Sun Pak, Juan, Yoko, Running Bear, and C.D.—were transfixed as the sun set and time as mankind had previously experienced time ended.

Birds stopped singing.

There was no wind.

Only stillness and absolute silence.

❋   ❋   ❋

The moment might have lasted forever.

It might have lasted less than a second.

No one would ever know.

The Mayan prophecy was complete. All had come to pass as eons ago had been predicted.

For Max it was a *déjà vu* of his near-death experience. Again there was light and love, and only the nurturing warmth from the human forms who stood with him, and the countless souls that surrounded the Twelve and rejoiced in the beginning of a new time for man and perhaps for the universe.

As time began again, Max spoke, but it was not the purely human Max. It was a Max imbued with his own awareness that he indeed was the One and that he had seeded the consciousness of each of the Twelve, millennia ago. He spoke with a gentleness and calm that was comforting to all who listened.

"Time has ended, and a new era will now begin," the One said. "The great shift has occurred. Nothing will change, and yet everything will change.

"The Earth remains and all its creatures, and yet the consciousness of all has shifted and will continue to shift in the times yet to come. As humans you will be entering an era of love, harmony, and freedom more suited to your destinies. Wars will cease as you discover the infinite bounty of all that has been created.

"There is no lack on this planet and no need for strife. The energy you have expended for survival and competition shall be directed into creativity and play. This is what was intended from the beginning and what each and every one of you shall now achieve."

He paused for a moment, then spoke again.

"This new era will last for one hundred and forty-four thousand years but may be extended endlessly, depending upon the choices made by you and by your descendants. There is always free will, and it is free will that has brought you to this place at this time. Each of you has played your role, as have all with whom you have lived and interacted. Although this moment was predestined, it was not predetermined that it would arrive.

"It has been your acts of courage, love, and choice that have brought these times of bliss upon the Earth."

The afterglow of the setting sun filled the clearing with pink and orange light. Every member of the gathering was glowing in the reflected joy of Max's awakening, and this joyful energy spread to every living creature on planet Earth. Instantly there was a new *aliveness* that could be felt in every tree and plant, and even the rocks and the soil upon which they stood became vibrant with shared consciousness and love.

The Thirteenth Apostle stepped back from Max and spoke again to the Twelve.

"I leave you now for realms beyond your current knowing but delight in all that you have done and will do," he said. "Know that in other dimensions we are already reunited, sharing the mystery of life and the great awakening that never ends.

"Max shall stay with you, and although he is the One, he is also— as a human—just Max. Do not draw attention to him as anything other than the being Max, for though he can leave at any time, his own desire was that he would walk among you as an equal and not be distinguished.

"Even as gods, our ultimate joy is experiencing the full breadth of human experience, including failure, disappointment, and struggle. Humans often seek to bury the shadow side of life, but as gods we rejoice in all that can be experienced. Even as awakened beings you will have your challenges, but rest assured that even in your defeats and failures, you shall be experiencing an ever grander and ever more complex human existence.

"Protect Max and protect yourselves and enjoy the lives that you were destined to create and live." He said finally, "May the joy of the universe be with you always."

With those final words, the Thirteenth Apostle was gone.

❋   ❋   ❋

Even as night fell, there was brightness in the faces of the Twelve and Max as they descended the still-wet path and reached the spot where Manuel was faithfully waiting.

There was a smile on Manuel's face as he greeted each of them. Even the drivers who had been waiting in the vans were smiling. No one spoke, and yet there was a silent communication among them all as they drove back to Tapachula.

The end of time had come and gone. The apprehension that all had shared was gone.

A new era had begun.

The Awakening

DECEMBER 21, 2012

B Y THE TIME THE VANS WERE UNLOADING THE TWELVE AT THE HOTEL in Tapachula, even in this remote Mexican town in Chiapas, news was filtering in that something extraordinary had happened.

Scientists had recorded a sudden change of the axis of the Earth. The magnetic fields had shifted. The very orbit of the Earth had shifted.

The consequences were still unknown but television, radio, and Internet sites were constantly updating with new speculation and new findings.

Although the result should have been sheer panic, while there was some apprehension among those who were reporting these events, the majority seemed calm, almost serene. Scientists expressed astonishment that such a shift could have occurred without warning and with no perceivable catastrophic impact.

There were no tsunamis.

There were no earthquakes.

In the Far East, where it was already the morning of December 22, 2012, the sun had risen on clear skies with a softness that was unusual.

Everywhere on Earth, it seemed like it was going to be a wonderful day.

*   *   *

When Max walked into the hotel, everyone from the bellmen to the desk attendants was relaxed and smiling. It was almost as if everyone was part of the same inner knowing, the same inside joke—secure in the knowledge that everyone was interconnected on the deepest level.

It was as if they were different cells in the same living body. And for Max, this wasn't a metaphor, but an actual fact.

Over dinner—the final dinner they would share as a group—Max revealed that it was only in the moment of his realization that he was, in fact, the One that the shift had actually occurred.

"It was never guaranteed that we would make this shift," he explained. "Throughout this lifetime of being Max, I've been more asleep than awake. I had to be, in order for the experiment to work.

"All humans are put to sleep when they incarnate," he elaborated, "so they can truly awaken. It's not enough for one or two to awaken, however, for consciousness to evolve and grow on a planetary scale. That's why it was necessary for *all* of you to participate. It was a group process—and a group awakening—that triggered my own realization.

"Each of you holds the energy of the One. As the Kabbalah and other ancient sciences have taught, the moment of Creation was a fragmenting of the consciousness of the One into infinite individual entities. Each of you—and every human being on the planet—cocreated the expanded consciousness upon which the shift depended.

"On this level, each of you and all who exist are equally the One."

Ever the practical inquirer Erol pressed the point.

"But if this was the case, why did you not become aware of who you were last August when we first met as a group and the energies were activated?" he asked. "Was there any purpose in having to search for you these last four months, or was it just a test of our belief and commitment to the mission?"

Several others nodded, as if he had given voice to something they, too, had been wondering.

"Nothing was arbitrary," Max replied. "I was not aware, but the plan required Max as a human being to activate all the energy vortices of the Earth, because it was the planet itself that had been suffering. The Gaia hypothesis really is true."

That yielded some confused looks from the group, and he explained.

"Gaia is a Greek goddess, and the hypothesis is that the Earth has a singular consciousness, and everything that takes place affects it. Over the centuries, every violent act has had its impact on the Earth, and above all on the sacred sites on the planet. The sacred sites themselves were chosen eons ago—sometimes consciously and sometimes not—by shamans, based on the powerful energies that appeared there.

"Each site is a vortex of energy, and it was necessary for me to journey to those places, to heal them. It was a long process that started when Max was a young man."

"But how did you know you would visit so many sites, spread so far apart across the world?" asked Melody.

"As Max I never had a clue," he replied. "The journey really started with my first trip as a student—to Peru and Bolivia, when I visited Lake Titicaca, and then even more while I was working on *In Search of Ancient Mysteries*. But I wasn't aware that anything extraordinary was occurring.

"It wasn't until I had made my initial trips as an individual, that all Twelve of you would enter the picture," Max explained. "That's why I couldn't know your names until I encountered each of you, one by one, and it wasn't until I met Running Bear that I could see the importance of the gathering."

"But what was the point of retracing your steps with each of us these last several months?" Sun Pak asked.

"First of all, there were places I had never been, which each of you identified as places of power—such as the monasteries in Tibet, the sacred Isle of Iona, the castles in Germany, and the remote springs in Vietnam and China," Max said. "And even if I had been there before, I hadn't been back for many years.

"When I returned with each of you, I was carrying the energy of each and every spot I had previously visited and was bolstered by your individual energies," he continued. "It was as if we ignited each site.

"But still my presence alone did not cause the shift. That could not occur until each and every sacred site had been given its charge. Once that had been done, all that was missing was the ignition key itself."

"What do you mean, the ignition key?" Chill asked.

"As Max, I was the ignition key. But it required a special type of current—a current based on integrating the highest level of consciousness into Max's being. This level of consciousness only took place for me when I finally realized that my very birth was linked to the date December 21, 2012, and that my only purpose in incarnating was to free humanity from a materialism that was dehumanizing each individual and debasing nature, the heart of creation on planet Earth."

He looked around the table at each and every one of the people with whom he had shared the adventure.

"Every one of you contributed to that final awakening. I could feel the desire and intent in each of your hearts, beginning with Maria, and saw it most clearly perhaps in the unconditionally pure love that always shines from C.D.'s eyes . . . from his entire being," he said warmly. "But it was most powerful in the collective energy of the group, the collective purity of each of you as members of the Twelve, seeking to help not just your individual families and nations, but all of humanity.

"It brought home to me—in the moment of numerical and vibrational connection—the pure base of love, which is, in fact, the essential element of all life. It is at the base of each conception and birth, both physical and metaphysical. Had I, as Max, not entered this higher state of consciousness, I would have been an ignition key without the power to heal the planet, and the great shift might not be happening."

He paused again, allowing what he had said to sink in, then spoke.

"There is more involved with human destiny than scientists can fathom." He held up the object that had been the key to his discovery. "Here in B.N. Mahars's notebook, there are equations that explain some of these connections, but even I as Max did not have the capacity to understand them. The calendars of the ancient civilizations, the legends of the twelve tribes, the twelve colors associated with each of you and with the cosmic energy of the universes beyond, all are linked.

"It is true that everything and nothing are the same, since the shift. There is no time. There is no space. And yet the illusions of life and death are real within the limits in which they have been created." He put down the book and peered at them, one at a time. "As you progress and become multidimensional beings, you will see that even these insights are but the beginning of a greater journey of awakening . . . a journey best explored at a future time."

Maria looked back at him, a mixture of love and awe reflected on her face.

"Yes," she said. "For now it seems enough to rejoice that humanity is saved. But before long the questions will begin again. Where do we go from here? What must we do with the remainder of our sacred lives?" she asked.

Before he answered, he smiled at her, and in his smile lay the promise that they would live and love together, just as they had pledged. And the human who was Max rejoiced.

"For the moment, and in fact for all moments, it's enough that you each experience the joy of who you really are. On the surface your lives may not change at all, but as you move throughout this vast and strange world, be aware that every human you meet—every animal, every plant, and even every object most think of as lifeless—is brimming with life.

"Challenges remain for all of you and even for me. For I desire nothing more than to continue on the journey of Max and discover what human tasks await me and how as a man with human needs and frailties, I will integrate the knowledge of who I really am with all whom I am yet to meet."

As he concluded, Max raised his glass in a toast to all assembled, as they continued on the strange journey that both man and God call "life."

Epilogue

NONE OF THE TWELVE EVER REVEALED THE ROLE THEY EACH HAD played in bringing about the great shift, and none of them exposed the true identity of Max as the One.

Meanwhile, the Earth flourished, and global warming slowed, then ceased. Perhaps more spectacularly, man found a balance with nature.

New technologies were invented, new forms of energy were found. Abundance became commonplace for all. Within just a few decades, the concept of war ceased to exist, and education and creativity became the battlefields of choice. There was no reason for crime.

Scientists continued to explore the dramatic shift that took place on December 21, 2012, but never arrived at a consensus. Some went back and studied the ancient Mayan beliefs, and it was proposed that the Earth—and Izapa in particular—were located at the center of the alignment of the great galaxy of the Milky Way and at the center of the infinite universes yet unnamed.

How this could be was the topic that was argued and never resolved, for indeed it was beyond human understanding.

Postscript

Though *The Twelve* is essentially a work of fiction, it contains more elements of reality than you might suspect. The belief in the great shift is reflected in aspects of several of the world's cultures, not only the Mayan.

And certainly, the current state in which we find our planet and its cultures would prove that something needs to be done. Whether or not you believe in a higher power—whether you consider yourself a Running Bear or a Dr. Alan—you can be a part of the solution.

Truth, integrity, and love are what will always matter most in life. The shift that is coming will highlight these simple values, which have been known throughout the ages.

As a species and planet, we are facing huge challenges, but the first steps are to wake up to who you really are and wake up as many others as you can. Reading and discussing *The Twelve* is a step in this direction, but only a step.

If you have connected with Max's belief that coincidences, serendipity, and synchronicities are embedded in every life, and that they can guide you to your higher purpose to serve others, then please go to http://www. planetchange2012.com, where you can connect with like-minded individuals.

Acknowledgments

I WOULD LIKE TO THANK THE READERS OF THE EARLY DRAFTS OF this manuscript including: Catherine Chiesa, David Wilk, Gayle Newhouse, Bob Holt, Linda McNabb, Cathy Montesi, Conrad Zensho, Thom Hartmann, Constance Kellough, Jose Arguelles, Cyrus Gladstone, Santos Rodriguez, and Dr. Ervin Laszlo. My thanks to my editors, Marie Rowe, Georgina Levitt, Kim McArthur, Amanda Ferber, and Stephen Saffel, who each added valuable suggestions to the manuscript, as did film producer Ian Jessel, my cousin Rhianne, and my film agent, Barry Krost. My appreciation to Waterside staff Ming Russell, Nathalie McKnight, and Carlene Hermanson, who spent many hours typing corrections and additions to the early and later drafts, and to copyeditor Claire Wyckoff. I have a truly wonderful publisher in Roger Cooper, who assembled a great team to edit and produce the beautiful book you hold in your hands. To all of them my heartfelt gratitude as well as to all those whose lives have intersected with mine from teachers and colleagues, to clients and golfing buddies, allowing me the privilege of living a life that stimulated the writing of this book.

Above all I must acknowledge my late parents, Selma and Milton Gladstone, who provided me both the intellectual foundation and inspiration to share my soul with others through the magic of writing.

© 2009 Doug Menuez

William J Gladstone

In Joy

I am deeply appreciative of the work that Dr. Jane Goodall and the Jane Goodall Institute have done and continue to do to educate young people on the importance and sacredness of their connection with the earth and all living things. A percentage of my author royalties are being donated to Jane Goodall's Roots & Shoots. I encourage you to visit www.rootsandshoots.org and to consider making a contribution of your own.

Recommended Reading

Argüelles, José. *The Mayan Factor: Path Beyond Technology*. Rochester, VT: Bear & Company, 1987.

Audlin, James David (Distant Eagle). *Circle of Life: Traditional Teachings of Native American Elders*. Santa Fe, NM: Clear Light Publishing, 2006.

Braden, Gregg, Peter Russell, Daneil Pinchbeck, et al. *The Mystery of 2012: Predictions, Prophecies, and Possibilities*. Louisville, CO: Sounds True Publishing, 2007. (Audio also available.)

Clow, Barbara Hand. *The Mayan Code: Time Acceleration and Awakening the World Mind*. Rochester, VT: Bear & Company, 2007.

Gladstone, William. *Legends of the Twelve*. New York, NY: Vanguard Press, 2010.

Jenkins, John Major, and Terence McKenna. *Maya Cosmogenisis 2012: The True Meaning of the Maya Calendar End-Date*. Rochester, VT: Bear & Company, 1998.

Laszlo, Ervin. *Worldshift 2012: Making Green Business, New Politics, and Higher Consciousness Work Together*. Rochester, VT: Inner Traditions, 2009.

Loye, David. *An Arrow Through Chaos: How We See into the Future*. Rochester, VT: Inner Traditions, 2000.

Márquez, Gabriel Garcia. *100 Years of Solitude*. New York, NY: Avon, 1976.

Melchizedek, Drunvalo. *Serpent of Light Beyond 2012: The Movement of the Earth's Kundalini and the Rise of the Female Light, 1949 to 2013*. Newburyport, MA: Weiser Books, 2008.

Michell, John, and Christine Rhone. *Twelve-Tribe Nations: Sacred Number and the Golden Age*. Rochester, VT: Inner Traditions, 2008.

Page, Christine R. *2012 and the Galactic Center: The Return of the Great Mother*. Rochester, VT: Bear & Company, 2008.

South, Stephanie. *2012: Biography of a Time Traveler: The Journey of José Argüelles*. Franklin Lakes, NJ: Career Press, 2009.

Whitehead, Alfred North. *Modes of Thought*. New York, NY: Fireside, 1970.